Shine On

Allison Jewell

*Best
Wishes,
Allison Jewell*

This is a work of fiction. Names, characters, businesses, places, events and incidents are either the products of the author's imagination or used in a fictitious manner. Any resemblance to actual persons, living or dead, or actual events is purely coincidental.

For my great-grandmother, Ina Mae, who teaches me about life, love, and laughter.

ACKNOWLEDGMENTS

I could not have created this book without the help of several people. Thank you to Daniel, my live in historian, for helping me research the prohibition era and all things moonshine; Karen Lawson, my amazing editor; Letitia Hasser, my wonderful cover artist; to Morgan Conwell, for creating the lovely artwork that first brought my characters to life; to Paul and everyone at BB eBooks for your guidance and hard work in getting this book formatted; to the members of my writing group for sharing your wealth of knowledge; to Tracey, who never hesitates to talk to me about fictional characters as if they are real people; to fellow author Laramie Briscoe for coffee, feedback, confidence, and friendship, and to my family for supporting me in the writing and publishing of this book. Last but not least, thank you to my two sweet boys, Elijah and Jonah, who inspire me daily.

Chapter One

Early Fall, 1924

Mr. Thomas's shadow covered the thin ribbon of light shining through the window. Emmie didn't have to look up from her embroidery to know he was staring down at her. She could feel him. He sat slowly on the faded blue sofa, scooting a little closer than was appropriate for a boss to sit next to his worker. But who was she kidding? A blind man could see he wanted to be more than her boss.

The wages she made sewing at the general store each afternoon gave her almost enough money to pay the mortgage on the little farmhouse Ronnie and Ma had left her after they passed. She needed to find another job to help make the difference for next month, maybe some cash for tuition, too. A few years back, the town's college had opened the Normal School for Teachers. Her mama had planted that seed in her head. It was the dream she wasn't ready to lay to rest yet.

"You're doing a fine job on those little girl dresses, Emma," Mr. Thomas said leaning into her.

"Thank you, Mr. Thomas," she said politely.

"Mr. Thomas," he chastised her, his voice smooth and cold, "I told you, please, call me Paul."

"I'm sorry, Mr. Thom… I mean Paul. It's just that everyone else—" she started.

He bent down so he was eye level. "Emma, darling, you know you're not like everyone else."

She sucked in her breath. "Mr. Thomas, I…" she shook her head anxiously, unsure what to say.

Ding. Thank God for the shop bell.

"I promised your brother I would watch the store while he was having lunch." She stepped around him.

1

She was sure he would follow her but at least in the store he would have no excuse to be so close. Making her way to the counter she glanced around the shop. She saw a tall redhead near the back looking at some canned goods. Emmie leaned in for a closer look. It was her.

"Ava. You're back." She hadn't seen her best friend in months.

"Emmie, it's so good to see you. I just went by your house. I'm so sorry I wasn't here when you needed me. By the time I heard Ronnie had passed away, we were already heading back. You've been through hell," Ava whispered wrapping her friend in a hug.

Emmie felt a prick of pain in her throat at the mention of her stepfather's death but she couldn't give into the tears now, so she smiled instead.

"What's that in your hand?" Ava frowned pointing to Emmie.

"Oh, this. It's a dress," Emmie answered sheepishly.

"I see that. Why do you have a baby's dress in your hand? Is there something you need to tell me?" Ava grinned at her joke.

"Oh hush," Emmie laughed in spite of herself. "I'm working here now. Smocking things for kids." She laughed nervously.

"You work for Mr. Thomas?" Ava looked disgusted.

"I needed a job," Emmie said.

"You know he's carrying a torch for you." Ava grimaced, "He could be your papa."

"Actually, more like an older brother... a much older brother. And I can't think about the torch he may or may not carry for me. I needed a job and he pays me well," Emmie said lifting her chin.

"Well, at least you're not having his baby." She pointed at the dress again. "That's probably why he makes you sew those things. The old coot's crazy, you know." She arched an eyebrow then continued. "Ma sent me for some things. She's dying to see you too. Can you come for dinner tonight?" Ava asked.

"Time is money, girls. Time is money." Mr. Thomas walked up putting his hand on her elbow.

"Emma, let me take care of Miss DeCarmilla. I don't want to keep you from finishing that beautiful dress." Ava gave him a look that said she didn't give a rat's behind about the dress or his opinion of time and money. But Emmie was thankful that her friend kept all snarky comments to herself.

Emmie stepped away from his grip, "I'll come over tonight after I get off work, okay?"

Ava pursed her perfectly glossed lips and crossed her long arms over her body. She patted her red pin curls, turned her attention to Mr. Thomas and gave him a wide smile. She sent him on a wild goose chase for supplies. Emmie did her best to focus on the smocking at hand but struggled not to watch the show in front of her. Mr. Thomas huffed as he retrieved the fourth item from the back room.

"Will there be anything else, Miss DeCarmilla?" he asked condescendingly.

"That's all," she answered sweetly. Then she moved to the counter to pay for her goods.

Time ticked slowly that afternoon. Emmie headed out the door as soon as the clock struck four. She uttered a quiet goodbye to Mr. Thomas, keeping her voice at a whisper. He sometimes liked to find reasons for her to work late and she didn't want to give him the opportunity make up some excuse for her to stay.

The DeCarmilla estate was grand. The house was white brick and decorated with rows of perfectly aligned windows. Two enormous pillars extended all the way up the three-story home and provided support for the large front porch covering. The huge carport on the side always held at least a couple of cars, thanks to Ava's older brother or friends visiting from Chicago. It was one of those houses that called the front porch a terrace. Gorgeous. Elaborate. Expensive. But Ava's folks weren't those kind of people. They were good to everyone. You'd be just as likely to see her ma, Molly, out in the flowerbed pulling weeds, as you would have one of their workers.

That was how Ava and Emmie got to be such good friends. Ruby, Emmie's ma, was a pretty good seamstress. One day when Emmie was about three, she tagged along with her ma on a trip. She had joined Ava playing on the tree swing in the back yard. The two were pretty much inseparable ever since. Except for the DeCarmilla family trips to Chicago, their hometown, the girls were almost always together. Molly invited

Emmie to visit Chicago with them this summer. Emmie had never been north of Louisville. She wanted to jump at the chance to go but didn't feel like she could leave Ronnie alone. He was drinking more and more. Emmie wasn't sure he would be able to get along without her. So, she turned the opportunity down. Then Ronnie had up and died less than two weeks after they left.

"Emmie girl, it is so good to see you again," Molly called from the front door. Emmie closed the space between them in a few steps. Molly wrapped her arms around her in a tight hug and whispered, "I'm so sorry you've been going through all this child."

It was not until that moment Emmie realized how lonely the past two months had been. Sure, she went to work. She had dinner a few times with her neighbors, Mae, Walter, and their young grandson, Max. But she was just going through the motions. Breathing in and out. Living each day as it came.

"Why didn't you call us?" Molly's big green eyes bore into hers. Her fiery red hair looked like flames, falling in curls around her face.

Emmie felt two strong arms pull her from Molly's embrace. Ava's papa, Al, always gave her the same greeting, a quick squeeze of a hug and a kiss on each cheek. "Good to see you, girl."

"Dinner won't be ready for another hour or so, Emmie. Ava thought you might like to relax out back, by the pool. She is upstairs changing." Molly led Emmie inside.

It felt like it had been ages since she had been in this house. There was so much change in the short time that had passed. Emmie stopped dead in her tracks at the sight of Ava.

"Good Lord, Ava DeCarmilla, what are you wearing?" Emmie snorted. "Your papa will kill you if he sees you walking around in that!"

Ava gave a slow spin in her new swimsuit. It was black and fit tightly against her body. It came a good seven inches up from her knee. A long drape of sheer fabric hung off one shoulder like a Roman goddess. White swim shoes laced up her legs like ballet slippers. They were striking against her dark charcoal stockings.

"Papa doesn't much care what I wear. It was Gabe that nearly died the first time I wore it on his boat this summer," she answered with a laugh.

"Gabe? So you and Gabe... you're a couple again?" Emmie frowned. Ava looked away sheepishly. She was avoiding this conversation. So, it must be serious.

Gabriel del Grande's family lived in Chicago most of the time. They teetered back and forth just like the DeCarmillas. Gabe's dad had a house just down the road from Ava's. For the last several years Gabe was the only del Grande in town. For a long time Emmie assumed Gabe's ma had passed away, but then one day he mentioned something about sending her a card for her birthday. She knew better than to ask him about it. Everybody's family had their own problems.

Gabe and Ava had been nearly inseparable for months last year. Then one day last spring he just up and moved back to Chicago. No word that he was leaving or why he was going. He phoned once to give some half-thought-out excuse about needing to be near his family but she didn't hear from him again after that. Ava was broken-hearted— cursed him, and swore him off forever.

Ava glanced down at her shoes and flipped with the ribbons that tied at her knees. "Well, you know. I mean... yeah... I guess we are... back together."

Emmie sighed and rolled her eyes, walking past her friend. Apparently, swearing someone off forever only lasted a few weeks now. Sometimes, Ava's drama wore her out.

Chapter Two

"Emmie, I was wrong about him. He did have a good reason to leave. He never dated anyone else that whole time we were apart, said he always felt like we were still together," Ava explained setting her jaw. "You know how Ma kept saying to give him time and if it's meant to be, he'll come back. Well, turns out she was right."

"Yeah, what was this good excuse he had for leaving and breaking your heart?" Emmie frowned trying to decide if this was worth the fight.

"I cannot say. I promised. You just have to trust me, please?" Ava looked dead into her friend's eyes. The two never kept secrets but Ava couldn't tell her this. She'd hoped that Emmie would at least respect her for not making up some lie.

For a split second Emmie looked hurt but brushed it away. "Okay, I trust you. Just be careful, alright." There were too many other things going on in her life right now to lose her best friend over a boy. In time the truth always came out.

"Want to borrow a swimsuit?" Ava asked, eyeing her friend's pale blue work dress. "Looks like you're a little over dressed."

"No, it's okay. Just your parents here tonight, right?" she asked. "No point in getting all dolled up. I'll just wear my slip."

"No, no one else… Vince is finishing up something at the office for Papa." Ava paused for a second then added, "I really do have this lovely swimsuit. It's just the berries! You would…" Her words trailed off as she headed back into the bedroom producing a navy swimsuit, if one could even call it that. Emmie had never seen a garment with so little fabric. It might cover Ava's stick-thin body but there was no way she would be able to squeeze her bits in that thing. She was all for the latest fashion but that new swimsuit was borderline indecent.

6

"Umm, no thanks. I'll be fine." Emmie slipped off her dress and laid it across Ava's bed.

The water was cool and refreshing in the sticky September afternoon. Emmie sat in her slip, dangling her legs into the water, taking in her surroundings. It was beautiful. A few big oak trees stood in the far backyard peeking over the white privacy fence that surrounded the massive pool. The white columns and arched roofline of the back terrace opened up to the shallow end of the pool. Sheer curtains framed the walkway from pool to patio. The pool itself was like a work of art, crystal clear water with dark blue lines dividing different swimming lanes.

Four Roman statues representing spring, summer, winter and fall stood guard at each of the corners of the cement path that enveloped the pool. Emmie craned her face up toward the setting sun and closed her eyes.

"Ava. Ava, are you out here?" a deep voice boomed from the other side of the sheers that separated the pool from the patio.

Ava looked at Emmie with wide eyes and smiled. "I am so sorry. I had no idea they would be back so soon."

"Ava, there you are. Hey, Emmie." Gabe walked right past Emmie and pulled Ava into a tight hug, and kissing like he'd just returned from war. Good grief. Emmie stared back out at the oak trees unsure where to look.

"Well, if it isn't little Miss Emmie Shimmy," Vince boomed, his dress shoes clicking closer to her on the pavement.

"Vincent, you hear me, you better not," she screamed scrambling from the side of the pool.

Anytime she was near a pool and Ava's older brother, Vincent, came up behind her, she knew her fate. It had been the same since they were kids. Emmie never saw his face, she just felt his huge hands lift her off the ground. In a matter of seconds, she was airborne. Her last plea was met with a mouth full of cold water and muffled laughter she could hear from above. Emmie popped her face out of the water and glared at him. If looks could kill Vincent would be a dead man.

But the look was in vain because, by the time she reached the steps, Emmie was laughing so hard she had a difficult time getting out of the pool. She walked right over to Vincent and smacked him on the shoulder as hard as she could. She still looked like the little mouse with big blue eyes to him that had peddled around the pool since he was ten years old. Unfortunately, that is not what she looked like to everyone else.

Emmie turned to head inside for a towel. She was surprised to find two guys in her path. She suddenly felt very self-conscious. One looked at her with blatant amusement like he had never seen a girl in a swimsuit before.

Oh My Goodness…

Her slip. She was in her slip, not a swimsuit.

The guy nearest her smiled, eyes wide with amusement. "Hi ya, Doll," he grinned.

Emmie rolled her eyes and walked right past him, still tugging on the hem of her slip. The second guy didn't have the decency to look away either. As she moved around him, she felt something drop on her shoulders. Emmie snapped back around, puzzled.

The guy pulled the collar of the jacket close around her neck and whispered, "Honey, there isn't any amount of pulling on that slip you can do to make it not cling to your…" he paused for a long second, "…your body."

Emmie wanted to find some cold dark cave and hide there for all eternity. Mr. Chivalry—I give my jacket to half-naked ladies all the time—didn't look the least bit flustered and she hated him for it. He pulled a cigarette out of his vest pocket and took a long, slow draw. His blue-gray eyes were staring into hers. A grin played at the corner of his mouth. Then he moved to her and headed toward Vincent, smacking the "Hi ya, Doll" guy in the back of the head on his way.

Her pride made her want to throw his jacket at him and walk inside with her shoulders back and chin held high. Her mousy modesty made her pull the coat tighter around her shoulders and scurry into the house.

Chapter Three

Emmie tiptoed through the house as quietly as she could, not wanting to catch the attention of Molly and Al. She was sure her face was flaming red and having to answer questions about her blush would only make her feel worse. She went straight to Ava's bedroom and changed into her dress. Ava entered the room a few minutes later with a smile painted on her face. Emmie looked away and continued pinning up her wet curls.

"I wish you would have just taken my extra swimsuit. You really are too old to be swimming in your underwear." Ava laughed.

"Yeah, says the girl who was outside in less fabric than a napkin," Emmie said.

"Yes, but my napkin isn't see-through when wet," Ava countered.

"Point taken. From now on, swimsuit it is." She nodded in agreement.

"So who is that down there?" Emmie didn't think there was anyone in Ava's family she hadn't met over the years.

"The first fool that talked to you was Patrick or Trick, ignore him. The guy that gave you the jacket is Silas. They're my cousins. Mom's brother's boys," Ava answered.

"Girls, dinner's ready," Molly called from downstairs.

"Are you going to be okay? No permanent damage?" Ava asked half kidding.

Emmie shrugged, "Not the worst thing that's happened in the last few months."

She grabbed Silas's jacket and headed down the stairs. The boys were already seated at the table when the girls walked in the dining room. Everyone's plates were already full and an easy conversation filled the air by the time they made it downstairs. Emmie nonchalantly dropped Silas's coat on the back of the chair and took her seat next to Ava.

Al's eyebrow arched in question. He opened his mouth to say something. Molly smiled and put her hand on his, silencing him with a look. He frowned, glancing at Silas but he said nothing. Molly formally introduced her nephews to Emmie, as if nothing had happened. Silas nodded hello playing along with the introduction but Trick was not so polite. Emmie swore his face may actually split open, he had such a wide smile. She felt shades of embarrassment coloring her cheeks again. Thankfully the phone at that moment started to ring.

The guys at the table visibly tensed as Al walked over to answer the call. His voice was clipped and quiet. She couldn't make out what he was saying. Vince and Silas moved nearer to him. When he put the receiver down he spoke to them quietly. They nodded. Silas motioned for Trick and Gabe to join him. Vince headed for the door.

"Excuse us, Aunt Molly. Dinner was great but we've got to head back to the office," Silas said.

"Oh Al, surely they don't need to go right this second. We just sat down," Molly sighed, annoyed with her husband.

Al put a hand up to silence her. Molly sighed and sat back down, "They'll be back soon."

Then he walked the guys outside, returning a few minutes later alone. Emmie looked over at Ava with an unspoken question. She shrugged. Dinner passed in forced conversation.

After the meal the girls relaxed on the upstairs sleeping porch. It felt so normal. Talking, laughing, and listening as the birds' songs turned into the hums of nighttime bugs. They relaxed in a comfortable silence for a while before Ava began to speak. Emmie expected her to turn the conversation to the pool shenanigans this afternoon but she didn't. Instead she focused on the topic that Emmie had spent the last few months avoiding.

"Emmie," Ava started, "what happened to Ronnie? We heard there was some kind of accident."

She took a long breath. "I don't really know, Ava. Sheriff Drake found him in his car. It hit a tree and caught on fire, I guess."

"Do you think he'd been into his 'shine again?" One of Ava's red pin curls came loose and fell into her eye. She brushed it back and looked at her friend intently.

"He was always in the moonshine. It was late at night. I was already in bed." She picked at a thread on the quilt she was wrapped in.

"You think he may have been up to something?" Ava arched an eyebrow. When Emmie didn't say anything, she continued.

"Remember that time we found those jars in your cellar? I'm sure they were moonshine," Ava said.

"Yeah, well. We know he drank. No surprise there, Ava," she said.

"I suppose you're right. I'm trying to think why he was driving around those fields after midnight." She pondered for a moment. Then she immediately changed subjects—as her brain was often inclined to do. But Emmie's mind didn't leave the topic so easily. Why was he in those fields so late at night? That was the question she'd refused to let herself spend too much time thinking about the past months.

****

Ava asked her to stay the night but she refused. Something about her house kept her grounded.

Spotty met them at the end of the road, barking a welcome. Her black lab mix had one large white spot on his right eye and another on his back. When she was a teen she decided she wanted a baby brother, so Ronnie showed up one day with a pup. He said it was the best he could do. It was the only thing he ever gave her.

The dog met her as she exited the car, licking her hand and sniffing at the leftovers Molly had packed up. The night was warm and the moon was full. Emmie waved bye to Al. She locked up, got ready for bed, and settled in, waiting for sleep to claim her. But it didn't. She closed her eyes and her mind played a picture show with vivid color—a perfect vision of the day Ronnie died.

"Emma," Ronnie shouted. Her pulse quickened. Was he already up? She hated mornings when he rose early. Usually his 'shine headaches kept him in bed until after dawn.

"Emma, you better answer when I call your name," he called from downstairs.

"Sorry, Ronnie. I was just on my way down." Her bare feet thumped down the stairs, trembling hands gripping the loose handrail.

"It's about time, girl," he barked.

Ronnie looked the same as he always had, maybe a little grayer around the ears, maybe a little more wrinkled around the eyes, but basically the same. His mouth was still set in a frown; his hands were calloused from working at the lumber mill. His dishwater-blond hair was cut short to his head. She moved around him to the old coffee pot.

"Ya ain't even started making the breakfast yet?" he sneered and jerked her back by the neck of her hand-me-down cotton dress. "Girl," he breathed in her ear from behind, "what'd ya think I keep ya around here for, hmm?"

Spotty came up and nipped at his hand. The dog yipped as Ronnie's work boot met his fur. Emmie grabbed Spotty and pushed him out the front door. When Ronnie was in this kind of mood it was better to get the dog away from him.

"Forget about it," he huffed as he put on his hat. "I'll be expecting supper tonight but I'll be home late. Gotta work outside on the farm for a bit. You can just leave my dinner on the stove."

Those were the last words she heard out of him. He was always working out on the farm but there was never anything to show for it. He let go of the garden six years ago after Mama died of the flu. He sold the only cow two years ago. The land was overgrown. She tossed and turned most of the night. Her brain wrestled trying to put it all together. She hung in the balance of sleep and awareness for hours, thinking it through.

"Oh my heavens," Emmie said aloud. Spotty turned his head listening for something outside.

When she did not speak immediately, he plopped back down on the covers. "The jars of 'shine, the late nights, always outside but nothing to show, the woods—that's it," she said aloud. Part of her wanted to toss off the covers and go look right this second. She knew it was a foolish idea. Dawn was approaching. So, she closed her eyes and made a plan instead.

Chapter Four

"What are ya doin' here in the middle of the night, girl?" Walter said, rubbing his long beard.

"I told you. I'm here to help. I've put it together. I know what Ronnie was doing out here. I'm not some kind of fool," Emmie said, looking around the dark cave that was hidden in the hills near the back of her property line.

This had been her third night out here roaming around the woods. She was about to give up when it hit her that she hadn't checked the only spot on their property that included a creek—the cave.

As she got closer she could feel it in her gut. She just knew she was right. Emmie did not know exactly what she was looking for out here: some old barrels, a still, or a person. Stumbling around the leaves she could see the faint glow of an old lantern coming from inside the dark entrance.

She'd never been so relieved when she smelled the familiar scent of Walt's sweet pipe tobacco and heard him whistling "Old Dan Tucker." He looked startled as she stepped into the mouth of the cave. Spotty ran right up to him, wagging his tail. Emmie wished she felt that at ease.

"You better get back to ya house. It ain't right for you to be walking around here at night. There's wolves in this forest, girl," Walter scowled.

"There are no wolves in my woods, Walt. You sound like that grandmother in Little Red Riding Hood," Emmie said, squaring her shoulders for the fight. Walter slowly closed the distance between them. The uncomfortable silence that passed almost made her lose her nerve.

"Does this look like a fairy tale to you? There ain't nothing for you in this cave," he said.

"I know what's been going on. I put it together. Ronnie's moonshine, all those late nights out here on the farm, with nothing ever to show. This is a still isn't it?" Emmie asked. When he didn't answer she continued, "You're gonna need help now that Ronnie's gone. You can't do all this by yourself. The way I see it you need help and I need money. Done deal."

"Emmie, I've known ya for a lot of years. You should know better than to walk up on a man's still. If it weren't me, you might be leaving with a hole that God didn't give ya," Walter started.

Emmie cut him off, "Walter, this is my land. This is my cave. That is my water you are pumping through that barrel. Part of that 'shine is mine the way I see it." She kept her shoulders square and looked him right in the eye and hoped he didn't see the way her hands trembled when she balled them up into a fist at her side.

"What do you know about 'shine?" Walter adjusted his pipe in his mouth.

Well, he had her there. She only knew three things about moonshine:

1. It was illegal.
2. It made Ronnie as mean as a snake.
3. It made fast money.

And none of those things she could say out loud. Well, maybe she could tell him the last one.

"I need the money, Walter," she mumbled relaxing her shoulders a bit.

"Emmie, you don't want this money. It's not clean. Ain't you working down at the shop sewing stuff?" he asked, pulling a long draw from his pipe.

"I can't make a living on that. I've been trying. I just need to build up a little money, then it's all yours again. I swear it," she said.

"You hungry, girl? Cause you know you are welcome at our table any time. I thought Mae done told you that?" He stood and started working on some copper pipe that was losing steam, only half paying attention to her. He didn't have time to be messing around out here with some half-grown kid.

"Besides, I hear Mr. Thomas has been trying to catch your eye. Why don't you just let him? You could do worse than a storekeeper," he added, never looking at her.

Great. As if this conversation wasn't bad enough now she had to talk about Mr. Thomas.

"No, Mae invited me for supper anytime I wanted. I appreciate it, really. I make enough money to eat. And I don't want to depend on Mr. Thomas anymore than I already do. He pays me for sewing and that's all I need," Emmie answered.

"You're talking out of both sides of your mouth girl." Irritated he started putting some goop on the pipe to no avail. It just kept running right down the side of the curved copper. "Ya say you got all the money you need from Thomas and ya got food. What do you wanna work out here with me and Ole Maizy for?"

"Maizy?" Emmie looked around. Was there another woman here?

"My still, Ole Maizy," he said with an odd sense of affection, like it was a pet.

Emmie blinked slowly and nodded. Had the old man gone off his rocker? Her face must have asked the question she held inside her mouth.

"Maizy's been in my family for years." He patted more paste on the copper pipe. She noticed how careful he touched it. "My paw told me they named her Maizy cause that was what them Indians called corn and bein' as we use corn to make the 'shine…" he shrugged then smiled thinking back on some memory leaving his sentence unfinished. He glanced back to Emmie.

"But that don't matter," he regained his gruff composure, "cause this is gonna be the first and last time ya see this here still. Now, tell me what's going on. You are a good girl. Why're you trying to get yourself all caught up in my business?" He hooked his thumbs under his overalls and waited for her to speak.

"Alright, here's the truth of it. I could use a little money to help make the difference in the mortgage. But mainly, I want to go to college. I want to be a teacher. I need to save up some money to pay for school. Please, I can help you…" She looked around praying to God she'd see something she knew how to do. But he was right she knew nothing about making moonshine.

Spotty stood and stretched his legs with a little groan. When she turned to face him she spied something out of place. Propped up on a large rock was half a sack of flour. She could tell it had been used because there was a little trail of white powder spilling out of the mouth. Why in the world would Walt have a sack of flour out here?

Walter was paying her no mind. He'd turned his attention back to Ole Maisy. He was worrying with the watery paste to no avail. The spot where the two copper pipes had been fused together was still emitting unwanted steam from the joint. His hands were shaking; he wasn't as young as he used to be. And this was hard work. Walter didn't drink this stuff like Ronnie, or much of it anyway. She believed him. He did this for tradition. No doubt his family had been making moonshine for years before the 18th Amendment made it illegal to do so. Truth be told, the little extra money he was getting from it probably didn't hurt his family either. He wasn't wealthy by any stretch. Emmie watched him as his brow wrinkled with frustration. Walter wiped the paste on his overalls and stepped back to see what was wrong.

"Here let me see your mix, Walt," she said. Emmie was surprised when he handed her the small bowl of paste. "This is too thin. Did you make this from that flour over there?"

"Who are you to be telling me what to do, girl? I've been doing this since before you were knee-high," he snapped but his eyes didn't hold any ill feeling toward her.

"Well, you're right. I don't know about moonshine. But I do know about baking and making a good batter. That paste is too thin. See, it's just dripping right down the sides. You're losing steam which probably means you're losing 'shine," she said, adding more flour to the bowl and giving it a good stir. "Try that."

He gave her an annoyed look then walked over to Ole Maizy muttering something under his breath. He carefully scooped some paste onto the joint, careful to slather it in each of the nooks and crannies. Sure enough most of the steam quit coming out of the sides of the pipe. Emmie grinned like the cat that swallowed the canary.

"My eyes ain't as good as they used to be. Can't see how thick it's getting anymore," he said, taking in her expression. Then he pointed a finger at her. "Just because you make a good paste don't mean you're my partner. I tell you what though, you're right. It's your land and so I'll make a deal. You mix me up some paste, I'll pay you one dollar each week."

"Walter, I'm not a child. I need more than that. I explained to you that I need the money. I can do more than make paste," she begged.

"Emmie get back to your house before I change my mind. I'm not playing at this game any more. I'll bring you your money soon as I can. That's four dollars a month. It's the best I can give ya right now." For the first time tonight he used a stern voice, he was serious now. He'd always been like a grandpa to her. She couldn't disrespect him now. He'd given her more of a chance than anyone else would have. Heck, some folks would have shot her for getting so close to their still. Folks around here didn't mess around when it came to their 'shine.

"Alright. Thanks Walter. You just let me know when you need me to mix more of that up for you," Emmie said and then turned and headed back toward the mouth of the cave. She patted her leg and Spotty trotted along after her.

"Um hmm," he answered as she was leaving. "Be careful on the way back to the house."

When she got back to her house it was nearly two in the morning but she couldn't sleep. It was good to finally figure out what Ronnie had been up to. Finally it made sense why Walter had been the one to find him that night. Emmie appreciated that Walter was at least willing to give her a few dollars a month. That would pretty much take care of the rest of the mortgage but there'd be no money left for school. Walter would come around, she just had to find a way to make him see he needed her help.

Chapter Five

N eedle in, needle out, change color. Repeat.

That's what her job felt like today. Monotonous. When Emmie used to help her mother with sewing and smocking, she loved it. It was creative, relaxing, peaceful quiet. Mama always hummed as she sewed. Church hymns, lullabies, classics, it didn't matter. She said it was impossible to be anything but happy when you're humming. It spoke louder than words.

Emmie started idly humming Ole Dan Tucker thinking back to her conversation with Walter a couple days ago. She had seen neither hide nor hair out of him since their midnight chat. She knew him well enough to know he wasn't going to skip out on the money he'd promised but Emmie wondered when he'd come for the paste. She'd worked every night practicing different ratios of flour and water trying to get a good thickness for the gooey concoction.

"Miss Emmie." Young Max peeked his head around the corner. "Mamaw Mae sent me to pick her up some stuff from the store but there ain't nobody in here to take my money." He held out a few dollar bills and some coins that were wadded in his left hand.

"Oh, I'm sorry. Mr. Thomas must be out back. What'd ya need Max?" She smiled down at him as she walked behind the counter.

Max was Walter and Mae's grandson, but he'd lived with them since before he was two years old. And from what she had heard that was for the best, his mama had died when he was born. Emmie barely remembered it but she remembered saying Mae and Walter like to have died right along with their only girl. When the boy never crawled or walked the boy's dad had dropped him off at Walter and Mae's. He never showed up again. Her mama said that's what brought the old couple back to life again, having a little piece of their daughter shining on in that baby boy's eyes. Max was growing up fine.

18

He dug down into his right pocket and put a crumpled list onto the counter. Then reached across and flattened it with his left hand. Max's right side didn't ever seem to work as well as his left. The gossipy ladies at church said he'd never walk, but Walter made a brace for his leg. Mae practiced with him every day and proved all those old biddies wrong.

He wasn't much older than six but read most of the words on the crumpled grocery list and figured the sum of the total cost before she did. Which was saying something considering half the people in this town couldn't read much more than their own name and address.

Emmie quickly got his change and boxed up the goods that he couldn't carry and put the smaller items in a couple of sacks.

"Wow, great job totaling out that sum, Max. I might have to ask Mr. Thomas to get you a job working at this counter. Is your Mamaw Mae going to be by later to pick the rest of this up?"

"Yes, ma'am. Thank you." Max smiled and headed back out the door. His limp was hardly noticeable. Sweet kid. She turned to head back into the side parlor she used for sewing and bumped right into something hard.

"Better watch where you're going Emma." Mr. Thomas smiled down at her, grabbing her elbows to steady her from stumbling.

She tried to step out of his grasp but he didn't let go. His fingers were digging into her elbows.

"Excuse me, Mr. Thomas."

"I heard what you said to that young gimp." He looked down at her.

"Gimp?" she questioned.

"You know, the handicapped child. You really do not have the authority to hire anyone. One—I would never hire anyone that young. Two—He would be of no use to me here. He can't even carry ten pounds of sugar and flour home to his grandparents," he added.

Emmie's mouth fell open and froze in a small O. "He is not handicapped, he limps. He's faster at sums than most adults," she spit at him. "And I was just kidding. I can't believe you'd say something like that."

His bony fingers dug deeper into her arm. "I will not have an employee talk back to me. I pay you to sew, not give me your opinion." His frown softened but his stare was as condescending as ever. "But I guess I cannot fault you for your big heart, my sweet Emma."

He released her arm and brushed the hair back from her forehead. Her skin crawled where his clammy hands had touched her.

My Sweet Emma, I'll never be your anything, Mr. Thomas.
Take this job and stick it, Mr. Thomas.
Stick this needle in your eye, Mr. Thomas.

There were so many things she wanted to say to Mr. Thomas but unfortunately she needed this job. She needed his money. So she said nothing, stepping around him, taking her chair.

Needle in, needle out, change color, repeat.

Never looking up at him again for the rest of the day. She tried humming to no avail. No amount of humming could cheer her up today. She wanted out of here. Walter was the only ticket she could see right now.

Chapter Six

Emmie walked into her house to the shrill of a ringing phone. She started to ignore it. The party line calls were rarely for her but it rang twice followed by a short pause. That was her ring. She rushed over and jerked the receiver off the hook.

"Emmie dear, I'm glad I caught you." It was Molly's soft voice on the other end. "How were things at the store?"

"Good," she lied. No point in telling the truth. It wasn't going to change the fact she still needed to work there. "How are you?"

"Well, Emmie I hated to do this to you but we are actually going to have to head back to Chicago," she started. Emmie's heart sank in her chest. "I am so sorry to leave you like this when we've only just returned. My uncle has fallen and has no family; so, I need to be with him. Al's got some work to do in the Chicago office and is going to let the boys handle things down here. We've told them they are to check in on you while we are away but I couldn't leave without talking to you. You're like my own, you know that."

Emmie nodded at the phone. Only after a few seconds pause did it occur to her that Molly couldn't see her actions. She smiled in hopes it would shine through her voice, "Yeah, I'm good… and I know. Don't you worry about me, I'm fine."

"I know you are, child. Are you sure you won't rethink staying at our house? I cannot help but think your Ma wouldn't like you living in that farmhouse all alone," Molly pushed.

"I've got Spotty. He's a good guard dog," Emmie laughed. "Thanks anyway. I just," Emmie shrugged then started again, "I just feel like I'm not ready to leave yet. Like if I leave for one night I may never stay here alone again. I know that sounds silly."

"No, I understand. Your mama would be proud of the lady you've become." Molly sounded choked up. After a short pause she repeated her question, "Do you need anything at all: money, food?"

"I promise, I'm fine. Go take care of your uncle. I'm sorry he's unwell," Emmie answered.

"You sound like your mama," Molly laughed. "Well, I've got to get to the train station. Ava's is pacing the floor to talk to you right now. Take care, Emmie."

"Did you hear the news? We've got the house to our selves. Get over here," Ava sang into the phone. Her voice was barely above a whisper; her Ma must still be in the room.

"Oh, Ava. I don't know. I'm beat. I think I'll just turn in early. It's been a long day," Emmie said, toying with the cord and slipping off her shoes.

"Come on, Emmie. You can relax here. It's not good for you to be cooped up in that house by yourself like some old bird," Ava begged.

Old bird. That's what she felt like lately. No one should feel like an old bird at her age. Ava was right, she refused to let this be the rest of her life. A bad, boring day at Mr. Thomas's was not worth a night of moping, no matter how tired she was.

"You're right. I'm too young to be an old bird. Are the boys there?" Emmie asked.

"Just us. I'm not sure when they'll be back. Are you hoping to see one of my handsome McDowell cousins? Hypothetically speaking, which did you want to see more Trick or Silas? I couldn't tell which you like best," Ava laughed.

"Ava, I was humiliated. I am interested in neither…" Emmie shouted into the phone and a traitorous grin escaped her mouth.

"Well, I guess I get to choose for you then when you get here. You'll come over right away?" Ava pushed.

"Yes, I'll be there soon," Emmie gave in.

Emmie smiled as she slipped into the dropped-waist sailor Ava had brought back from Chicago. The fabric was so soft and light it felt more like a nightgown than clothes. Ava or her ma always brought her back special things from Chicago. Clothes from the city always looked and felt a bit different than what you could find here. It was one of the few things she had that really made her feel special.

She was unpinning her hair when she heard a knock at the door. Spotty jerked up from his pallet on the floor. Standing at attention, he took his spot and barked a warning at the front door. Emmie brushed him to the side. A quick peek out the window and she found Walter staring back at her. He was carrying a sack of flour.

"Howdy there, Emmie. Brought you some flour for the paste. I'll be needing it tonight," he said, dropping the sack by the kitchen table.

"No problem, Walter. I've got something I want you to try though." She couldn't keep the excitement out of her voice. He was going to be so pleased, she just knew it. "Do you have a minute for me to mix it up?"

He merely nodded. He still wasn't really happy with this arrangement, but he wanted to help the child out. For a good girl like her to come find him in a cave in the middle of the night and ask to help make 'shine… something wasn't right. It liked to have broken his heart when she told him she wanted to go to school to be a teacher. She was a smart girl that'd just been given a hard row to hoe. Four dollars a month wasn't going to get her to college but it was the best he could do right now. She scurried around the kitchen mixing up some concoction and… putting on a pot of tea?

"Emmie, I ain't really got time to have tea. Mae's cooking up supper. Ya hungry? She and Max would love to see ya," he said, rubbing his gray whiskers. Poor girl must be lonely.

"Oh, I can't. Thanks anyway. I'm actually just getting ready to head over to Ava's. This'll just take a minute. I'm not making tea. I'm going to use that pot to show you something." She gave the mixture a final stir, scooped some up and beat the side of the bowl with the spoon testing the consistency. Then looked up at him with a grin, eyebrows raised.

"That looks fine Emmie," he answered her unspoken question and sat down in one of the kitchen chairs. Walter wondered what was she playing at.

"I put some holes in this spout see." She held the teapot up close for him to get a good look. Sure enough somehow she'd worked little dings and holes into the pot.

Her nimble fingers spread the paste thick over the broken spots. She added water to the pot and put it on the stove. "This'll just take a minute. I've been working ever since I met with you. Trying out different ratios of flour and water. Yesterday morning I was eating breakfast and it hit me. You need more than flour to keep that steam in." She studied the pot like some mad scientist. Such a good, smart girl. He couldn't let her get mixed up in this mess. What was the old coot thinking?

"Heard Max saw you today. Said you bragged on him for his number smarts," Walter said, looking down at his calloused hands.

"I did and I meant it. Max's a smart boy, Walt. You and Mae have done a fine job with him." She smiled at him.

Walt nodded. "Said he came back to get the grocery list and heard you talking to Mr. Thomas."

He looked up at her for the first time. Her eyes were huge. Pain pricked at her throat hoping the boy hadn't heard Paul call him a gimp. But she didn't have to ask. She could tell by the look on Walt's face that he had.

She closed her eyes and let out a sigh.

"Thanks for taking up for him. He said he heard you say he wasn't no gimp and he was a smart boy," Walter added.

"Oh, I really think Mr. Thomas is some kind of ugly. Just a big ole bully. Wish I could tell him where to stick his opinions." She saw fire thinking about that sweet boy hearing a grown man call him names.

"You've got a good soul, Emmie. I'm not sure it's right to get you mixed up with any of this." He pointed at the pot that had just started to whistle.

Sure enough almost no steam was coming out the cracks and holes she had made in the spout. It was all pouring right out the top, just as it should.

"That looks pretty good there, Emmie." He took a closer look at the bowl. "What'd you do?"

"Well, like I was saying I was eating breakfast yesterday and it hit me… oatmeal. I mixed a little of oatmeal in with the flour and tried it out on the pot and it worked like a charm." She grinned.

"Did you beat the heck outta your teapot just to learn to make good paste?" he asked, then chuckled, not sure if he was laughing because she'd outwitted him on the paste he'd been making for forty years or because she was so happy with the results of her experiment.

"Fine job, Emmie. Right fine job," he said as she covered the bowl of paste with butcher paper. "That should keep it fresher for you. Is that enough or do you need me to mix up some more?" she asked.

He assured her that the bowl was plenty, gave her a dollar with the promise of another next week. Then he paused for a moment like he had something else to say but thought better of it.

Chapter Seven

"Where in the world have you been? I was getting worried about you," Ava asked as she opened the door. She was wearing a large feathered headband, an obnoxiously large feather headband.

"Ya been plucking a chicken, Ava?" Emmie laughed, pointing to her friend's forehead. Spotty made an attempt to walk into the house with her. She gently pushed him back to the porch.

"Wait, here." He flopped down on under the chair nearest the front door with a disapproving sigh. When Emmie turned back to the door Ava was standing with a hand on her hip, glaring down in her direction. Apparently, she did not find humor in Emmie's joke.

"I'm sorry. It's lovely." Emmie smiled but then couldn't help but add as she walked by, "I'm just saying it's a good thing the dog is staying outside. Or he may try to eat your hair."

Ava frowned and patted her curls. "It's the latest fashion you know—all the rage in Chicago."

"Hmm…" Emmie smiled and nodded. "Well, if anyone can pull off hair of feathers, it'd be you. But really you needn't get so dressed up for me."

"Looks like you got pretty dressed up, yourself, there Emmie," Ava said, straightening the collar on her dress. "And it's a good thing too."

Emmie looked confused but, in that moment of silence, noticed she could hear music from a record player in the distance.

Ava continued, "Because my feathers aren't for you and I'm guessing this pretty dress isn't for me." She smiled.

"You said the boys were out," Emmie said quickly and quietly. Her heartbeat pulsed in her ears.

"They were but you took a long time to come over and they came home. What took you so long anyway?" Ava asked.

"I ran into Walter and he wanted to talk to me for a bit about Max." Emmie then recounted the story of what had happened earlier at work.

There was no way she could tell Ava about the paste she was making for Walt. She'd thought about it the whole walk over to her house.

To tell Ava or not to tell Ava. She'd decided not. What she was helping with was illegal. She wasn't selling the 'shine but she was sure there were laws about helping someone make it. Not that she thought Ava would tell on her. Emmie just didn't want her to be caught up in it. Heck, as soon as she could save up a little money she'd be done too. So she shared as much of the truth with her friend as she could. Ava was disgusted at what Mr. Thomas had said about Max. She said someday he would get what was coming to him.

"Let's not think about the crazy ole man tonight. Come on." She grabbed Emmie's arm and led her down the hall to the parlor.

Well, one of the home's parlors anyway. This was the "boys" room as Ava called it. A dark wood desk sat in the front of the room with leather couches and chairs, and blue striped curtains framing the floor-to-ceiling windows. They were actually one of the sets Emmie's mama had made all those years ago. In the back of the room, a heavy wooden pool table was adjacent to the fireplace. That's where the boys were playing billiards. They looked like some ad in a magazine. Posed laughing, smoking, playing pool, drinking… wait… drinking?

Trick froze when Emmie entered, glancing immediately from Vincent to Silas with an unspoken question, obvious to all. She had never felt so unwelcome walking into a room. It was like the life had been sucked out of the place.

"Take it easy, Trick. She's fine," Vince added, barely looking up from his shot at the back corner of the pool table.

Silas put his cue down on the floor and looked right at her with a smile that made her feel uneasy. "You're not gonna be calling the buttons are ya?"

"Sorry?" Emmie asked genuinely confused.

"The police," Ava laughed at her expression. "Give her a break, boys. Sheesh."

Ava walked over and helped herself to a drink. This wasn't the stuff that Walter made. Walter's moonshine was clear. This was dark caramel brown and didn't come from an old canning jar—it had a real bottle sealed with dripping wax.

"Since when do you drink?" Emmie asked, sitting next to Ava to get a closer look at the glass.

"Since a few weeks ago. It's more of just something to hold in my hand. It's the entire buzz in Chicago. They have whole clubs for it and everything," Ava explained, sloshing the drink around as she spoke.

"Well, this isn't Chicago." She instantly felt like she was talking out of both sides of her mouth. She wasn't a fan of drunkards, but was prohibition right?

"Just take a sip. It's not that bad. It sort of tastes like that cough medicine that Dr. Baker used to mix up," Ava said.

"What is it?" she asked.

Trick answered right away, clearly this conversation had peaked his interest. "It's bourbon. Kentucky is famous for it, you know. I heard this story of some man that came down here right after the start of prohibition and bought a whole distillery, disassembled it, put it on a train, and moved it to Canada. Now he's selling all kinds of bootleg liquor, taking money away from the people of your state."

Ava just raised her eyebrows and smiled behind her glass. She still had yet to take the first sip. Gabe walked over and took the glass from Ava's hand and set it on the table, tsk-tsking in mock disapproval. Louis Armstrong belted out an upbeat song and he pulled her up for a dance. She twirled, kicked her legs, and waved her hands like a mad woman. Emmie couldn't help but laugh at her erratic movements.

"So, you're a good girl after all." Silas plopped down on the couch next to her.

"Yeah, what makes you say that?" she wondered.

"You didn't take more than a sniff of that whiskey but you didn't run out the door either. You're alright, Emmie." He pushed her with his elbow.

She felt her body turn red from toe to nose. What was wrong with her?

****

Silas tried not to laugh at her blush. At first yesterday, out by the pool, he and his brother had thought she was some sort of floozy. He could see now he was wrong. She had been genuinely embarrassed. Vince had told him she was a friend of the family. Silas knew from experience that just because someone was a friend of one family didn't mean she was a friend to them all. He knew he should just walk back to the pool table and keep playing. So why couldn't he move from this couch? He grabbed her hand and pulled her into a loose embrace, his feet moving quickly to the music. Silas could tell by how tense she was that she'd not had much experience with dancing, she was so stiff. Maybe she should have had the bourbon.

"Relax, Emmie," he whispered.

"I don't know that crazy dance." She nodded over to Ava and Gabe.

He laughed out loud. "Who would want to? It's ridiculous."

At last she threw her head back and laughed, relaxing around him for the first time. Silas pulled her in closer. Wrapping one arm all the way around her waist while his other arm held her hand tightly to his chest. This was the best he'd felt in a long time. He'd deal with the consequences tomorrow. He was going to enjoy this tonight and with that thought he leaned down and brushed a quick kiss on her lips.

****

Spotty entered the mouth of the cave and plopped down at Walter's feet. Walter walked over and scratched his ears. *Silly name for the dog. Not a damn spot on the thing,* he grinned. *The girl must be at that Del Grande house if the dog was out roaming around.* He didn't know if that was good or bad. *Talk about wolves in the forest. Them people were wolves, keeping more skeletons in their closet than Red Riding Hood's grandma, if ya ask me. I suppose it weren't none of my business though.*

Walter stood back and watched little to no steam escape his makeshift pipe. Emmie was good at making paste for the still pipe on Ole

Maizy. Maybe if he could just get a little more business he could give the girl a couple more dollars each month.

He had just dropped off a dozen ears of his best corn on her porch. He didn't exactly know why he felt like he needed to raise her. Their families had been neighbors for years. Her mama, Ruby, was a sweet little thing that could barely raise her voice enough to shoo away a fly. He didn't know how she did it. She lived there alone on that farm with a toddler and did it with a smile on her face too. The townsfolk talked about her having a baby with no dad. He never knew if she was a widow or just a young mom that got herself in trouble. He never cared to ask, either. The way he figured it wasn't any of his business.

It wasn't long after Ruby had moved to town that she'd married that good-fer-nothin' Ronnie. Always had been a thorn in his side. He must have convinced her she needed him, having that baby and all. He probably weaseled his way into her life just like he did Walt's.

For all Ronnie's faults he was a stiff negotiator. It was a few years ago he had come toting a gun to Walter's barn. Mouthing off, saying he'd found Walt's still on his land.

"I know it's yours Walt. No use in lying to me," he'd boomed arrogantly.

Walt had tried to play it off like he didn't know what he was talking about. But Ronnie had pulled out Walt's pipe and tobacco. Damn it. He was getting too old for this. It was a fool's mistake leaving something like that behind.

"Alright, I admit it. You better get to shooting me Ron or get outta here. I ain't got time for your games," he'd said.

Ronnie laughed at him then. Told him he wasn't going to shoot him, put his gun away, and started acting like they were best friends or something. He said the gun was just to get him to own up to the fact the still was his. Ronnie said he never would hurt a friend. But his smile was too big, too fake. He'd seen enough marks on Emmie's mom's cheek to doubt his story about not hurting a friend.

"Let me help," Ron had begged. Said he needed the money to support his family. Walter doubted that his intentions were that honorable.

More than likely he just wanted the extra cash to buy more booze or invest it in some gambling scheme.

"Ronnie, I ain't really in the business. I mean I just make a few quarts here and there for some friends. This ain't how I make my living. You know I'm just a farmer," Walt had explained.

"You make more than a few quarts, my friend. Remember I saw your still and your mash. That's gonna make more than enough for your friends. And anyway, that's why you need me. You know I've got connections. With the seclusion of my cave and your knowledge we can grow this into a real business," he had promised.

When the old man had looked skeptical Ronnie pushed him further. "Walt you know you are going to be needin' more money as that boy gets older. The brace you got on his leg barely fits him now. How long you think you can keep just making those things for him? He needs to see a real doctor. Sure you and Mae have done your best, but don't you want more for him? Trust me, doctors aren't cheap. I can help you. We can do this." He stuck out his hand for a shake.

Walter had thought about it for a moment. He remembered it felt like he was making a deal with the devil but he'd agreed to give it a try anyway. So he shook his hand and bought into the promise that Ronnie had offered.

Surprisingly enough, Ronnie came through. Within weeks business picked up tenfold. They were selling jars even before they'd finished making them. Walter hadn't ever heard of selling stuff before it was done, but Ronnie assured him this is the way business worked now.

One of the weirdest things about partnering was Ronnie would never tell Walt who all the jars was going to. Said the less Walter knew the better it was for him. But other than the secret customers, he was more honest than Walt expected him to be. Nearly always paying him on time, for the first two years anyway. Until he got into drinking more and more of the 'shine himself.

By the time Ronnie had died they were selling more jars of 'shine than ever, but he was barely breaking even. Something wasn't right. Promises of cash that never arrived. Walt had confronted him about it once but had woken up a few hours later in the cave with a large gash to his head. Ronnie was mean when he was drinking. Walt had decided to just up and quit on him. Find some other place to work, there was plenty of little spring caves around the country he could use. He would just go back to making for his friends. But, he never got the chance to talk to Ronnie again. The next night he'd found him dead in the fields… in his truck. Walter never told anyone, but it didn't look like a car accident to him, didn't believe it was suicide either—Ronnie was too vain for that.

That night he'd been out checking on the mash. He'd heard the shot and had gone running as fast as his old legs could take him. It sounded like it was at the house and he knew that girl was in there. Coming down the backside of the hill he stumbled upon the car. He didn't see anybody at first, just the outline of Ronnie's lifeless face smashed up against the steering wheel. Turned out the sheriff and his boys were already there. They crept out of the trees. Sheriff Drake looked calm, greeted Walt like everything was just normal. Told Walt he was handling this investigation and he should just head back home. He didn't know if they were the ones that killed him but something wasn't right. Walt had been living around those hills too long to make the mistake of questioning what the sheriff and his boys had said. So, he played dumb the next morning when they'd found the car scorched beyond recognition. The sheriff had told Emmie Ronnie had a car accident. Walter guessed he was one of the only people to know Ronnie had not died in some fiery crash. He intended to keep that to himself until he met his maker.

Chapter Eight

"It's been two weeks, just let it go okay?" Emmie hated talking about this. Apparently Ava loved talking about it. Loved making Emmie feel stupid. Well, that probably wasn't true but it was how she felt. Stupid.

"Emmie, it's complicated, he's complicated. Trust me," she begged.

"Look, I'm fine with trusting you about Gabe. You're right, he's been good to you since you've been back. I'm trusting you there. No problem. Because that's your life. This is mine. So you trust me. He's a jackass," Emmie spit.

Ava's mouth flew open in mock horror. "Such language. My ears will bleed."

"Your ears are fine. I don't want to talk about him. He's nothing to me." Emmie pretended she didn't care and continued stirring the sugar into the apples that were simmering on the stove.

"Okay, I'll let it go," Ava conceded.

Emmie sighed. Finally. Her friend had been talking about Silas for days.

"After I say this one last thing," Ava added.

Emmie knew the promise of silence was too good to be true.

"I had Gabe talk to him," she smiled sheepishly.

"You what?" Emmie shouted.

"Well, I couldn't let him think it was okay just to kiss you then not call for a couple weeks. I mean for goodness sakes, Emmie, had you ever even let a boy kiss you before?" Ava continued. Emmie was too gobsmacked to answer.

"Gabe said that Silas said he just didn't have time to get all wound up with some 'good girl' down here," Ava smiled like that was the best news she'd ever shared.

"And you're happy to relay that message to me because?" Emmie arched an eyebrow, thoroughly irritated.

"Because it means he likes you," she testified, throwing her arms up in the air. Sometimes Ava really acted like she was about twelve years old. Emmie turned around and continued stirring the pot with more force than was necessary to break up some of the apples.

"Don't you see? He just doesn't think it's worth the effort because he lives up there and is only here for a short while. But that doesn't really matter does it, Emmie? We can show him he's wrong. Marry him and we will be real cousins." Ava laughed at her timeline.

"Well, maybe not quite that fast," Ava corrected, "but it could happen. We can have fun trying anyway. Just come over for dinner tonight. The more you are around each other the better. I don't like you avoiding the house anyway. Things are always better once they're all out in the open."

"Alright, I'll come over, but just to be clear, it's not for him. It's just because you're right. I'm tired of avoiding your house," she clarified.

"Do you mind getting me a couple of jars out of the cupboard under the stairs?" she asked.

Ava moved around the corner toward the pantry. "Lord have mercy," Ava shouted.

"What is it?" she called to her friend, only to receive no answer. She turned to see Ava emerge with a jar of moonshine in each hand.

Chapter Nine

"Oh." Emmie looked taken aback for a moment.

"I really didn't take you for such a drinker. Living a double life here, Emmie?" Ava teased. "Guess we found where Ronnie hid his stash. Last time we stumbled on it, a few years ago, it was just two jars in the barn. His habit must have picked up... A LOT."

"How much was in there?" Emmie tried to remember the last time she'd dug around in that pantry. It had been months and there wasn't any 'shine back then just stacks of old mason jars.

Ava didn't answer her. She just sat the jars on the table and pulled her friend around the corner to peek into the small closet. Spotty's toenails clicked on the wooden floor as he followed to see but quickly looked disinterested and went back to stalk the pot on the stove.

"Two, four, six, eight rows of ten. Good night, Emmie! You have eighty bottles of moonshine," Ava said.

"Eighty-two counting those two on the table," Emmie corrected.

"What are you going to do with them?" Ava picked up a bottle and eyed it suspiciously.

"I have no idea. Pour them out? I guess that'd be the right thing to do." She took the other jar and put it back in the pantry, then went back over to give the apples a final stir.

Ava gave her a wicked grin. "Then why are you putting that 'shine back in the pantry?"

"I just don't want mess around with it right now. I thought you wanted to head back to your house soon anyway?" She did her best to sidetrack her friend. She knew what she had to do with that 'shine but had no intention of telling Ava.

Pop!

She spun her head around from the stove to see her friend with a jar in one hand and the cap in the other. Ava took a big sniff and drew her head back with wide eyes.

"Just a sip to see what it tastes like, okay? Then we can pour the rest out. Promise." Ava held the jar of 'shine over her heart like she was making a vow.

"Oh, alright." One sip wasn't going to hurt anyone. She got out a couple glasses and poured a tiny splash into each one. The girls clinked glasses and tipped their heads back.

Ava immediately sprayed hers back into the glass coughing like she had ingested some type of rat poison. Emmie forced hers down her throat. FIRE—it felt like fire. Burning all the way down to her gut.

"Oh my gosh," she screeched, running to the sink to fill her glass with water. She drank the entire cup in an attempt to put out the burn. It sort of worked. When she finally caught her breath she turned to find Ava in fits of laughter.

"Your face..." That is all Ava could get out before another swell of laughter took her over.

"That stuff is disgusting. Why in the world people would spend their hard-earned money on that I have no idea," Emmie laughed.

Ava picked up the jar to give it a closer inspection. Spotty barked and stood at attention, his ears cocked sideways. He ran to the front door before they ever heard the knock. All traces of humor left the room.

"Get rid of that. I'll go see who it is," Emmie told her friend.

****

"Hey Miss Emmie." Max waved before she got the door all the way open. Spotty bounced from foot to foot until Max reached down with his good hand to scratch behind his ear.

"Hello, Max, Walter," she smiled at her neighbors. "Come on in."

The three of them walked into the house and stepped into the kitchen.

"Sorry, Emmie, we didn't realize you had company," Walter said, tipping his hat and wiping his hands on his blue jean overalls.

"Oh, it's fine I was just leaving. See you tonight, Emmie," Ava said. She turned on her way out. "Oh, and I added that last ingredient to the applesauce."

Last ingredient? Oh, you have got to be kidding me. Emmie thought.

"Max you look mighty handsome in that hat. You know, those are all the rage in Chicago this summer," Ava added, touching his newsboy cap on her way out the door.

Max's mouth split open with a grin from ear to ear. "Thanks Miss Ava."

She waved like a movie star and headed out the door. Just as dramatic as ever.

"What can I do for ya?" Emmie said, making her way over to stir the applesauce-moonshine mixture. Mainly just to be sure it wasn't emitting some odd smell. The good news, it wasn't.

The apple and cinnamon seemed to cover it up well.

"Sure smells good in here Miss Emmie," Max added licking his lips.

"Well that's because I got some delicious apples from some young kid this morning. You stop by the store tomorrow and I'll have some for you, if you'd like."

The boy nodded his head excitedly.

"Tell her why we're here, boy," Walter prompted.

"Well, I have an offer for you." Max said, looking nervously at his feet. "You said the other day you seen how good I am at my numbers. That's because Mamaw Mae practices with me every night. She helps me with reading too but I've been having a harder time with it. School don't start for another couple of weeks and I..." he paused looking up at her. "I want to be good at this Miss Emmie. I'm not so good at some other things but I am good at book smarts."

That just about broke her heart. She hated for him to think about the things he wasn't good at. Who cares if he had a limp or one hand that worked better than the other? Some of the kids were so hard on him for it.

Max went on, "I figured since you want to be a teacher, that working with me on my reading might be good practice for you too. I can bring you more of them apples if you want? Or Papaw said we could get you some extra ears of corn," he pleaded but kept his chin held high.

"I thought you might be interested in hearing his business proposition." Walter's eyes smiled at the way the tables had turned.

Emmie answered, "Of course, Max. I would be honored to work with a smart, hard-working young man like you. How often were you thinking we should practice together?"

They settled on twice a week for an hour. Emmie was excited about it. Tutoring him really would be good practice for her, if she ever got to enroll in that new teacher's college up on the hill.

"Walt, can I talk to you a second?" she asked.

She led him over to the small pantry and opened the door. He bent down and peeked his head in. When he came out his eyes were wide and he nodded but didn't say a word.

"Think you can get rid of it?" she whispered.

He didn't answer just shrugged like he wasn't sure.

"Maybe we can talk about it?" she whispered, a little annoyed.

"Later," he said, heading back into the kitchen.

She said bye to Walter and Max went into her room to get ready. She put on a dress Ava had given her that she said just didn't fit right anymore. It hung just past her knees with a drop waist, and a beautiful Irish lace overlay. Sometimes Emmie was pretty sure Ava was lying about the clothes not fitting her anymore, it was just an excuse to keep her friend up to date in the latest fashion she had seen in Chicago. Fashion usually took a couple years to make its way down to Kentucky.

The applesauce had cooked to almost nothing while she was getting ready. She had just let it go since Ava had ruined it. When she went over to turn it off, it surprisingly still smelled delicious. Out of curiosity she tasted a spoonful of the concoction. It was phenomenal, so much better than that disgusting fire alcohol she'd had earlier. It still tasted just like applesauce with a hint of the kick that set her mouth on fire earlier. She rinsed out the empty jar on the counter and filled it with the moonshine applesauce she had made. She covered the lid with a square bit of red gingham fabric that she usually used on jams to make it stand out from the other jars in the cupboard. Emmie wasn't exactly sure what to do with it but she'd save it until she figured it out.

Chapter Ten

Silas saw her walk up to the house from his bedroom window. She was dressed up for him. He knew it. Damn it. He didn't have time for this. Silas bent down tied his brown lace-up boots and buttoned his vest. If he could have just kept himself under control a couple of weeks ago he wouldn't have been in this mess.

Now he was walking some tightrope between breaking this girl's heart, which in turn would piss off his cousins, and just trying to get his job done. He was ready to get back to Chicago already. He had been sent down here just to take care of one simple job… one simple task turned into a huge cluster now he was back down here dealing with three-tooth moonshiners for God knows how long.

And to beat it all now he was going to have to spend the days working at his uncle's law firm since apparently the family was telling everyone he was down here for work. Not that Silas really minded helping out. He had a degree and everything. It was just that when he spent the day at the office his brain wasn't always as clear at night as it needed. He couldn't afford sloppy mistakes.

Throw that girl into that mix and he was destined for failure.

"Hello, Emmie." He gave her an easy smile or tried to anyway. Was she this short two weeks ago? He could have sworn she was taller.

"Hi, Silas." She moved past him with barely a look in his direction and walked over to where Ava and the rest of the group stood.

That went well, he thought.

Silas reached down and pulled a cigarette out of his vest pocket and lit it, breathing in deeply and squinting to keep the smoke out of his eye while the flame took.

"Who's cooking tonight?" Emmie asked, looking around for Ms. Jackson, the housekeeper/cook/everything else that was usually on hand when Ava's parents were out of town.

"Oh, Applesauce," Ava cursed with a wicked smile.

Emmie's heart pounded and she turned to look at her friend before she realized Ava was using it as a swear word. Silly flapper lingo nearly gave her a heart attack. She was sure her friend was getting ready to spill her guts about the moonshine applesauce they had just created. Ava always had a big mouth.

The look in Ava's eyes said she thought her little joke was funny. Then she continued, "I completely forgot Ms. Jackson is off this week. Well, I'm sure we can throw something together."

"Doll, when is the last time you threw anything together in the kitchen?" Gabe laughed.

"That's pollywampus. I can do this. We can do this." She held out a hand to Emmie.

The girls entered the room twenty minutes later with a couple trays of meats, cheeses, and crackers, after raiding the cabinets.

"We didn't have much to choose from. You need to go to the store tomorrow. Or I could bring some things by after work for you," Emmie said.

"That'd be great if you wouldn't mind," Vince agreed.

Gabe and Ava went out for a walk after dinner. Vince excused himself to call his fiancée. Which left Trick, Silas, and Emmie in an awkward silence until Trick walked over to the piano. He sat down and became Beethoven Jr. Clearly showing off. It worked.

"Wow. That is amazing." Emmie walked over and sat on the bench next to him.

"Do you play?" he asked.

"Oh, no. Always wanted to though." She stared down at his hands.

"Here you can do this," he said sincerely. "Just do what I do."

He sat on one end slowly playing a couple notes at a time. Then she finger-pecked following his lead, mimicking a nursery song. Silas watched as her brow creased in concentration. Her face was beautiful as she studied his pattern and tried her best to match his brothers' motions.

Trick reached his arm around her to correct the finger placement on one of the keys. He left it longer than was necessary. Silas fought the wave of jealousy.

This shit was ridiculous. He should just leave the room. Go about his business. But he couldn't bring himself to do it.

"Attagirl." Trick bumped her shoulder.

She threw her arms up in a cheer. Then gave him a sideways hug. "Thanks Trick. You have no idea how long I've wanted to play on this piano. It's been here for years and I've always been too afraid to ask."

Trick smiled like a dog with its head out the window. Silas swore his brother's tongue was getting ready to roll out of his mouth. The worst part was Emmie noticed it because her grin got even bigger. Their flirting was painful to watch—annoyingly painful.

"Give it a rest. Good God," Silas heard himself say.

They looked at him bewildered like they'd even forgotten he was in the room.

"She barely pecked out four notes of that song. I am not sure that calls for such a celebration," he sneered.

Trick looked amused and scooted closer to Emmie. Pushing his brother was one of his favorite past times… but Silas wasn't in the mood tonight.

"Excuse me for boring you with my lack of piano skills," she spit back at him and moved to get up from the bench, stumbling on her dress as she spun.

He walked up to her and grabbed her elbow to help. Emmie quickly jerked away from his hold. That pissed him off more.

"Your piano playing wasn't half as annoying as your skill-less flirting with my brother. First me, then him. Vince and Ava are right, you really are a friend of this family," he said quietly.

Trick opened his mouth to speak but was quieted with a sharp look from Silas.

Emmie's mouth fell open and froze there, unable to think what to say next.

So she said nothing. Just grabbed her bag and headed out the door.

"I'd say you screwed that up completely," Trick said walking up behind his brother.

"Shut up, Trick," Silas answered.

****

"Why do you have your sewing chair in here Emma?" Mr. Thomas asked, pointing to the small wooden rocker he all but required her to sit in while she worked. He was a weird man.

"Sometimes I can't hear the bell in the side parlor. So, it made sense to bring it in here, if that is okay with you," she said.

Lately, Emmie had taken to sewing in the store. It seemed so frequently without a shopkeeper that she was doing both jobs, which was getting to be ridiculous. She'd been toying with the idea of asking for a raise. If she was going to be doing two jobs she may as well be paid for them, right?

"I actually wanted to talk to you about that… Paul." Why was it so hard to say his real name?

"Yes, dear?" he asked.

Dear—that caught her off guard. She sucked in a breath for courage. "Since I'm spending about half my time watching the shop lately while your brother's been out, I wondered if I might be able to get a raise."

"A raise?" Mr. Thomas laughed. "I think we both know I pay you well enough and all you've given me so far is a little bit of sewing," he added in his natural condescending air.

"You know the deadline for tuition is next week. I was just thinking that since I'm doing both jobs that maybe you could advance me…" she continued, protesting.

"We've had this discussion before, Emma. I don't pay you to think." He arched his brow to see how far she was going to push him. "Whoever filled your pretty head with thoughts of college should be tarred and feathered. Come and sit." He pointed to the chair.

"My mom, Mr. Thomas. She's the one who believed in me," she whispered.

"Well, a pretty girl like you has no reason for books. You should be kept like fine china," he said, touching her cheek.

I'll show you fine china. She turned and moved back to her chair.

"Excuse me sir, can I help you?" Mr. Thomas was clearly irritated that their moment had been interrupted.

Emmie was relieved until she heard the voice of the customer ask for her—his voice.

"Silas?" she asked, startled.

Chapter Eleven

"I'm sorry. Emma is busy right now. How can I help you?" A fake smile was plastered across Mr. Thomas's face.

Silas stared at him for a moment. Emmie was sitting three feet to his left. This was ridiculous. He glanced at her. She shrugged her shoulders and rolled her eyes in reply. He wasn't sure if the eye roll was for him or the storekeeper.

"Look, Paul is it? I just need to have a quick word with Emmie. And I can see her…" He pointed a finger in her direction. "She's sitting right there. It will just be a second." He looked right at Mr. Thomas.

"I said, she's busy and time is money, son. What can I do for you?" Mr. Thomas said, taking a step closer to Silas.

Silas tried to decide if it was worth the fight.

"No thanks, Paul. I can take care of myself." He turned and walked to the nearest aisle and started looking through cans.

What in the world is he doing? Emmie wondered. Mr. Thomas had stopped her from having to talk to Silas, so there was at least one redeeming quality to him. She smiled to herself.

She went back to smocking a rose pattern, stealing glances at Silas as he slowly moved around filling his basket with this and that.

"Look," he said, slamming a can down on the shelf.

Mr. Thomas was more than annoyed.

"I just came in to say," he paused and swallowed hard, "I'm sorry. I said things I shouldn't have." Everyone in the shop was listening. Emmie felt red moving up her neck. Shades of embarrassment were coloring her face.

He looked over at her. "You're a good girl. I shouldn't have said otherwise. I acted like some kind of fool." Silas shrugged his shoulders and shook his head like he didn't know what to say next.

Emmie dropped the toddler-sized dress she was working on and stepped away from her chair. Words always failed her at times like this. Unfortunately, she didn't have time to think of what to say.

She may have been turning red but it was Mr. Thomas that saw red. "Out," he screamed, pointing at the door. Spit flew from his lips. Then he composed himself and looked around at the two ladies who has just entered the store. "Customers only, Mr. McDowell."

Silas walked over and grabbed two more things off the shelf and took them to the counter, letting the basket smack down. "Well, you got yourself a customer right here." He spread his arms wide over the goods.

Emmie had never seen Mr. Thomas look at someone with such animosity. He quickly started totaling the cost without so much as looking up in his direction. She walked over to the counter next to Mr. Thomas and started putting the items in a bag. He turned around slowly and grabbed her hand.

"Go. Sit. In. Your. Chair." Then he whispered, "My Emma."

She closed her eyes and sucked in a breath.

It wasn't worth it.

She sat down in the chair like a whipped pup.

She glanced up at Silas and mouthed a simple, "Thanks."

She felt like a child.

People of Mr. Thomas's generation were so controlling.

Just like Ronnie.

Silas's eyes flamed with fire. He opened his mouth to speak but closed it, clenching his fist. Mr. Thomas counted out his change. The other customers went back to their shopping.

"Thanks, Paul," Silas said, grabbing the goods with one arm. "Oh, and you're wrong you know."

"Enlighten me, Silas. What am I wrong about?" he whispered leaning across the counter.

"Overheard your conversation earlier. She should go to college... she's smart enough. It'd get her away from Daddies like you," he spit out the last part. Emmie stopped sewing; she'd already screwed up the pattern anyway. Her eyes opened wide. She wasn't sure if she felt happy or offended at his comment.

"Get out," Mr. Thomas shouted. "You are no longer welcome in this store."

Silas smiled and touched his hat to say goodbye. "See you tonight, Em," he shouted as he turned and headed out the door.

"Emma," Mr. Thomas started, then was distracted by something behind her. She turned to see his brother Will coming through the parlor.

"Where in the hell have you been? We need to talk, now." Mr. Thomas met his brother in the parlor. "Emma, watch the shop." She folded the dress and put it in the basket with her sewing things and walked to the counter to help an older lady waiting patiently to buy some sugar and a bolt of white fabric.

Her mind was still reeling from the scene just minutes ago. But the thing that stood out most... Silas believed in her. He believed she should go to school... and he told Mr. Thomas. That was better than any apology he could have given.

****

Gabe and Trick picked up speed to keep up with Silas as he walked out the store.

"How'd the apology go?" Gabe asked, smashing out his cigarette.

"Fine," Silas answered, passing the bag of groceries off to his brother.

Gabe nodded, not wanting to push his friend any further. Silas wasn't really one to be pushed.

"That's all you're gonna say?" Trick didn't mind pushing. "My big brother, that I have *never* in my life heard say he was sorry, is only going to give me a 'fine'?"

"Shut up, Trick," Silas smiled and lit his own cigarette. They walked the next block in silence. He knew they wanted to know what had happened in there. Damn, in this tiny hicktown they'd probably know before this weekend anyway.

"I don't know if the apology took. She heard it though, so Vince and Ava should be satisfied," Silas added. They'd given him seven kinds of hell, discovering she'd left when they were out of the room last night.

Gabe nodded again, accepting the information without asking for more. That's why their friendship had worked all these years. Trick looked eager for more. Dumb kid. Silas grinned. He would tell them one more piece but that was it.

"I didn't make any friends outta her boss Mr. Thomas though. That guy hates me," he laughed. Just when Trick looked like he might ask why, Silas cut him off. "I gotta go check on Uncle's firm. I haven't made an appearance in a couple days. Tell Ava I asked Emmie to come over tonight."

****

When Will came out of the office he looked all flustered. He just started opening crates of goods without saying anything as he walked past her.

"Emma, I need to speak to you," Mr. Thomas barked. She knew she was in trouble. Although she had done nothing wrong, she hated this feeling. Her hands started to tremble, like always. Even when she was younger and Ronnie had some halfhearted excuse to spank her, she had felt half scared to death. This was why she'd spent most of her life trying to be as perfect as possible. If you were what everyone else expected you to be, you didn't have to feel that awful trembling feeling.

When she walked into the parlor he patted the couch for her to sit down next to him.

"Emmie, we need to talk. I don't like what happened here today. You cannot bring your personal life here to work."

She nodded.

"I'm just going to lay it all out here Emma." He looked at her right in the eyes. "I can understand why you have a soft heart for Walter's family. I understand why you have taken such a liking to that little..." he paused, thinking of the right word, "the little boy, Max. But I must say something about your choice of acquaintances. You are better than your friends."

48

"What friends?" Emmie asked puzzled, "Silas?"

"All of them Emma, dear. The whole clan of them: Ava, her parents, Vince, Silas, the others. You know you are better than them. They are no good." He touched her knee. "They are one step removed from immigrants. Half of them Italian, the other half Irish heathens."

"Mr. Thomas," she started then paused when he arched his brow, "...Paul, they are Americans." He snorted at this. "And they most certainly are not heathens. They go to church more than I do." She threw her arms out exacerbated.

"Dear that is not church. They don't even call it going to church. They are Catholics," he spit out like he'd just told her they were atheist.

She actually laughed at this. "Oh, Mr. Thomas. I have been with them. I assure you it is in fact a church."

"This is no laughing matter, Emma. Show me your friends and I'll show you who you are. You don't want your reputation tainted with the likes of them. I won't have it," he said.

"Well, thank you for the warning," she huffed. "Anything else? I am very busy."

"Don't be upset with me. I have your best interests at heart. Surely you know that," he pleaded. "Besides, do you know there is a rumor they make all of those trips to Chicago because their business is on the wrong side of the law?"

She opened her mouth to speak but stopped. It wasn't worth dignifying his stupidity with a comment. Ava's father's firm had represented local police officers and city officials. People were always just jealous of those that were successful.

"Well, I actually have to get going. I was supposed to be off thirty minutes ago," she added snidely.

"Remember my advice, Emma," he called after her.

Her hands were still shaking... her heartbeat was still pounding in her ears... but she didn't stop. Emmie just kept on walking right out the door.

Chapter Twelve

"R...o...b...i...n..." the boy paused sounding out each letter.

She showed him how to chunk the word into two words and a light bulb went off. "I know it, Miss Emmie. I know it. Rob...in... Robin. Like the bird and it matches this picture." The boy jumped up elated with himself.

"You did it, Max. See I told you that you'd make a great reader. You just have to know all the tricks," she smiled up at him. They were sitting on a bench outside the store. This bench had turned into a classroom two days a week and it was so much fun for both of them. Sadly, it was more fun than he'd probably have once he finally started school. Then it'd be all about memorizing and copying things from the board. Emmie knew from experience. When she graduated, she would do her best to change that.

"I never knew big words was just made up of small ones," he said, thumping the book with his good hand.

"Well, what in the world is all this racket?" Walter walked up and stopped in front of them. He hooked his thumbs under the straps of his overalls like he always did.

"Pawpaw I just figured out a big trick in reading," he said, holding the book up.

"Trick?" Walt questioned.

"Yep, Max just figured out that sometimes there's smaller words in the big ones," Emmie answered.

"Hmm," Walter thought, unsure what to say. "Well, good job Max. Mamaw Mae is headed home and needs you to help shuck some more corn she's putting up. Tell Miss Emmie thank you."

The boy did as he was told and turned to head home with a little pep in his step.

"Wait," Emmie called after him. "Would you mind walking Spotty home? I'm heading to Ava's and he will follow me."

"Sure, Miss Emmie. Me and Spotty's good friends, ain't we?" Max patted his thigh with his good hand and whistled. The dog looked up at Emmie reluctantly.

"Go on. I'll be home later." She smiled pushing him toward Max. The lazy old thing stretched then took his time walking over to Max.

When Max and the dog made it to the end of the row of shops, Walter spoke, "He really learned good for ya? Think he's gonna make it at school?" Walt laid it all out on in the line.

"Oh yes. He's a really fast learner," Emmie assured him.

"That's real good." He looked relieved. "I appreciate what you are doing."

"Honestly, he doesn't need my help, really. I think I'm learning more from him than he is from me," she said.

Walter nodded and looked down at his feet.

"What ever's affected his moving… it hasn't hurt a thing in his mind. That boy is smart." Emmie reached up and touched the old man's arm.

Walt bit his bottom lip, causing the gray hair that surrounded it to stand straight up. He only nodded. Too many emotions to speak. Emmie got that.

"Ya got time to walk with me a minute?" he said, glancing at Will and Mr. Thomas through the shop windows. "I need to tell you a couple things."

Emmie fell into step with him as they headed out of town. When they had walked past a few shops he started speaking again.

"I've been thinking about what you found. You don't need to be stuck with that stuff in your house. Part of me hopes maybe you've had the good sense just to pour it down the sink." He looked at her for an answer. Her eyes let him know the jars of moonshine were still there in the pantry. "That's what I figured. Well, the bigger part of me thinks that would have been a waste of money anyway," he said.

"I guess I've been having the same battle. I don't know which it is," she started.

"Just hear me out." He stopped walking and turned to look at her. "If I had the money outright I'd just buy that 'shine from you and give you your money so you could get yourself into that school and outta thinking of all this mess. But here's the kicker—I ain't got it and I ain't got no way to get the money quick neither. I've been thinking about it since you showed me them jars."

"Really it's fine, Walt. I should have thought before I asked you. That would be a lot of 'shine for you just to sell all at once. You can just have it. I can move it to the cave for you. It's probably yours anyway, right? I mean you and Ronnie worked this thing together."

"See that's the thing Emmie. That's why I ain't got no way to unload 'em. I got a few folks on my list. That's how I got into doing this, just a few friends that like to wet their whistle every now and again. That's pretty much all I been making for these last few months," Walter explained.

Emmie nodded trying to understand where he was going with telling her all of this.

"See, I ain't got no way to get money or sell all them jars because I don't know who we was selling 'shine to. Ronnie liked to drink but he didn't take all that you found for himself. He'd always hide a big mess of it, sell it, and then come back for more when the next batch was done. Ronnie didn't want me to know who he was selling to; said that wasn't how our business was gonna work. His job was to sell and my job was to make. To tell ya the truth I never had no reason to question it. I figured if he ever got busted by the revenuers the less I knew about any of it the better. And then last spring when Cliff's barn got burned down—well, I figured all the better that I didn't know nothing about it."

"Cliff Harris's barn? What's that got to do with you and Ronnie making 'shine?" Emmie asked, thoroughly confused.

He swore under his breath. "I shouldn't have said that. I thought everybody knew Cliff was making money on the side with the revenuers. He was a fool bragging about it to everyone… Making 'shine, used to be about tradition. Family heritage. Now, I don't know… I didn't want no part of those moonshine feuds."

"Walt, the only thing I knew about 'shine until a couple of weeks ago was that Ronnie was as mean as a snake when he drank it," she laughed then thought a moment about what he'd just told her. Her brain was trying to fit all the pieces together. "Wait, Walt, are you telling me you think Ronnie had something to do with Cliff's barn getting burned? Was he involved in these 'shine feuds you mentioned?" she whispered.

"No, no. I ain't saying that. They already laid blame on the Johnson's. They are saying that old man is the one that burned his barn," Walter said, looking off in the distance.

"Johnson. You mean Bo's folks? Are you saying his family is mixed up in all this too?" Emmie asked, trying to piece it all together.

"I don't know what I'm saying. More than I should, I guess. I just know there is stuff going on that I don't want no part of... and I sure don't want you to have no part of," he said. They walked on in silence for a few minutes, each lost in their own mind.

Finally Walt continued, "Well, I guess my point is I really ain't got nobody much to sell this 'shine I been making to... much less what you found in your pantry. I am going to get that out of your house though. I don't like you having it," he said.

"Sure. You can just have it. You have helped me more than enough already. Want me to help you move it to the cave?" she asked.

"No, I don't want you to touch it. I'll bring my truck over to your house and pick it up tomorrow morning, okay?" he asked.

"Sounds fine. And Walter, thanks for all your help so far. I know you don't have to take on my troubles," she added and meant it. If he didn't have a way to sell the moonshine he'd made in her cave, then he was paying her to make a paste these last couple of weeks that he didn't really even need. It must have been his way of trying to help her. She'd have to think of some way to make it up to him.

"One more thing Emmie." He started walking again.

"Are you sure there is no hope of you just taking up with Mr. Thomas?" he asked. "I know it's none of my business. He could probably just pull the money you need right out of his safe, if he thought you might be Mrs. Thomas someday. It'd keep you out of all this 'shine talk." He kept looking straight ahead.

"There is not a snowball's chance in Hades that I will *ever* be Mrs. Thomas, I promise you that. Anyway, he's not too keen on the idea of me going to school. He thinks it's a waste of time." Emmie arched a brow hoping to end this part of their conversation.

"Well, can't say I'm surprised to hear it. I understand." He ran his hands over his whiskers while he thought of what to say next. "Then I'll just say, be careful around him. Don't bring up nothing around him that relates to 'shining or would even make him think of 'shining. He don't think much of it."

Emmie waited for Walt to go on but he didn't seem to have anything else to say.

"I gotta head on home. I'll see you tomorrow. Thanks again for working with Max." Walt turned and headed toward his house. Emmie hadn't walked another twenty-five feet when she heard a car slow down next to her.

"Headed my way?" Silas asked leaning out the window of his car.

"Actually, yes I am," she said.

"Want a ride?" He opened the door.

"That'd be nice." She stepped into the black Model T Ford and closed the door behind her.

"So this is why your shoes are always dirty. You don't have a car," he smiled, changing gears.

"My shoes are not always dirty." She looked down at the layers of dirt creeping up her soles. *Are they?*

He smirked, never looking up from the road.

"And even if they were. It wouldn't be a very gentlemanly thing for you to point out." She crossed her arms trying to decide if she was mad or teasing him.

"Sweetheart, make no mistake—I am not a gentleman." He shifted gears again and the car picked up speed as it took them to Ava's house.

Chapter Thirteen

They drove for a bit in silence while she thought about what Walter had said. Who in the world would burn down Cliff's barn? She knew Cliff from Ronnie's church. He seemed like a nice enough guy. Did Ronnie have it in him to do something like that? Emmie also wondered how Walter knew Mr. Thomas's opinion on moonshine. What she did know was Mr. Thomas would never tell her. She leaned down and started casually brushing the dust off her black Mary Jane heels.

"Now don't be getting all that dust in my car." Silas glanced over at her, a smile peaking out the corner of his lips.

"Oh shush, you infuriating thing. I can see you smiling, you know." She pointed at his mouth. "Right there, I see the start of the forbidden Silas grin."

He laughed.

She was starting to feel more at ease around him. In the last couple weeks since his apology they'd seen each other nearly every day. She had been going to Ava's almost every night. Her house felt too dark and lonely. Ava had asked her countless times to pack up and stay with her but she just wasn't ready yet.

"You should do it more often, you know," the words escaped her lips before she even had the chance to think.

"Talk about your dirty shoes?" He loved to keep her riled up as long as possible.

"No, smile. Makes you look years younger." She tried to turn it into a joke but wasn't as witty as he was.

"I'll keep that in mind." And just like that he looked more serious again.

"Oh, come on. I was just teasing. You know you don't look old." She smacked his arm playfully.

He rubbed his arm and looked genuinely surprised. "I never took you for a violent girl, Emma Talbot."

"Only when forced," she smiled.

"I'll remember that," he answered.

"And please don't call me Emma. My mama only called me that when I was in trouble... and even worse than that... it's what Mr. Thomas calls me." She faked a shiver for effect.

"Why don't you just tell him you don't like it?" He arched a brow and glanced over at her as they turned into the driveway.

"I did correct him once when I first started working there. He told me 'Emmie is a child's name and you are a lady now, Emma,'" she mocked his voice perfectly. "It wasn't worth the argument, so I let it go."

Silas shook his head. "He's a real pain in the ass isn't he? Why do you work for him?"

"Ronnie took out a mortgage against the house last year and I'm trying to pay it off. Mr. Thomas pays me better than I deserve, so I put up with it. And you heard the rest the other day. I'm going to go to school and I'll need money for that too. Doesn't look like it'll happen this semester but I have to keep trying, right? And I never really got to say thanks," Emmie added.

"For what?" He looked puzzled.

"For telling Mr. Thomas that I am good enough for college." She looked right at him. Her big blue eyes wide and honest.

"Oh, well it was the truth. You shouldn't have to listen to someone put you down like that," he shrugged.

"Well, thanks. Nobody really understands why I want to do it go to school so badly." He looked over at her again as she spoke. He was surprised she was telling him all this. He wasn't the type of person that people usually felt comfortable opening up to. She just kept talking and talking. Odd that he didn't mind. He didn't really want to think about that too much.

"See my momma wanted to be a teacher. But then she had me, married Ronnie, life happened. Mama put her dreams in me. She believed in me then I started to believe in me too. It wasn't until this summer when

Ronnie died and all the expenses fell on my feet that I really got scared. I may not be able to do it. I went to Mr. Thomas and told him about my plan. He laughed but said he'd give me a job to help pay for the house. He pays me too well and I hate it. I hate feeling like I owe that crazy man something."

"Maybe you could find another job. Have you thought of talking to Uncle Al? I bet he could get you some secretarial work, answering phones or something," he suggested.

"I really don't want to ask him for that. If something came open there, I'd apply in a heartbeat. But I really don't want any special favors," she answered.

"Swallowing your pride might be worth it to get outta that shop." He pulled into the carport on the side of the house and turned to face her.

Emmie thought for a second. "You might be right. I swear the next person that asks me if I've ever just considered marrying Mr. Thomas will get more than a soft smack to the arm like you got." She tried to joke but he didn't laugh.

Marry Mr. Thomas. Marry Paul Thomas. He'd seen girls back home do that before. Mr. Thomas was just the type of leach that would feed off her desperate situation too.

"You're right. You'll never have to marry that man. If I ever hear anyone suggest it you won't have to be the one hitting. I'll take care of that for ya." He tried to smile but it didn't reach his eyes. He was too annoyed at the thought of someone taking advantage of her.

Why do I care? he inwardly shouted.

But he knew why he cared. No use kidding himself. If he was going to hell anyway he might as well ride this thing out till it was over. He scooted closer to her and brushed a loose strand of hair from her eyes. The color that crept into her cheeks was beautiful. She did this every time he touched her. He ran his fingers down the side of her face and leaned in and kissed her.

Heart pounding.

Intense.

Soft.

Sweet.

It was all those words mixed into one. She ran her fingers down the stubble that darkened his cheek. His eyes looked so alive, so warm, so kind when he was here with her. She could live in this moment forever.

"Whoo Hoo, it's about time you two just got on with it. We've been about to explode from the tension around you both lately," Trick shouted, jumping up and down on the side rail of the car—causing it to jerk side to side.

Emmie and Silas looked up to see they had not just one spectator but an entire audience.

Chapter Fourteen

"**G**et off the damn car, Trick," Silas laughed, then reached around Emmie and thrust open the door with more force than was necessary, knocking his brother off the side rail.

"After you." He motioned for her to exit.

"How kind of you to open my door... and you said you weren't a gentleman?" Emmie smiled sarcastically and stepped out of the car. She walked over and helped Trick up off the ground. "Sorry. He doesn't like to be teased, I guess," she apologized for Silas.

"Actually, I don't like you teased." Silas put a hand on the small of her back and led her through the door.

She arched an eyebrow. "I seem to remember you poking fun at my dusty shoes?" she made the phrase a question.

"That was different. It was me," he shrugged then added, "I don't like you teased about kissing and stuff."

When they got into the house Ava was all smiles but she didn't say a word about the moment they'd just seen. "So, what's the plan for tonight?"

"Swimming?" Trick suggested.

"Too cool. That water was like ice this morning. I think it's about time to close it down." Ava answered.

"I'm gonna take it easy tonight. I've got to head back to Chicago early tomorrow. I promised Kate I'd meet her this weekend to listen to something about wedding plans she'd made," Vince said then pretended to hang himself.

"Oh! I wish I could go." Ava pouted. "But I hope to be planning my own soon. Won't that be so much fun, Gabe?" she squealed.

"Yeah, can't wait babe," he said with a laugh.

Well that was news. Emmie thought. She had somehow missed when they'd gotten that serious. A glance around showed no one else looked so surprised.

"I probably should have directed that question at Emmie. Lord knows she will probably be more help planning than you will," Ava added.

"Can't wait," Emmie repeated his answer but with a much more excited tone.

"As exciting as this conversation is," Trick added, "we still don't know what to do tonight. I am so tired of just sitting around here. There has got to be something to do in this town."

Gabe walked over and said something to Silas that the others couldn't hear. Silas thought about it for a minute and then nodded in agreement.

"You all go get ready. We're going out," Gabe said with a sly grin.

"Where?" Emmie asked.

"Surprise. Can you all be ready in half an hour?" Silas answered.

Ava clapped her hands excited, grabbed Emmie's hands and pulled her upstairs before she could ask any further questions.

"Ava I don't have any clothes here. Can I borrow something? I'm not sure my work shift is going to be fitting for where we are going," Emmie said, looking at herself in Ava's full-length mirror.

"Of course! I have just the thing. This is way too short on me, so it should be perfect for you. And here put these on." Ava tossed a dress and what seemed to be fifteen pounds of pearls on the bed next to Emmie.

"All these?"

"Yes, and this is for your head," she added, throwing a brown headband with a cluster of white beads on the front.

The girls got ready with lightning speed, barely talking as they rushed around the room. Ava stood in front of her friend, gave a little spin and put her arms out for inspection.

"You look gorgeous," Emmie said because she did. Ava had the body and personality to pull off this crazy eclectic look. Her dress was black lace dropped and cut out in all the right places.

"What about me… are you positive I don't look ridiculous?" Emmie asked.

Emmie was stunning; Ava could never understand how she didn't see this about herself. She could wear men's overalls and have dirt caked on her hands and still be pretty. Emmie didn't need all the makeup and fancy clothes but she wore it well.

"Will you believe me if I tell you look amazing?" Ava questioned.

"Probably not," Emmie smirked.

"Then let's just see what Silas says… So, are you happy, you know about you and Silas?" Ava asked, leaning in to her friend.

Emmie fidgeted with her beads. "Yeah, I mean it's kinda early…"

"Pish Posh. It's not early. Silas kissed you, again. That was a real kiss. He's crazy for you, I just know it," Ava bounced.

"It was real, wasn't it?" Emmie touched her lips.

****

Silas drove. Ava and Gabe took the back, which left Emmie smashed next to Trick in the front.

"Where are we going?" Emmie asked for the hundredth time. They'd driven away from town toward the north end of the county.

"Patience is a virtue," Silas replied.

"If we are going to some field party, we are all sorely overdressed," Emmie warned.

"I promise you that we will not be partying in a field tonight," Gabe laughed.

The drive was long. It seemed they had been in the car forever. Emmie was sure she would have a permanent imprint in her leg from whatever Trick had in his pocket.

"Ooh…" she called out when they went through a particularly sharp curve and she was slammed into him.

"Good grief, Trick. What is that?" She felt around on the outside leg of his pants.

Trick just smiled, "That's a little personal don't you think?"

Silas tried to look disinterested in their conversation. He failed.

"Really Trick, what in the world is that?" It tinged when she tapped on it. They went over another bump and it... sloshed?

"Patrick McDowell! I know what that is," she laughed.

He faked his best innocent smile then took the flask out of his pocket and had a sip. "Sweetheart if that bothers you, you're not going to like where we are going," Trick said.

"Shush, Trick. You'll ruin our surprise. And I just love surprises," Ava cried.

"It doesn't matter. We are here anyway," Gabe said, pointed to the row of shops in the small downtown area.

"This is the surprise... Smith's Grove? You wanted to eat here? What does this tiny town have to offer that we don't have in Bowling Green?" Ava asked confused.

"Just trust me, eh?" Gabe said kissing her hand.

They pulled up to a row of three connected buildings: a bank, a general store and a run-down restaurant.

Emmie looked up at Silas with her eyebrows raised in question. He decided not to say anything. Her curiosity was a part of the fun for him. He wondered how she would take this. It would either a wonderful night or a total disaster. Either way he needed to know this about her. She was such a good girl but if she was really going to be with him, he needed to see how she would handle the unexpected. This was definitely going to be unexpected. Silas smiled in spite of himself, looking forward to her reaction.

"Looks like they have a frog legs special tonight! Yum," Trick said, walking up to the sign out front and rubbing his belly to add emphasis to the words.

"I am not eating in there." Ava looked thoroughly disgusted at the grimy windows of the restaurant.

Emmie elbowed her friend. Honestly, she could be rude. The guys had put thought into this outing, so there must be a reason they wanted to eat here, even if it didn't look like the most appetizing place. "I'm sure it will be really good. Can't judge a book by its cover, right Ava?"

"Emmie this book has a really bad cover," Ava snarled, reading down the sign. "Chicken livers platter. I can't do it. I'm sorry."

Gabe belly-laughed, grabbed her hand, and led her around the edge of the building. Ava's mouth dropped open and a light bulb of awareness flashed in her eyes.

What in the world? Emmie wondered, as she stood by the door and watched Gabe, Ava, and Trick disappear around the corner.

Silas walked up, put his arm around her waist and pulled her close to his body, "Don't let go of me, okay?"

She nodded completely confused.

"Trust me?" he asked sincerely, his deep blue eyes searching hers.

She nodded again.

Chapter Fifteen

Silas left his hand around her waist as they walked on. He wanted any wandering eyes to understand that she was there with him from the minute they walked through the door. Emmie looked confused as they walked past the entrance to the greasy spoon that fronted the real establishment. He couldn't believe she was willing to eat here in this horrid place and never complain.

Her shoes sank into the mud as they rounded the building. Maybe they had planned a picnic out back? She looked around for a blanket or table but there was nothing. They turned the corner and walked around the back of the building. The stench of garbage was repulsive. She did her best not to make a face as they walked around it because she could feel Silas watching her. Emmie didn't want to be judgmental and hurt his feelings but she was starting to agree with Ava—this book did have a really bad cover.

The rest of the gang was huddled around the doors of the cellar. "Ready?" Gabe asked Silas.

Silas looked around and nodded.

Gabe pulled open the cellar door and laid it flat on the ground. "Quick." Ava opened her mouth to say something. "Now, quick," he repeated and walked ahead of her down the stairs. Ava followed behind holding onto the back of his jacket.

"Come on." Silas pulled Emmie forward never letting go. She could feel her heels sliding on the damp concrete stairs as they descended deeper into the cellar. It was cool, damp, and dark.

Trick grabbed the doors and pulled them closed as he stepped down the stairs. Just before it completely snapped shut Gabe reached up and pulled a chain. A single bulb emitted a yellow light that barely saved them from the pitch black.

Emmie felt her heart pounding in her chest. What in the world was she doing? Anything that leads you into a dark cellar cannot be good, right?

"Trust me, remember?" Silas looked down at her and brushed a hair off her cheek.

"Silas, I…" she started, then broke off. He was so calm, relaxed. She found peace in his demeanor. "Okay," she nodded.

"Alright. Knock three times," Silas told Trick.

Trick did as he was told.

"Sorry. No deliveries today," a muffled voice called from the other side.

"Knock twice," Silas whispered to Trick.

At once a small peephole opened and a large brown eye stared back at them waiting.

"Shine on," Silas said to the eye.

The peephole snapped shut, followed by a series of creeks, flips, and knocks. The door squeaked open to reveal a short man with dark skin and the most beautiful deep brown eyes. He was barely Emmie's height. He reached up and pulled the cellar's light cord leaving them with only thin strip of light spilling out from where he stood in the basement.

"Welcome Mr. McDowell. We got your call and everything is ready for you." He turned and nodded at Gabe then Trick.

As they walked into the cellar, they were surrounded by restaurant goods: boxes of corn, sacks of potatoes and flour, broken chairs, and old tables. They must be under the restaurant.

"Right this way. Watch your step ladies," he said stepping over a broken pallet.

They stopped when they reached the heavy steel door in back of the cellar. The small man reached up a tightly balled fist and knocked on the door five times. The sound echoed through the small basement.

The door opened and Emmie could not believe her eyes. It was a full restaurant. There were ten square tables draped in white cloths and a couple of larger booths in the back corners. The soft lighting of the chandeliers added a warm orange glow to the stonewalls that enclosed them. They must be under the store… maybe the bank too.

This was so weird. Why would there be such an elaborate hidden restaurant under that grimy one upstairs? The tall blond that answered this door was talking feverishly with Silas and Gabe. He was all smiles and pleasantness as he led them to one of the booths in the back. "We're so glad to see you've brought these lovely ladies. Everything is ready for you at the back table." He held an arm out to the large booth to the right.

That's when it caught her eye. Half of the length of the stonewall to the right was an honest-to-goodness bar. There wasn't liqueur on the shelf behind the bar. It was just filled with some glasses but she could see a man in a long white apron stirring some concoction. Although she wasn't sure whom it was for... this place was like a ghost town other than her party and the staff.

She scooted around to the center of the round bench as full awareness dawned on her. She'd heard ramblings of places like this in big cities, whispers of blind pigs or underground saloons. Places that didn't give up the nightlife just because of the 18th amendment. Of course, when she'd read about them it was usually because they'd been raided and carts full of people had been taken to jail.

Her pulse quickened at the possibility. She looked around at her friends. Ava was elated, smiling, lighting a cigarette, and saying things like amazing and wonderful place. Gabe looked happy he'd pulled off a good surprise. Trick hadn't sat down yet. He'd stopped off at the bar and was engaged in conversation with the man in the long white apron that worked there. Silas, well... Silas was watching her look at everyone and everything around them.

"You brought me to a blind pig?" she asked.

"A blind pig? No," he laughed, "I wouldn't take you to one of those rough places. This is a restaurant and I promise the food is much better than it looked upstairs."

"But I see a bar over there," she questioned, "and we had to go down through a basement and speak passwords and knock special ways.... It feels like a blind pig."

"Honey, a blind pig is a roughneck saloon. Yes, there is one of those here but I would never let you go there. This is just a restaurant that is private. Members only. A speakeasy. Not as nice as what we have in Chicago but pretty good for a little country one."

"Speakeasy." Emmie tried the word out. She had heard the word. "What do we do here?"

He laughed at her question. "Emmie girl, we eat. We relax." He rubbed his brow in exasperation. "Whatever you usually do out with friends. You just have the option of having a drink if you want." He wasn't sure how this was going.

She nodded her head and took a long swig of the water that the waiter had just put down on the table.

"Can I get ya something else to drink?" the waiter asked.

Emmie looked at Silas, leaned in, and whispered in his ear, because she was too embarrassed to ask aloud. "Like moonshine? Is that what he's asking me? Because I really don't like the taste of that stuff."

"We're going to need just a minute." Silas sent the waiter away.

Chapter Sixteen

"Sure. Sure. Mr. McDowell. I'll just get Mr. Del Grande's drinks and be back shortly," he said with only the faintest southern drawl.

The waiter walked away from the table to give them privacy. Gabe and Ava were into their own private conversation, faces close, Ava was giggling. Silas scooted closer to Emmie.

"Em?" he made her name a question.

"Yeah," she answered, wide eyes still periodically glancing around at her surroundings.

"Do you want to leave?" he asked sincerely.

She thought it over. He could tell she was having an internal debate. He could almost imagine the little angel and devil on her shoulder arguing with each other. After a few moments she closed her eyes in silent resolve. He wasn't usually a betting man but he would put money on the fact they were not eating here tonight. It'd been a piss poor idea anyway. What was he thinking?

"No," she said quickly, like she was afraid if she didn't answer fast she would change her mind.

"No?"

"Yes.... my answer is no. I want to stay but I'll need you to help me understand some things, okay?" she asked.

"On a scale from one to ten how much trouble would I be in the if the police or revenuers showed up?"

"Zero," he said honestly.

"Zero because it's not illegal?" she asked.

"Zero because I have this under control and that's all you need to know. You said you trusted me." He set his mouth in a firm line showing that he wasn't really going to be pushed any further with the legality question.

He helped manage a law firm for goodness sake how could he skirt this issue?

Well, she wasn't going to be pushed either. "There is a difference in being trusted and being plain ole stupid, Silas."

His eyebrows rose with surprise but he said nothing else. He hadn't expected that. Usually when he told someone that's all you need to know they stopped talking.

"Okay, next question. What kinds of drinks will that man make me?" she pointed to the bartender.

"To answer your question earlier, yes, they do have moonshine, 'shine, white lightning, what ever you want to call it. However, since you've already told me you are not a fan of that," he paused thinking and then added, "which, by the way, I may have a few questions of my own later… You may want to consider a soda pop and bourbon, beer, wine, or a mixed 'shine drink."

Uh oh… she was an idiot. Why did she tell him she didn't like moonshine? Now he was going to ask her questions and she was the world's worst liar. So, she chose to avoid that little comment. "What's a mixed 'shine drink? And how does this place get all of this stuff?"

"Mixed makes the moonshine easier to drink. Takes away some of the burn… Georgia's peach 'shine is sweet… tastes like peaches, if you'd like to try that. It's kind of like a punch. And for your second question… It's not my job to know where it comes from." The lie rolled off his tongue easily. She did not need to know that; it was for her own good.

"Why is it so dead in here?" she looked around at the empty place.

"Gabe and I wanted to take you all somewhere nice and private. So, when you were getting ready we made a couple of calls. You'd be surprised what a few dollars can do in this town," he smiled.

What he didn't tell her was he really just didn't want her first experience in a speakeasy to be crowded with people she was going to have to walk past on the street, see at the store, or sit next to in church. He didn't know how she was going to react to this place. He wanted it to be as comfortable and relaxing as possible.

"So, do you want something to drink or is it just dinner?" he asked.

"I'll give the peach thing a whirl. I like peaches," she said with more confidence than she felt.

Partly she wanted to give it a try in hopes it would relax her nerves but a second part of her wanted to give it a taste. It sounded somewhat familiar to the applesauce concoction that Ava had accidentally made a couple of weeks ago. And that got her wheels turning. Although her gears were somewhat conflicted. Why was she so nervous being here, yet helping Walt make paste or thinking about a new recipe for 'shine didn't bother her a bit? It made no sense.

The waiter came back with what looked like two sodas for Ava and Gabe but she was sure there was something more in them by the way they were sipping. Trick sat at the bar, he didn't want to be surrounded by couples.

"Nothing but water for me tonight," Silas said. "She will have the Georgia's peach."

They never ordered food but filet mignon wrapped in bacon with sides of mashed potatoes and peas alongside the biggest buttery yeast roll she had ever seen arrived at their table at the same time as Emmie's drink.

"Oh, this looks wonderful," Emmie said, smiling down at the plate. She couldn't remember the last time she'd had a real meal like this.

"I'm glad you are enjoying it," Silas commented halfway through their meal. He liked eating with her. The girls he was around back home cut their food in small pieces and then spent most of their time moving it around on their plates rather than actually swallowing it.

Emmie had put down more food than he had. Ava on the other hand was more of the pushing food around variety, which explained why she looked like a walking stick and Emmie... Emmie had curves. Good curves. He had a mental flash back of the first day he met her when she was dripping wet from the pool. He smiled at the memory.

"I'm sorry." She put her fork down and looked up. "I haven't eaten today, I guess I was starving."

"Why have you not eaten?" he asked concerned.

"We've been so busy at the store lately and with Will only showing up here and there now, I haven't had much time to eat. I guess I just forgot. But my gosh, this is good."

"Eat up. If you're gonna drink that later," he pointed to the Georgia's peach, "you're going to want something in your belly."

She glanced over at Ava's still nearly full plate and felt too self-conscious to continue eating like a pig. "Don't look at me Emmie. I had a big lunch. You eat up."

Emmie laughed at her friend. "You're lying. I haven't ever in my life seen you eat a big anything."

"Well we can't all be so fortunate to eat what we want and stay a beauty like you. Your food goes to the right places..." She touched her friend's arm and smiled.

Ava remembered when Emmie's mom had first died. They were only fifteen. Ronnie had once let her go days with almost no food in the house and no money to get it before Emmie asked if she could come over for dinner. She never wanted Emmie to feel bad about eating anything. Ava had always felt herself lucky to have the luxury to be a picky eater. Most people around here didn't get that chance.

Emmie's face flushed at her friend's complement. "You know that's not true but thanks for not making me feel like a hog," she laughed. "So, what's in this thing?" Emmie swirled the drink around in the glass and gave it a good sniff.

It smelled like peaches and something else that burned her nose a little. That was the 'shine, no doubt.

"Fruits and vegetables mostly. It's good for you," Trick answered, finally joining them. And he wasn't exactly lying. Most of the moonshine around here was made from corn. "Give it a taste."

Emmie tipped her drink up a tiny bit, expecting the white lightning experience she'd had with Ava not long ago. However, she was pleasantly surprised. The peaches made it taste sweet, tart, and cool. It only had the faintest burn as she swallowed it down.

"Wow, that wasn't half bad," she said.

"Yeah, well just take it easy. That kind of 'shine can sneak up on ya," Silas warned, stretching his arm around her shoulder.

She was handling this well... better than she seemed to at first. Silas pulled out a cigarette put it in his mouth and then fumbled with his lighter, never moving the other hand from her shoulder.

"Let me do that before you burn your face off," she said, taking his lighter from him.

She sparked the lighter and held it up to his hand-rolled cigarette. He breathed in deeply to give it a good flame then blew the smoke away from her.

Never in all his years had anyone lit a cigarette for him. Hell, last month he probably would have sent someone packing that took something out of his hand like she did. But she was different... and he wasn't sure how he felt about that.

By the time Emmie finished the small glass of Georgia's peach, she could feel the warmth in her face. She was having a hard time taking the smile off her lips. Every joke Trick told was funny even if she didn't completely understand it. She had somehow leaned into Silas's chest like she had never been so relaxed in her life. She wasn't drunk... she didn't think. But she wasn't quite herself either.

"So, Emmie do you like that 'shine better than what we had at your house a couple weeks ago?" Ava laughed.

Ugh. Ava had the biggest mouth sometimes.

Chapter Seventeen

"**M**r. Del Grande, Mr. McDowell someone is on the phone for either of you," the waiter said as he came to the table.

Thank God for small favors. Perfect distraction from Ava's big mouth. The guys walked over to the far end of the bar where the bartender held out a black phone.

"Ava, I'm gonna kill you," Emmie whispered, sitting closer to her friend.

"What?" Ava looked confused.

"I did not want to bring up the moonshine," she spit.

"I didn't know that was a secret. Emmie, you had one sip then... you drank a whole glass sitting here tonight. What's the difference?"

Well Ava had a point. "I just don't want him to know I have all that 'shine at my house, you know. He might think I'm some kind of saucy lady."

"Saucy lady... Em, there is no chance you have to worry about him thinking that. He's got you on a pedestal. We'll just tell him the truth... that it was Ronnie's."

Emmie nodded. The truth was more complicated than Ava really understood. "Yeah, well. I just want to be careful. I don't think I'm ready to fall off that pedestal yet."

"Are you girls about ready to go? I think there ready to close up for the night," Gabe said.

"Yeah, sure. It's really getting late," Emmie agreed, scooting out from the bench.

Silas led the way out of the restaurant. Getting out proved much easier than getting in. All of the security checkpoints were now just a quick walk through. They piled back into the car and headed towards Ava's house.

The warmth of the Georgia's peach 'shine had worn off and just left Emmie feeling sleepy in its wake. She leaned her head over on Trick's shoulder and rested her eyes.

"Emmie girl, wake up," Silas repeated softly until her eyes opened. It was odd how at times his phrases could sound so Irish.

"Oh, sorry. I didn't know I fell asleep," she said sitting up. Looking around she was surprised to see the others were already making their way to the house.

"It's probably Trick you should apologize to. It's his ear you've been snoring in for the last forty minutes," Silas teased.

"I did not snore. Did I?" she asked.

Laughter was his only reply.

"Let's get you in," he said, opening his door.

"Actually, I think I'm just going to walk on home tonight," she answered. Her bed was calling her name and she had promised to meet Walt tomorrow morning.

"Em, it's after midnight. You are not walking back to your house. Just stay here," he pushed.

She smiled at his protectiveness. She hadn't had anyone worry after her since her mama had passed. "I'll be fine. There's nothing between here and there to worry about. Everyone in this town is in bed but us."

"Come on, don't fight me on this." All trace of humor was gone from his eyes.

"Well, maybe you could just drive me home? That's a compromise, right?" she suggested.

He sighed, "Alright, compromise." He wasn't a fan of compromise. It meant he wasn't getting all he wanted. There was a lot more going on in this town at night than she knew and he didn't want her accidentally caught in the middle of something on her walk home.

She could tell he was upset. They drove most of the trip in silence. He stopped when they got to the intersection that would lead them into town. "I just realized this is where I picked you up earlier... I don't know where you live."

She showed him where to make a couple turns.

"Right here, down this drive," she said.

Silas stopped the car just short of the drive. "You live here?" he breathed in deeply through his nose, knuckles tense on the steering wheel.

"Yep. Is something wrong?" She looked out the window to see if there was something she was missing.

"Ava said you lost your stepfather recently. So, you'll be here alone?" he asked.

"Yes, Ronnie died a few months ago… but I'll be fine. I've got good neighbors. They live just down that path not half a mile away." Emmie wondered why in the world was he behaving so strangely.

He nodded. His hands never relaxed on the steering wheel the whole time he pulled up to her house.

"What's wrong Silas?" she asked.

He shook his head. "Nothing, nothing. Just tired." He stopped the car, walked around, helped her out, and led her to the front door.

"I'll call you tomorrow, okay?" he said, while she fumbled with the key to unlock the door.

Then he leaned in and brushed a kiss on her forehead then walked back to the car. She stood waving at the door. "Lock up," he shouted as he started to pull away.

He didn't like this. Not one bit. Why did no one think it was important to let him that she was Ronnie Talbot's stepdaughter? Vince had to know but he was probably halfway back to Chicago by now. He didn't like being kept in the dark especially when they were mixing his personal life with his work. And why the hell was everyone okay with Emmie staying in that house alone? He punched his steering wheel in frustration but that accomplished nothing. When he got home he was pulling Gabe's ass out of bed. He had some shit to explain.

Chapter Eighteen

Silas's boots thumped loudly on the wooden floors of the DeCarmilla house. He balled up his fist and beat on Ava's door.

"Gabe." There was no reply.

"Gabe get your ass out here," he repeated. Just as he reached down to turn the knob the door popped open revealing a very confused, very tired, and very angry Ava.

"What's wrong with you?" she asked, pulling her robe up around her shoulders.

"I need to talk to Gabe. Now," he said, pushing past her to walk into the room.

"Gabe's not here. He said he had something to take care of and he'd probably just sleep at his house. I assumed he was with you... it was something to do with the call you got at the speak." Ava's eyes widened and he could almost hear her thoughts.

"What's he out doing if he's not with you?" she asked.

"You're right. I was supposed to meet him," he cursed. He knew getting all mixed up with some girl down here was going to cloud his head and damned if it hadn't already happened.

She looked relieved instantly when he admitted he should have been with Gabe. Looked like they were still working out some trust issues. Silas wasn't touching that. Not his problem.

"Silas," she said, touching his shoulder, "what's wrong?"

He turned and paced, rubbing his jaw. He shook his head. He couldn't tell her.

"Nothing. It's fine. Look, I gotta go meet Gabe," he said and turned to walk away from her.

"Is this about Emmie?" He paused with his back to her and nodded. "What ever it is... she's crazy for you, ya know," Ava added, "and she's like my sister. So, take care of her, okay?"

He turned his face and looked right at Ava, nodded, then walked back down the stairs and out the door. He would take care of her. Despite all this shit… he would take care of her.

****

He parked his car at the office and made his way down the deserted street to the blind pig that was above Dillard Brother's Shoe Store. The crowd was a little larger tonight than usual. Some of the regulars of the Smith's Grove speakeasy had to come here because he had closed access to the nicer joint for the night, so he could take Emmie out without her running into folks she may know. Next time he'd probably leave it open to a select few but he had needed to test the waters with her tonight. He wasn't sure how she'd react to the speak. She did fine once she got past her questions. Silas couldn't believe that she drank that peach 'shine. He smiled at the memory. Which reminded him Ava had said something about it not being her first time. Now it kind of made sense. If she was Ronnie's daughter then she'd probably been around it all her life. Up until a few months ago he had made quite the name for himself in this town. Something that brought him recognition, power, respect, and death.

"Silas, over here," Gabe called from behind the bar.

Silas weaved in and out of people as he walked over to Gabe and the manager of sorts, James.

"What's the problem?" Silas asked.

Gabe pointed to a man sitting near the end of the bar. He was a short, gruff-looking man. He had about a week's growth of brown beard covering his face and neck.

Silas looked back at his friend with his eyebrow arched in question. How was this guy worth the drive out here in the middle of the night?

"He says that he knows we recently lost our 'shine flow and thinks he can help us out," James answered.

So, that's why he was worth the drive.

The man was staring a hole through the guys. Something was wrong with this guy.

"We will take him to the office," Silas said to James then added, "give us about five minutes first."

James nodded in understanding.

Silas shut the door to their meeting room. It was a small room that held a couple of chairs and a small metal table. The walls were painted stark white leaving a feeling of emptiness.

"We will deal with that guy in a minute," Silas started. He paused for a minute trying to keep his composure. Turning his back he started talking, "Gabe, tell me why we are here."

Gabe looked confused, "Because James called and asked us to come in about something important."

"No, no. Think further back. Why are we *here?*" He emphasized the last word raising his arms at his surroundings as he turned back to face Gabe.

Gabe stood there staring in surprise. Finally he shook his head. Silas was pissed but he had no idea what was going on. "I don't know what you're talking about Silas."

"Why the are were here, Gabe? Why are we here in this tiny little podunk moonshining town?" he voiced, eerily calm.

Gabe looked at the ground like he was expecting the answer to be written on the floor under him.

"To figure out what was going on with the 'shine flow to the speaks in this area?" Gabe made the phrase a question.

"That's right. We had a huge increase from a supplier at a cheaper price. Things were good, right?" Silas smiled but it didn't reach his eyes.

"Yeah, until we checked the books," he answered.

"That's right, the books... Gabe, what was going on with the books?" Silas asked, still smiling that same odd grin.

Gabe felt like a child at school being quizzed by the teacher. He knew Silas could be set off but he'd never had his anger directed toward him. Where was all of this headed? They'd had such a good night out with Trick and the girls.

"Well, they were short money. Money that was supposed to go to Ava's pop and your dad for taking care of the speaks and blind pigs down here," Gabe answered.

Silas smiled and motioned his hand for him to continue talking.

"Okay," Gabe breathed deeply unsure if he was scared or angry. "The books were short because James had fronted the 'shiner a lot of cash for moonshine that was never delivered."

"Right again, my boy. Keep going," Silas said.

"Your dad told us we couldn't come home till the money was back," Gabe said. "But we never found it because..." Awareness shown in Gabe's eyes as he trailed off. Ugh. He told Vince Silas was going to be pissed about this.

"And there it is..." Silas smacked his hands together dramatically in the air. "Finish."

"We never found it because the 'shiner was killed the night we got to town," Gabe's voice came out barely a whisper. "Look, Silas, I told Vince we needed to tell you but..."

"And what was the bootlegger's name?" Silas asked refusing to listen to Gabe's excuse.

Gabe shook his head and looked down again. When he started to apologize Silas cut him off again.

"What was the fucking bootlegger's name?" Silas shouted, flipping over the chair he was standing next to.

"Ronnie Talbot," Gabe answered.

"So, answer me this, Gabe. Why in the hell didn't anyone tell me Emmie's family was involved in all this shit?" Silas shouted.

"Silas, we don't think she's involved. You've met her. She's one of the most naive people I've ever met. Ronnie was no good but that's got nothing to do with her," Gabe started.

"He was her father! I don't care if she knew about it or not—she is too close to it for me to be with her." He turned back to the wall again.

His friend walked up behind him. "You know how Ava's family treats her. They really don't believe she had anything to do with any of it. That's why Vince didn't want you to know. They want her left out of it. Besides the trail ended with Ronnie. Whoever killed him that night probably took the money. Vince searched Ronnie's ground for days afterward and found nothing. But that man waiting out there... he might know something—that's what we need to focus on, not this." Gabe tried to refocus the conversation.

"Did they really think I wouldn't find out who she was? Stupid…" Silas started but Gabe cut him off.

"Look, don't get involved with her then, if you don't think it's right, then don't do it," Gabe shouted.

Silas rubbed his brow and paced the length of the table. "I'm already involved." Then he turned and walked out the door slamming it behind him.

Chapter Nineteen

Spotty lay in a pallet in the corner chewing on an apple core. Emmie simmered the last of the apples in a mess of sugar and cinnamon. Her house would smell like heaven for at least a couple of days, maybe a week with as much applesauce as she had canned this morning.

Max was getting a couple jars as a thank you for all the apples he had picked. Since Ava had ruined Emmie's last batch, she made him some more. Well, maybe she couldn't quite say ruined, especially after she had the Georgia peach 'shine last night it had given her a new idea. She had a plan that was going to help her and Walter sell all that moonshine quickly.

Walt showed up at nine o'clock on the nose in his old truck.

"Whoo-ee, Emmie your house smells good." He walked in and put his hat on the kitchen table. "Max would die if he was here right now. Not much he likes better than your applesauce."

"Well, it was Mama's recipe and, of course, I've got some for him." Emmie produced a basket with two big jars full of the warm applesauce. "He picked all these apples, it's only fair."

"Thanks, Emmie. I appreciate all you are doing for him," he said.

"You know I'm happy to," she said. "I've got something else to share with you too."

She walked over to the counter and strained what looked like the last few spoonfuls of a very watered-down applesauce. "Now just hear me out before you give me opinions, okay?" she asked.

Emmie took a small cup down from the cabinet and poured a little of the liquid into it. Then she sat the cup down next to him. "Taste it." She had that same mad-scientist look in her eyes as she did the day she made that first batch of paste for him.

He picked up the cup and threw back the drink. Sweet, warm, spice. It was good. "Ya making drinks now, girl? Cause you'll want to be careful with this stuff."

"Walt, it's not for me. It's for you. To help you pick up business. I figured if you had something better to offer it might take out the competition."

"Competition," he laughed at first then fell stone silent thinking about Ronnie. "You don't even know what you're talking about. This ain't some kind of baseball game, child."

Emmie was so tired of hearing that she was a child. She was twenty-one years old for goodness sake. Most girls her age were getting married, having kids. She did know about this—he was wrong.

"You think I don't know? I know what this is. I also know this will sell. Last night I drank something called Georgia's peach 'shine at a…" she started to tell him everything but stopped herself not wanting to get anyone in trouble. She didn't really know if he was supposed to know about the speak. "Well, it doesn't matter where but it was good. People are buying this stuff, Walt. I promise." Her eyes widened as she spoke. She pulled out a chair and sat at the table across him.

If he were a younger man, he'd be angry with her for her mouthing back at him like that. But he was old enough to know she was just a child—just a child without a clue about the road she was driving herself down. He had to do the right thing and get her out of this.

"Emmie, I appreciate you trying to help out," he paused, "but I don't know nobody that's looking for apple pie tasting moonshine. You know I'm selling to people my age that like the burning taste of this white lightning. No matter how good that stuff is, they wouldn't touch it with a ten-foot pole."

"But you could find new clients. Try to sell it to people like Ava or me that don't really drink much and don't like that strong taste. Just social drinkers, ya know?" she suggested.

Walter looked mildly amused. "You want me to walk around town and ask young girls if they want some of my apple pie 'shine? I'm pretty sure that wouldn't have a good ending for me."

She looked at him annoyed. "You know that's not what I meant."

"Yeah, I know what you meant. But there's stuff about this business you don't know and I don't want you to know. I appreciate you looking out for me and trying to boost my sale but you're staying out of it. Here's the new plan..." He took out his pipe and lit it, taking a few puffs before he finished speaking, "I'm gonna take that 'shine outta your pantry because you don't need that in your house and I've got a place to hide it. When I sell it, half the money is yours. That should knock a dent in that tuition money that you need for next year. In the meantime, you're gonna have nothing to do with any of this. We're just going to go on living our life like normal. I'm going to keep doing what I do and you're going to keep working there at Mr. Thomas's store and tutoring Max. You'll get to start that college next year. That's the best I can do Emmie. I hope you know that."

"Walter, I cannot just take your money," she started quietly.

"You're not. It was Ronnie's 'shine too. Think of it as an inheritance. He didn't leave you anything else."

"What about the paste?" she asked.

"Child, with as much 'shine as you have in that pantry, it's gonna be awhile before I need to make more." He then added, "It's better this way, trust me."

She nodded but she sure wished they could have had this conversation yesterday.

He stood and walked over to the pantry, opened the door and looked back at her confused. "Emmie, what happened to the 'shine?" It was gone.

"Well, I guess I should have asked you first but..." She turned to look at the floor next to the stove. He followed her eyes.

"Oh for Christ's sakes, Emmie. What in the world have you done?" he sighed, walking over to the stacks of amber-colored liquid.

"I'm sorry Walter. I really thought I was helping." She felt her eyes well up. That made her angry. Really, of all the things she'd been through in the last few months, this was what she was going to cry over. The fact she made some apple moonshine that Walter didn't want. But she couldn't help it. Her throat swelled so she could no longer speak. She'd screwed up big time. Ruined no telling how much money of

Walter's 'shine all over a stupid idea. The whole thing was dumb. He was right. What did she know about any of this?

She walked over to the pantry and pulled out one of the empty crates she'd found in the barn. She neatly packed a few jars of the applesauce she'd made for Walter to take home to his family. Emmie got them all packed and loaded carefully in the front seat of his truck. As she walked back into the kitchen she found Walter holding a bottle of the apple pie 'shine. He was inspecting it like it was a fine piece of china. Running his wrinkled fingers over the smooth glass and the little scrap of blue-checkered fabric she had added to the top, just to pretty it up.

"It's the nicest looking 'shine bottle I've ever seen. I know you was just trying to help," he said, looking at her. He walked over to the pantry, grabbed a few more empty crates and started filling them with the apple pie 'shine.

"What are you doing?" she asked.

"Packing up the moonshine like I came here to do," he answered.

"You don't need to take this. I can figure out how to get rid of it."

"Emmie, I am not leaving you with this 'shine in your house. I'll figure this out. My friends like apple pie so I'm sure they'll like this too," he smiled at her.

Emmie was pretty sure there was nothing else he could say to make her feel any worse. She knew better than to offer to help solve this again. There was no way he would let her. "Can I keep a couple jars? I mean for Ava and her brother?" she added.

"Sure, just keep them hidden until you give it to them." He handed her two of the jars. She set them on the counter.

Together they carried the crates to the truck, covered them with blankets, and then stacked some bales of straw on top to hide the glass jars. He probably wouldn't run into anyone on the short drive to his home but you couldn't be too safe. The eighteenth left no loopholes for a farmer hauling moonshine.

"I'm sorry, Walt," she said again.

"Shush. I ain't listening to your apologies. You was just trying to help. I've been around these hills long enough to know things always works out," he said then climbed into the truck and drove away.

Emmie waved goodbye until she could no longer see his truck. She stepped off the porch, walked up the hill, sat on her Mama's grave, and let the tears flow freely down her cheeks. Not even bothering to hold back. What would her mama think of the person she had become? It was so far from the life she had planned.

Chapter Twenty

Silas was exhausted. Thank God it was Saturday and he didn't have to spend this morning at his uncle's law firm. He brushed his teeth and splashed water on his face in an attempt to wake up. It didn't seem to be working. His bare feet led him downstairs where he could smell freshly brewed coffee. Trick must already be awake.

"You look like death, brother. What happened last night?" Trick asked with a smile. The last time he saw Silas he was driving away in the middle of the night with a beautiful girl. Death was not exactly what he had expected Silas to look like this morning.

Silas just shook his head and rubbed his jaw. He helped himself to a cup of black coffee and sat down across from his brother.

"Did something happen when ya dropped Emmie off?" Trick pushed further.

"No… yeah. But it's not what you are thinking, I'm sure," Silas answered, still fidgeting with his coffee cup. He took a few drinks before he went on. "Remember that man we found dead… the one that took the money and never paid us back or delivered the moonshine?"

"Yeah," Trick answered.

"That was Emmie's stepfather. She lives there… in that house, on that land, where we torched the car." Trick's mouth fell open while Silas explained.

"Guess that explained why Vince hightailed it down here when we called him that night. Also tells us why he felt he was the only one that could deal with Ronnie's family and ask about the cash. They are so damn protective of her they never even told me who she was, like I wasn't going to put it all together eventually." Silas shook his head.

They sat there in silence for a second before Trick spoke, "Damn. I don't know what to say. What are you gonna do?"

"Well, Gabe got a piece of my mind last night. Vince and I will talk when he gets back. And that's not even the worst thing that happened yesterday."

That piqued Trick's curiosity. "Something worse than Gabe and Vince not telling you Emmie's dad was the guy who took our money and ran… and now we are stuck down here till we can find it? I can't wait to hear what else happened last night."

"This hillbilly that looked like he hadn't showered in a month came in running his mouth about our joint. Says he knew we recently lost all of our moonshine flow, that we'd recently been stiffed some money, and that our businesses were looking for some new partners," Silas explained.

"What did you tell him? How did he know all that? Did a lot of folks around here know that James was buying from Ronnie?" Trick fired off the questions without giving him time to answer.

Silas shrugged his shoulders. "Wish I knew more than I do. I don't like him knowing all that shit though. Makes me wonder if he was talking about the money Ronnie owed. You know all along Vince has been saying he bets our money is in the hands of whoever killed Ronnie. This guy maybe is the lead to follow."

"Did you get any info outta him?" Trick asked.

"Not much. We know that man was just a mouse sent in to test the waters with us. Roughed him up a little bit and he squealed like a pig. Sam Young is the man we need to talk to. Gabe is going to set something up the end of this week. You want to come?"

"Wouldn't miss it," Trick smiled. "I think you're right, especially now that we know Emmie is Ronnie's only family. If she is hiding that money, she's got nothing to show for it."

Silas nodded, agreeing with his brother. Last night he remembered a conversation he'd overheard between Emmie and Mr. Thomas. She had asked him for a raise, talked about needing money for the mortgage and school. If she had the money she wouldn't be begging that man for extra cash. Vince was probably right. But that didn't make it right that they had lied to him.

"So what are you doing to do about Emmie?" Trick asked, finishing the last drink of his coffee.

"I don't know. You think I should cut it off with her? I mean that'd be the best thing to do, right?" Silas asked.

Trick wouldn't have been more surprised if pigs had flown through the kitchen. His brother had never ever, in his entire life asked him for advice. "I think you should do whatever it is you want to do. But I will say this, would you have even questioned what to do with any of those other gals you've been with?"

Silas thought about it for a second. "No, I would have left without thinking twice," he shrugged.

"So maybe this is different, you said yourself you wouldn't have even questioned it before... Maybe you should just stick with it." Trick really thought his brother deserved a little something good in his life. He'd really never seen him as happy as he was last night at the speak and Emmie seemed like a good girl.

Silas stood, nodded, and walked out the kitchen door without another word.

****

By the time he got dressed and made it to Emmie's, it was nearly eleven. He knocked on the door only to find no answer but a barking dog. He knocked again harder and this time the door actually squeaked open.

"Emmie.... Emmie...." he called a few times before he crossed over the threshold. He let himself in and closed the door behind him. She was gone but couldn't be far. Her purse was sitting by the door and there was a cup of coffee on the kitchen table. And the dog was locked in the house.

"Easy there boy," he said. The dog stood at attention and barked at him. Clearly he wasn't a fan of strangers coming in his house. Silas eased past the dog into the small kitchen. He found some apple scraps on the counter and handed them over.

"See there boy, I'm a friend." He approached the dog cautiously. The dog took the treat and wagged his tale. "Some guard dog you are," Silas laughed then took in his surroundings.

The farmhouse was small. Downstairs there was a kitchen, staircase and then a small sitting room. In the back of the house there was a tiny bedroom barely big enough for a bed and a chest. It didn't look like a woman's room though. There were no powders, shoes or dresses. He spotted a pair of men's work boots in the corner.

This must have been her stepfather's room. He walked back to the front of the house and went up a couple stairs until he was tall enough to see the loft. This was her bedroom—still small but full of her things. He recognized the shoes she wore last night. The slip she wore the first time he saw her at the pool was draped over a chair in the corner. There was a stack of books next to her bed. He smiled, glancing around. This space fit her. Simple, eclectic, and it smelled like heaven in here. What in the world was she cooking? He stepped down and walked back to the kitchen. The kitchen table was stacked with jars all covered with a little blue checked cloth.

Silas picked one up and held it in his hand. It was still slightly warm. How early had she gotten up to start canning? He hadn't dropped her off until after midnight. She'd probably gotten up and started cooking before daylight. He smelled the pot that was still dirty on the stove. It only had the a little bit of applesauce left. Mmm... that smelled delicious.

He sat down at the kitchen table and waited. The dog whimpered and Silas found more apple scraps. She surely wouldn't be gone long. His eyes glanced back to the end of the house again, Ronnie's bedroom. His mind flashed back to that night. There had been four of them on this property that night: Gabe, Trick, Sheriff Drake, and himself. He had come to this house that night but it was all locked up. James had told them he was pretty sure Ronnie's still was on this land by the way he'd been bragging about it at the pig. They'd been walking around searching for it when they heard the gunshot. By the time they got to the car Ronnie was already dead. Shot in the chest right there in the driver's seat of his car. The old man had stopped dead in his tracks when he saw them—Strangers, Suites, Guns, Badges. He looked scared to see the four of them standing there. When he composed himself he said he lived just down the way and had come running when he heard the shot. Silas never believed that. That old man was out in the woods for something that night.

Sheriff Drake, an old friend of the DeCarmilla family (meaning on their payroll), had assured them that the old man was no threat. So, they had let him go. It had been Silas who convinced the sheriff to start the fiery crash, after they checked the car for the money. He didn't want folks around town to start asking too many questions about the murder. Silas needed to be able to handle this one without the hassle of dealing with the local police. Ronnie had a reputation as an alcoholic; it was better that everyone just thought he'd had an accident.

Without realizing what he was doing, he found himself in Ronnie's old room. The dog followed him, cocking his head to the side. Silas ignored him, glancing around for anything that looked odd. He looked in the drawers for false fronts, nothing. He quickly looked under the mattress, nothing. Double-checked the pillows, nothing. He was getting ready to leave when something on the floor caught his eye. Next to his work boots one of the wooden slats of the floor was slightly raised. He bent down and slid his finger along the slot until he could pry it up. Sure enough there was a small box. Opening it up there was a letter to Emmie and under the letter was a stack of cash. A quick count of the money showed it was over $700. It wasn't all the money he had owed but it was a pretty good chunk. He quickly stuffed the money in his vest pocket. But then he couldn't move. He should just take that money and leave. It was their money... his money. It was not hers. He flipped the envelope with her name on it over and over in his hand. He wondered what the note said. Should he read it before he took the money? No, of course not.

He reached in and took the money out of his vest and put it back into the box and replaced the floorboard. What was wrong with him? He just needed time to think through all this. It wasn't all of the money anyway. He'd follow the hillbilly's lead to this Sam guy and then decide what to do with all of this.

He walked back to the front of the house as quickly as his feet could take him, before he came to his senses and tried to get that money again. As he reached down to grab the knob of the front door it popped open smacking him right in the face.

Chapter Twenty-one

"**D**amn it," he shouted. That was a pretty good hit.

Emmie stared back at him with her mouth open wide. "Oh Silas, I am so sorry!"

Spotty danced from foot to foot barking for her attention. She reached a hand down but he jumped away from her. He padded back to Ronnie room, barking at the door. She shushed him, leaned up and gently touched Silas's face.

When she came into focus he noticed her face was red and splotchy. Her eyes were swollen and glassy.

"Emmie girl, what's wrong?" he asked, his tone softer now.

She shook her head and felt her eyes fill up with unshed tears again, as she turned and walked away from him.

"Nothing. It's nothing," she repeated.

He didn't believe that but was unsure how far to push her. Had she somehow seen him digging through her stepfather's room? An unexpected wave of guilt rushed through him. He did his best to brush it away. He hadn't taken the money… and even if he had, it was his. There was no reason to feel any shame. He made a halfhearted attempt to reason with himself but it did no good. He still felt bad and he didn't like it. The dog barked again, prancing in front of the bedroom door. Apparently the dog didn't like it either. Silas glared down at the dog, willing it to shut up.

Silas walked up behind her at the stove, put his hand on her shoulder, and rubbed it down the length of her arm.

"You can tell me things, you know." He hoped she found those words comforting. He never really knew what to say at times like this.

She nodded, keeping her back to him. Emmie was having a hard time keeping the tears that threatened to leak over to her cheeks at bay.

She grabbed the applesauce pot and quickly put it in the sink. She plunged the cooker into water and began rinsing it out.

Fear. She felt fear. Fear of being caught, fear of her mistakes, fear because she didn't know what in the heck she was doing with anything in her life anymore... Fear overtook her and came out as a sob. She rested her hands on the counter to stop their shaking.

Silas pulled her into his arms, saying nothing. Sometimes if he couldn't find the right words to say in a situation, he would just jump to action. Granted, if he couldn't find the right words the next action was usually more violent than hugging... but it was the same principle. To his surprise she hugged him back. He felt her hands dig into his vest. He rubbed her back, then her hair, brushing the ebony waves away from her face. When she finally calmed he pulled away from her a little bit, put his hand under her chin, and brought her eyes to his.

"Whatever it is, it will be okay. I promise, Em." And that's when he knew without a doubt he would weather whatever this storm was through to the end. He didn't make promises to anyone that he didn't intend to keep.

She swallowed hard and nodded. Just when he was sure she wasn't going to tell him anything she started to speak, "I've been up on the hill. At my mama's grave, talking to her a little."

Silas only nodded. He'd learned from working with people at the law firm, and in other affairs, that when people started talking it was best to shut up and listen, even if it left long awkward pauses. Which is exactly what was happening right now. It was a good three minutes before she started talking again. She just pulled away from him and continued cleaning up her canning mess.

Emmie sighed and continued scrubbing the pot. She washed it much longer than necessary. She just couldn't quite get it clean enough to convince herself there was no way Silas was going to smell the moonshine in it. Maybe she should just tell him. Secrets never led to anything good. She knew that. But after he hugged her so tight and made her feel so safe, Emmie was afraid to risk what might happen if she told him what she'd been up to. She knew there was no way he expected what she'd actually been up to this morning. It wasn't really her character, so she didn't have to feel guilty about it, right? Wrong. She felt awfully guilty. Maybe Walt was right. It was time to just put this ugly mess behind her.

"Ya ever feel like you're just messing things up over and over again? Like when something bad happens and then you just make the wrong choices trying to make it better. Then find out you are in even worse shape than when you started?" she asked, drying the dishes.

The dog started making an awful racket in Ronnie's room. He was whining and clawing at the floor. She pulled him by the neck and closed the bedroom door. The dog sighed and lay down in front of the door.

"You have no idea," he muttered under his breath staring at the dog. He opened his mouth to try explaining his comment but was startled at her reaction. She was smiling. "Misery loves company?" he asked.

"Something like that I guess. I just let a friend down today and I feel awful. That's just one of a thousand things lately. Mr. Thomas is a horrible man to work for and I dug myself into that deep mess. And school… I'm starting to think that dream's already set sail. I mean I'm already twenty-one. Ronnie wasn't a fan of the idea. Then when he died… I thought, maybe I could work it out," she paused for a second looking up at him. "Isn't that awful that I thought that? Of course, I was sad that he passed but I need to take care of myself." She tried to explain and hoped that he understood. He nodded in approval of her thoughts. "You know, I think today's just turned into an Emmie pity party," she laughed trying to make a joke of all the things she'd just told him.

Only he didn't let it go at that. "I can't really speak to your problems with your neighbor but I'm sure it will work out. Mr. Thomas… that may be a better discussion for another time. But about school, you are certainly not too old. I had people in class with me that were much older than you are and they did great. There is no timeline for life, Emmie, other than a starting and a stopping. What happens in the middle are your choices," he said.

They sat in the quiet of the moment again for a bit before he went on. "I believe you can do this, you know. I could probably get you in this semester. You wouldn't have missed that much yet and I can get the cash. All you need to do is to say the word."

"I appreciate that, really. It's just that this school thing… I want to do it for myself. That's why I found the job at Mr. Thomas's, then it turns out I needed the money for the mortgage. But I'll work it out. It's not your problem. I'm sorry that I started all this…" she let her words trail off.

"I thought you'd probably turn me down. But I just want you to know the offer is out there," he said and she nodded.

The dog sighed and plopped down in front of the bedroom door. Barking one time in Silas's direction. "Spotty what has gotten into you?" Emmie laughed.

"Spotty?" Silas questioned. "There isn't a spot on that dog."

"Yes there is. He has two. His eye and his back," Emmie answered with a laugh.

"If you say so." Silas shook his head. "I just stopped in to check on you and make sure everything was okay. You know, make sure that we were okay after last night."

With everything that had happened today she had practically forgotten about last night. "Yes, I had the best night. Maybe we could go out like that again sometime?" she asked.

He smiled from ear to ear. "You just let me know and I'll set it up."

"Well I'm pretty much ready to go again whenever," she said then worried maybe that was too forward. She wasn't really sure how she was supposed to act.

"Actually, I wondered if you would want to go to St. Joseph with me sometime for Mass. I know you're not Catholic but in a couple weeks they're having some kind of dinner after and everyone is supposed to bring something. I'm not much of a cook and if this applesauce tastes half as good as it smells, I sure would like to take it to this potluck with me." He reached up grabbing one of the jars from the table giving her one of his million-dollar smiles. "And you too, of course."

She laughed out loud. This sure was the start to an interesting relationship. "My applesauce would love to go with you… and me too, of course."

Chapter Twenty-two

The alarm rang early the next morning but she was already awake. Spotty was barking at the window. The dog had been acting crazy since last night. Emmie let him outside and headed back upstairs to get ready. She dreaded the workday that awaited her. Emmie put on her baby blue work dress, grabbed purse and started into town. She was just moving through the motions. Her heart wasn't in this job. When she stepped out onto the porch she let out a sharp high-pitched scream as a man came into focus. Even after she recognized him, her heart still pounded out of rhythm.

"Good Lord, Gabe!" She grabbed her chest. "Are you trying to scare me to death?"

"Sorry, Emmie. I wasn't sure what time you woke up, so I thought I'd just wait out here until you left for work," he said with a grin. "Not much a guard dog, this one?" He rubbed Spotty's belly.

She was glad her heart attack had amused him.

"Now, please don't take this the wrong way because you know you are always welcome at my house… but why are you here?" She glanced around at the car and rocking chair on the other end of the porch just to be sure he was alone, which he was.

He ignored her question and asked one of his own, "Do you have time to talk to me a minute?"

"Well sure. If you'll give me a ride to work, I should have about twenty minutes. What's going on?" she wondered. She was pretty sure this was the only time she had ever been alone with Gabe.

Emmie still wasn't a hundred percent sure about his character. What kind of man pulls a disappearing act with no word sent to the person he supposedly loves? That still felt like trouble to her. But, in fairness, he had seemed sincere since he had come back to town.

Emmie took in the sight of him as she walked closer to the swing. He was tall, about the same height as Silas but his shoulders were broader. His face was sharply angled with a wide jaw. She noticed for the first time the depth of the scar that pulled down from the center of his nose to his full upper lip. On some men a scar made them look weak but that wasn't the case with Gabe; it made him seem stronger. Most days he wore a suit like the other guys but today it was just a white button-down shirt and navy pants. His shirtsleeves were folded up to his elbows. She'd never noticed his hair was nearly as dark as hers.

He slid across the swing and patted for her to sit next to him. She sat close enough to the edge that her toes brushed against the porch as she pushed them back and forth. He didn't start talking right away, which made her feel even more anxious.

She turned and looked at him square in the eyes, "Are ya all right, Gabe?" This was beyond weird.

"Yeah," he nodded. "It's just... I know you don't think much of me."

He was direct and honest. She guessed she had to admire him for that. She opened her mouth to correct what he had said but he cut her off.

"When I left Ava like that," he nodded again to himself, "I screwed up. No matter how important things were I should have called her. But I don't pretend to be perfect."

"Gabe really, you don't need to come here and explain yourself to me. We each have our own cross to bear, really," she said.

"I know. It's just... she thinks a lot of you. I've already had to face her family. And they all understand because they know my business," he attempted to explain but fell short because all the things he couldn't tell her. He ran his hands through his hair like he might pull it out. She'd never seen him so uncomfortable.

"Gabe let's just let this one go. You two seem to be fine. I've got no judgment on you. Lord knows, I've had my share of screw-ups. Ava's happy, you're happy, I'm happy. It's fine," she shrugged her shoulders.

He let out a long sigh and plopped his feet down abruptly stopping the motion. Emmie lurched forward. She had to grab the chain to steady her. Gabe stepped out of the swing and turned to face Emmie.

"I need your help," he said quickly. Like if he didn't say the words they would get hung in his throat.

"Okay. What can I do for you?" she asked genuinely. He smiled in relief.

"I want you to help me pick out a ring," he said. As soon as the words came out of this mouth he immediately looked like he might toss his cookies.

Emmie's eyes widened with surprise. Ava had nonchalantly talked about marriage that night before they left for the club but she wasn't expecting it this soon.

"You... I mean you are going to..." Emmie was having a hard time spitting out the words.

"Yeah. I'm going to ask her. I've got it all planned." He smiled, proud of himself. "I want everybody there. I've talked to her folks. My parents are happy. Her parents are happy. You think she'll be happy?" he asked, looking sick again.

Emmie thought for a minute still trying to process all of the information he'd thrown at her. "Are you kidding me? Ava's been planning her wedding since she was about two years old."

He nodded soberly. "That's why I need ya. A ring is going to be the first part of this wedding, right? And Emmie, you know how hard she can be to please. I'm not sure I'd ever pick out the right one. But you know her better than anyone. So if anybody can get it right, it'll be you. Plus, she already said it. You know more about this stuff than I do. As soon as those words came outta her mouth, I knew I had to ask you."

"Okay." Emmie put all of her effort into a smile. Really, she felt as uneasy about this as he did. What did she know about weddings? She had only been to a handful in her whole life. But her insecurity wasn't going to make him feel any better, so she faked it.

She stood from the swing and slowly closed the distance between them. She grabbed his arms and looked up at him. "But you have to answer this for me, honestly before I will help you."

He was serious again. Lines of concern marked his face and he almost looked like a boy.

"You promise me you didn't go up there to Chicago for some other girl. Because you know how Ava is. She acts all confident but inside she can be a mess. If you were up there hanging around some floozy and she was down here just trying to put one foot in front of the other..." Emmie started with the toughest voice she could muster.

Gabe laughed, literally he belly laughed. "I wish I'd have just had to go up there for some floozy."

Emmie put her hand on her hip and stared at him incredulously.

He quickly held up a hand and tried to back peddle. "No, that came out wrong. I'm just saying, I didn't have time for another woman. I was up there for business. I swear, Emmie. I don't want anyone else or I wouldn't be doing this."

She let out a breath. "Alright. I believe you," Emmie said, and realized she did. "She is going to be ridiculously excited. Where do you want to pick out the ring?"

"There's that jewelry store on the square," he suggested. She was impressed that he'd noticed it. He really had been thinking about this.

"Yeah, that's a good one," Emmie smiled. This might be fun after all. "It's not cheap though."

"Well that's good because I don't plan on buying anything cheap. You do know Ava, right?" he laughed.

Gabe leaned over and gave Emmie a hug, squeezing her much harder than necessary. For the first time he reminded her of Vince. As he pulled back the lines in his face were gone. He looked so relieved. "I do love her."

Without waiting for Emmie to say another word he turned and headed to the car and opened the passenger side door for her. As she settled in for the short ride it was on the tip of her tongue to ask when he how he planned to pop the question but she didn't have the chance.

"So, you and Silas huh?" he said, never looking up from the road.

Emmie really didn't know what to say... or even what he was asking. So she just smiled and shrugged her shoulder, "Yeah..."

"Well, that's good. Got to admit though, I wouldn't have put you two together," he said, grinning. "I mean because you're so... Emmie." His voice was kind and soft. "And he's so... Silas." His voice was sharp and mockingly deep. "But eh, it's good, right?" He looked over at her to see her reaction.

She had absolutely no idea what all of that was supposed to mean so she just nodded, "Yeah."

He kept talking, "You know I told Ava to stay out of it. But oh, she was so excited when she got back to town and saw the Silas and Trick here." He laughed and mocked her voice, "Oh wouldn't it just be perfect if she fell for my cousin? We'd be a real family."

Emmie's eyebrows knitted together thinking through what he'd just said, but Gabe just kept talking.

"The truth is she'd picked out Trick for you first. She thought you'd think he was funny. And maybe he'd help you lighten up a bit. But then, things didn't work out like that did they?" He laughed out loud remembering something funny. "Silas dropped that coat on your shoulders and I knew he'd never let Trick have ya." Gabe glanced over and grinned at her.

"Okay, wait." Emmie shook her head trying to process one thing at a time.

"She planned to set me up with Trick? She planned all this?" Emmie asked as they pulled up to the store.

Gabe laughed out loud. "She did pretty good with it too, eh? Even if she does stick her nose where it doesn't belong."

Emmie was livid. She was humiliated that night and Ava knew all along. She was going to be in so much trouble.

"You can't tell her you know though. I don't want her to know I came to see you. She'll get all suspicious. I want to surprise her," he said.

She sighed and pursed her lips annoyingly. "Alright, but after you pop the question she is going to have to answer to this."

He slowed down the car as they neared Mr. Thomas's store. "Can we go at lunch today, to that jewelry store?" he asked, looking nauseous again.

"Today," she shrugged, "I don't see why not."

"Thanks a million, Emmie. You're a good friend," he said through the open window as he pulled away from the curb.

She walked into the store to see a vase of fresh cut flowers sitting next to her chair. Lying next to the flowers was a card bearing her name in a small unfamiliar handwriting.

This was going to be an interesting day after all.

Chapter Twenty-three

Emmie walked over to the vase. It was filled with a beautiful mix of wildflowers. Yellows, oranges and greens spilled out of the clear glass into a late summer rainbow. It was beautiful and organic. The smell was earthy and fresh. This was certainly going to make her day better here at the shop. She tried not to get her hopes up as she pulled open the small card, but really, who else would have brought her flowers?

She inwardly screamed and wanted to dance around when she read the note.

"Dear Emmie, I saw these as I was leaving the house today and thought of you. Hope they made you smile... sorry I wasn't there to see it. Maybe you'll save a smile for me at dinner tonight? Ava's house 6:30 pm. Yours, S. M."

She read the note, once, twice, maybe a hundred times before she returned it to the envelope. She closed her eyes and lifted the vase up to her nose again taking in the beauty.

"Uh hum," Mr. Thomas cleared his throat behind her.

She spun around, the card flying out of her hand in the process. Mr. Thomas bent to pick it up. He obviously read the card... he didn't even try to hide it. As his long willowy arm stretched out to hand it to her, his face went sour.

"Time is money, Emmie," he said, indicating she needed to be busy.

She turned and put the vase on a table in the side room.

"I really don't have room for that. I don't want to risk a water stain on my furniture," he said, pointing at the table.

She walked over and moved them to the floor near her chair.

"Really, Emmie. Those ugly weeds are right in the way. We may trip over them," he huffed.

"Where would you like me to put them, Mr. Thomas?" she asked because she could tell he was in one of his moods.

"S.M. Is that Silas McDowell?" he asked, arching a brow.

"It is really not any of your concern, Mr. Thomas," she said, putting the card in her purse.

"A woman brought them in this morning. He probably didn't even pick them for you," he said. "You know you cannot trust him"

Emmie refused to talk to him about this.

"Where shall I put them, Mr. Thomas?" She held her shoulders high.

"Outside," he said with a smile. "They may aggravate customers' allergies. We wouldn't want that."

She rolled her eyes. "I cannot put them outside, they'll wilt."

He shrugged his shoulders. "That is not my problem. I guess you could take them home. But I know you need the money. Time is money, my Emma, and I'm already going to have to dock your pay, as you have been here fifteen minutes and not even started working."

Her mouth fell open. What a jerk. "Fine. I'll be back and you can dock whatever you like."

She grabbed the flowers and headed out the door. Mr. Thomas was right, she needed the money. He knew she wouldn't take the fifty minutes it would take to walk home and back. What he didn't count on was she could walk to the law firm and back in fifteen minutes. The flowers would keep there as well as they would in the store and she may even take a little time to say a proper thank you to Silas.

****

"Miss Emmie," the young receptionist smiled. "Didn't you just love your flowers? If that wasn't just the sweetest thing. He had me run them over this morning before he headed into his meeting." She smiled and leaned forward to confide in her, "He was pretty hush-hush about it too."

Emmie smiled. "Is he still in his meeting? I'd like to say thank you." And... tell him what a jerk Mr. Thomas was being. She knew that was immature but she wanted to complain and knew he'd be more than willing to listen.

"Let me just call up and check." The other woman actually winked as she picked up the phone.

After a quick conversation she ushered Emmie to a small waiting room on the first floor. Silas walked in with a shy smile. He pulled Emmie up and brushed a quick kiss on her temple.

"Did you like them?" he asked.

"They are lovely," she smiled.

He glanced at the vase on the table, then back at her confused. "Is something wrong?"

She rolled her eyes. "Mr. Thomas made up some excuse for why I can't have them. He's just jealous. I was hoping I could keep them here until after I've gotten off work."

Silas looked annoyed but only shook his head. "Yes, I'll have Victoria keep them at the front desk and bring them to you at dinner tonight."

Emmie agreed and volunteered to cook the meal that night at Ava's house. By the time she got back to the shop she had been gone a total of twenty-five minutes. Will, Mr. Thomas's brother, was at the register taking care of a customer. Mr. Thomas crept close to Emmie, so no one could hear his words.

"That will be a total of forty minutes docked, Emmie. Now, if you would like to work through lunch or stay late to make it up, you may." He walked over and touched her shoulder. "Because you know I am always too lenient with you." Mr. Thomas smiled like he had offered her a new car.

"I'm sorry. I have plans. Thanks anyway." She turned away from him without waiting for his reaction. Then she sat in her chair to begin a project for a new baby. Luckily the work was quite intricate and took concentration. When Gabe arrived at noon to pick her up for the trip to the jewelry store, she hadn't even realized it was lunchtime. Emmie grabbed an apple out of her purse and ate it as they walked to Moore's Jewelers.

Gabe offered to take her to a restaurant as a thank you for the help but she didn't have time. He really wasn't so bad once she got a chance to actually talk to him. Their conversation was easy and comfortable. Even the silent parts, which she always thought was a good sign. If you can't be comfortable with folks in the stillness of the conversation, something is wrong.

"So, do you want to give me any parameters?" she asked, walking up to one of the two long cases that lined the wall of the store.

Gabe shrugged, "Nope, just as long as she likes it... it works for me."

Emmie had never been in this store but always wanted to know what it was like inside. She scanned the cases for the perfect ring. She felt like a raccoon, her fingers itched to touch all the sparkly things encased in glass. A small balding man walked up to them and offered his assistance. She was surprised that he let her try on different rings to see the "whole picture" as he kept calling it. They looked at many beautiful rings but none of them felt like Ava. When Emmie was just about to suggest they call it quits for the day she saw it in the very top shelf of the farthest case. It was the sort of ring that made you ask, "Is that too much?" As soon as the question popped in her head... she knew they'd found the one.

It was a platinum band with a brilliant center-cut diamond. Smaller emerald-cut diamonds were set against the side and tiny round diamonds snaked around the whole set forming a large wavy line. On Emmie's finger it took up nearly the entire area from knuckle to finger joint. But it was perfect for Ava. Even Gabe whistled as he saw it. And then... he almost fell over when he saw the price tag.

"Really Gabe, there are a lot of lovely rings here, if this is too much," Emmie assured him. She knew Ava wouldn't mind.

"No, this one is really her. I'll just get my dad to wire some money from my bank account in Chicago," he answered.

Emmie wondered what that would be like... to run out of money and just have it wired to you from somewhere else. She wasn't jealous exactly, just curious.

He walked her back to the shop on his way to the bank. Gabe thanked her again two or three times for her help. He was so anxious. Emmie nearly asked again how he planned to pop the question, but he didn't seem to want to talk about that. It wasn't really her business anyway, so she didn't push.

When Emmie walked back into the store, Will met her in one of the aisles.

"Hey Emmie, come here," he whispered.

She followed him to a trash bin in the storage room without talking. She peeked over into the can and saw a fresh bouquet of white and green flowers dumped in the bottom. There was a hothouse tag from Deema's Florist. She looked up at Will with an arched eyebrow.

He leaned, over picked a card out of the wastebasket and handed it to her without saying a word.

Maybe Silas had sent her another bouquet?

"My Dear Paul, Emmie mentioned you were jealous of the flowers I picked for her this morning. My sincerest apologies for excluding you. I never meant to hurt your feelings. So, I've sent you some of your own. - S.M."

Chapter Twenty-four

Emmie had never in her whole life been so glad to see the end of a workday. She could not get out of that tense air fast enough. Of course, Mr. Thomas had never admitted to the note or flowers. It was just that every direction or question he asked was belittling and his voice was laced with sarcasm. Not just with her, with everyone: his brother, customers, deliverymen—it didn't matter, everyone was treated the same.

When Emmie reached her house it dawned on her that she had volunteered to cook for all her friends, which she didn't mind doing in the least. However, she knew for a fact that Ava's house would have no groceries and she was expected to cook for three grown men and two women. Emmie dug around her house and tried to find enough odds and ends that would work together to form a meal. She'd just paid this month's mortgage and unfortunately she was going to be cutting it pretty tight the rest of the month, so there was no money for an extra shopping trip.

After scrapping around in her cupboard and pantry, she was pretty pleased with her loot. She had plenty of beans, salted bacon, butter, eggs, and all the dry goods she needed for cornbread. She loaded a crate with groceries and an old iron skillet. Emmie ran upstairs and pinned up her hair, changed clothes, and then headed out the door. The dog followed closely behind her.

When she rounded the corner of the road leading to Ava's, she could feel the heavy wooden crate biting into her fingers. She should have called someone to pick her up. By the time she reached the driveway she was sure she had blisters, but it was only after dropping the crate on the porch that she actually noticed they had already formed and popped, leaving behind ugly red scrapes in her skin. She flexed and released her fingers while she waited for someone to come to the door. Spotty took his favorite spot under the chair.

It was Trick who answered. All at once the conversation with Gabe flew through her mind. This is who Ava had picked out for her... and set her up to meet... in her underwear at the pool. Shades of humiliation burned in her cheeks. She tried to give him a polite smile but was struggling severely.

"Emmie." He bent down, scooped up the crate with one arm, and led her into the house with the other. "Are you alright? Your face is burnin' up. You should have called me to pick you up instead of carrying this." His genuine concern made her feel even more embarrassed.

"I'm fine. If you'd just carry that into the kitchen for me. I told Silas that I'd cook supper tonight." She tried to turn the conversation away from her blush.

Trick looked down at the contents of the crate. "Well, I'm sure it'll be great, Emmie. Nothing like a good skillet," he said, pulling it out of the box confused.

Ava walked through the swinging door of the kitchen right on cue, "I have pots and pans. That must have been ridiculously heavy."

Emmie felt a bipolar range of emotions. She honest to goodness didn't know whether to tear into her friend for the matchmaking pool shenanigans or dance around her about the awaiting proposal. Unfortunately, she couldn't do either. However, as soon as this was all out in the air... until then she would just have to pretend.

"You know I can't cook cornbread without Mama's skillet," Emmie said, continuing to unload.

As soon as the heavy cooking started Trick excused himself from the room. Apparently he needed to go make some phone calls. Ava offered to help but her services ended up being limited to boiling a pot of water for tea and bringing Emmie a ridiculously fancy apron to wear. It was one Ava's mother had made for Ava in an effort to entice her into the kitchen. Even a frilly apron couldn't do the trick. Emmie boiled the beans in some water and stock, adding a good bit of salt, pepper and spices. Then she set her sights on the cornbread. This is why she lugged the heavy skillet... to make cornbread in anything other than an iron skillet was blasphemy to Emmie's mother. It was a tradition that had been ingrained in her since she was old enough to mix cornmeal and flour. She got the skillet piping hot in the oven then set it on a warm burner on the stove to melt the butter. When the butter had just started to pop she added the cornbread batter. She loved the way it sizzled and rolled slowly across the pan. Whenever she made cornbread, she could feel her mother surrounding her. The sizzling, the smells, the warmth— that's what made it one of her favorite things to cook.

After popping the cornbread in the oven, stirring the sugar in the tea, and giving the beans a final stir, she ran upstairs to double check her hair and borrow a bit of Ava's powder. She did not want to look like a sweaty pig when Silas arrived. When she made it back downstairs, she pulled the cornbread out of the oven to cool and set her sights on washing the dirty dishes. Over the sound of sloshing water she heard someone sit a heavy glass on the counter next to her. Her first thought was Ava had returned to help but when two arms snaked around her waist, she felt her breath catch in her throat.

"Looks good," Silas's voice whispered close to her ear.

She smiled, proud. Some part of her needed to hear his approval of what she'd worked so hard to prepare for him.

"Thanks. It's not much. Just some things I had around the house, beans with bacon and cornbread." She tried to act nonchalant.

Silas's arms made a quick motion of spinning her around and pulling her in close for kiss. She felt herself relax in his embrace. One arm still firmly placed around her waist, he cradled her neck with the other as she tilted her face up to look in his eyes. He leaned down and whispered, "I wasn't talking about the food."

He gave her a devilish grin, stepped back, and took off his jacket. She got lost in the meaning of his comment for a moment and smiled, feeling her blush return.

Silas spread his arms wide and looked around the kitchen. "What can I do for ya?"

Her thoughts faltered. She couldn't think of a single thing to tell him that she could actually say out loud. What was this strange power he had over her? She quickly turned back to the dishes and scrubbed the mixing bowl vigorously.

"Umm… you can cut the cornbread. It's in the iron skillet." She pointed to where it was cooling on the stove.

He reached for a knife and grabbed the pan's handle before she could utter a warning. Silas set loose with a string of swears that would make a sailor blush. Emmie put a hand over her mouth and closed the distance between them.

"Oh my, Silas, I am so sorry. That pan just came out of the oven." She looked up with wide eyes and reached out to take his hand. Sure enough a perfect outline of the panhandle was forming on his hand.

"No shit," he said sarcastically.

Emmie led him over to the sink and plunged his hand in a pan of cold water. After a quick scan around the kitchen she spied what she was looking for. Under a large window in the corner was a small aloe plant. She broke off one of the spiky leaves and brought it over to him.

Silas had turned and reached for the butter.

"No butter. This will be better." He looked up at her surprised. His brow creased with confusion as she snapped the leaf in two.

Holding his hand out carefully, she milked the leaf until a few dabs of the clear gel dropped onto the burn. With a soft touch she spread the aloe across the red welts.

"Does that feel better?" she asked, still holding his hand.

He smiled like he was seeing her for the first time. His gaze was so sincere, so honest. "It's fine." He paused for a minute then added, "I'm impressed, Emmie. I don't think I've ever been with a girl that knows how to milk medicine out of a plant."

She really wasn't sure how to take that but was pretty sure it was a compliment. "I've had a lot of burns. I can wrap it… to keep the aloe on, if ya want."

Silas composed himself. He shook his head and shrugged brushing off the suggestion. Clearly needing to look extra manly after making a mistake in the kitchen, he said, "Nah. I'll be all right. Thanks anyway."

Emmie noticed that her vase of flowers was sitting on the counter near the sink. She grabbed them along with some dishes and made quick work of setting the table. Silas brought out the cornbread, using a potholder this time, and called everyone to eat. After they were seated and the food had been plated, Silas said a quick prayer and everyone turned to their food.

Gabe dug right in. He'd spent some time in Kentucky and was used to the cuisine. Ava picked and pushed her food around… but that's what Ava always did. Trick choked on a drink of the tea. He nearly spit it out on the table.

"Oh my…" he cut off and puckered his lips together. His face set in a deep frown. "What is in that? It tastes like syrup."

Ava laughed out loud at his reaction. "Trick, it is sweet tea."

Silas stomped his brother's foot under the table. Trick tried another sip and kept his disgust down this time. "Sorry, Emmie. It's not bad. I've just never…" he stammered as he ran his tongue over his teeth, "had tea leave a film over my teeth before. But this…" He pointed down to the bowl of beans. "…this looks delicious." She could tell he didn't think so, but she appreciated that he was trying.

Silas glared at his brother across the table like an alpha dog waiting for another member of the pack to back down. Eventually, Trick looked down at his plate and stuffed his face with cornbread and beans. He looked up at Emmie and gave her a thumbs up and smiled with his mouth full.

Gabe went on and on about how beans and cornbread were an acquired taste, which he enjoyed. Ava mainly sipped the tea, saying over and over what a great cook Emmie was and she was saving room for the applesauce. Silas drained his glass of tea and fed himself heaping spoonfuls of the beans and bacon. Every time she stole a glance at him he was swallowing and smiling. So much so that she knew it wasn't real.

He was pretending to like it and somehow that was worse than Trick's boast earlier. The rest of the meal was an eaten in an uncomfortable silence. She should have known better than to cook such a poor, country meal for four people who could have hundreds of dollars wired to their bank account anytime they wanted.

She wasn't bitter. She wasn't even embarrassed. Emmie just realized for the first time how different their life was from hers.

Chapter Twenty-five

Before the dishes had been cleared Ava's father called to check on things. He was uneasy that she had been left behind without any of her immediate family. To him she was still a child. Once he'd gotten the all clear from Ava that everything was going fine, he asked to speak to Silas. Emmie was surprised to see that he took the call in her father's office—he obviously wanted to be away from the others. Gabe followed behind him but Trick hung around to help clean up the dishes. From the bits of conversation that Emmie had picked up, it seemed there was something important going on with a court case. Al was depending on Silas to help close it out, since he was stuck in Chicago.

The girls and Trick headed into the kitchen. Ava and Trick were masters at easy conversation. But their attempts to draw Emmie into their antics were met with nods, smiles, and shrugs. She wasn't angry, just lost in her thoughts.

It was like her eyes had been opened for the first time. The house was too grand. Their clothes had real labels. They had cars. They knew how to drive. They went to college (except Ava… she had no ambition for that and no need for the money). They had real families. They did not work in a general store. They did not wake early to can applesauce. They did not make moonshine in the hopes for a few extra bucks. They did not eat beans and cornbread.

"Earth to Emmie," Trick repeated. A quick scan of the room showed that Ava had left and she hadn't even noticed.

She smiled over at him, shaking her head to clear her thoughts. "Sorry."

"I'm sorry if I hurt your feelings. It really was good. I know you worked hard on it." He took a step closer to her. He put a kind hand under her chin and lifted it so she was looking straight at him. "We all really appreciate it, okay? Just needed you to know that." He tried to give her a carefree grin but came up short.

Emmie nodded, "I know, it's fine. It's even okay if you don't like it. I'm not pouting, cross my heart. I've just had a lot on my mind lately."

Trick nodded and thought for a second. He leaned down and whispered in her ear. He wanted to be as close to her brain as possible, in hopes it would take. "Don't think about it too much."

Emmie looked back at him with wide eyes. What was he talking about... how could he know her thoughts? "Excuse me?"

He gave her his crooked grin and cocked his head to the side staring down at her. "Don't overthink it Emmie. Whatever's going on in your pretty head." He touched one of her curls with his pointer finger. "Just go with it. He pining for you, ya know? Whatever is on your mind..." he took a step back, "let it go."

"Who's pining for her?" Silas's voice boomed from the doorway of the kitchen.

Trick's grin turned into a wide smile. His eyes were amused as he opened his mouth to speak. "You are, brother."

Startled, Silas's mouth fell open for a brief second before he composed himself. "Yeah, what's your point, Patrick?" he spit his brother's full name. "I'm pretty sure she doesn't need you to tell her that."

He cleared the space between them in a few short steps. "You don't, do you?"

Words failed her, so she just shook her head quietly, "That's not what I'm thinking about."

Trick left the room. Neither of them noticed his exit.

"What's on your mind?" He sat on a chair at the small table in the kitchen and pulled her into his lap. She felt her heart rate pick up. Never in her life had she ever sat in man's lap.

"It's fine. I'm fine." She smiled and hoped it was convincing.

"Let's not lie to one another," he said. But as soon as the words left his mouth he felt like a hypocrite. How could he tell her that? After he'd, just days ago, rummaged through her house and contemplated taking seven hundred dollars from under her floorboard. How could he say let's not lie after he had set the fire that torched her stepfather's car and sat by while she believed in an accident that never happened. Silas swallowed hard.

"Okay, I'm not fine. I don't fit in with you... any of you really," she answered honestly. "I'm not..." She shrugged and paused unsure what to say. She looked down at her hands and picked at her cuticles. "I have never been out of Kentucky. I haven't been to college... and I eat beans and cornbread."

His brow creased deeply in-between his eyes. He rubbed his jaw trying to decide what to say next. "Em, sweetheart." A nervous laugh escaped him. "You'll go to college. And none of what you just said matters. You think I care what you eat?"

Emmie stepped out of his hold, paced across the room and threw up her arms. "It's not about what I eat... that's just an example," she sighed. "I'm just saying I'm not like you."

He laughed again. "I'm pretty sure if you were just like me, then I wouldn't be pining for you." His sarcasm didn't slip past her.

"I am not kidding. It bothers me," she sighed. "If you run out of money, you make a call and it comes through a wire and into your bank account. Like, like..." She threw her hands up again. "Like a magic trick." She touched her chest. "Me... I need money... I get a job, and if that's not enough, I eat beans and cornbread until I get paid again..." She was fully aware that her argument really didn't make much sense. Emmie was metaphorically on her soapbox now and knew she needed to step down.

A glance in his direction showed his feathers were up. He was proud and no doubt didn't like having his money thrown in his face... or compared to magic.

"Emmie. I work for my money. I. Work. Hard. Day and night. Things you don't even know." He rubbed a hand through his hair and then continued, "Don't put me in a box. Rest assured, if I need money wired, it's my money. What's this about? Do you need money? Because if you do..." He started but she cut him off.

"No, I don't need your money. That's not what this is about." She shook her head and tried to gather her thoughts. What was this discussion about? That's when it came to her. This wasn't about them as much as it was about her. She didn't know who she was anymore.

"Sorry," she rubbed her face, "it's just that I am working through some things. Everything is changing so quickly… too quickly. Like I can't figure out which end is up sometimes." *Like Ronnie's death, jobs, moonshine, engagement rings, Silas, college, money.*

"Now that," he said, pointing his finger at her from across the room and nodding as he walked slowly over to her. "That I understand. Now, listen to me." He touched the fabric of her dress directly above her heart. "This is what I care about."

He pulled her close to his chest and wrapped his arms around her. He still didn't really understand what the outburst was about earlier, but he did know she never needed to feel less than him.

He put a hand on each of her cheeks and pulled her face up to his. "And you're wrong about that stuff you said earlier. It's me that doesn't deserve your beans and cornbread." That was one of the most honest things he'd ever said to her.

Chapter Twenty-six

Emmie laughed and rolled her eyes. She wasn't sure if she was rolling her eyes at his comment or at herself. He had sent her flowers and had been so good to her today and she freaked out on him. Needless to say, she was beginning to feel a little embarrassed. Flowers. She hadn't even mentioned the flowers he'd brought back home to her. How ungrateful.

"Thanks again for the flowers. I loved them," she said honestly.

He smiled but said nothing. She waited for a few moments for him to brag or laugh about the flowers he'd sent to Mr. Thomas but he never said a word. He wasn't going to tell her. Should she bring it up to him?

"Emmie I have the most exciting news. We are going to have a HUGE celebration. But we have so much work to do between now and then... You must help me," Ava shouted as she danced into the kitchen. Gabe was close on her heels.

Oh my God. He had done it. He had proposed to her. Emmie didn't even think he'd had time to get the ring but he must have. She smiled and grabbed Ava's left hand. Gabe appeared in her peripheral vision shaking his head no, he may have been silent but he was very animated.

Emmie recovered. She shook Ava's hand and danced with her. "A celebration," she exclaimed. Ava was so excited that she never noticed her friend's mistake.

"Yes, we are going to an early Halloween party. And get this—we will wear costumes. Emmie, will you make them for us? Please, please?" she begged her friend.

"Sure, of course," Emmie nodded. Us, where in the world was Emmie going to find money to buy fabric for a Halloween costume?

Ava pulled Emmie into the living room and shared all of the details about the upcoming celebration. Apparently Ava had spoken with her mother after Silas got off the phone. October thirty-first was on a Friday this year and they were going to meet in some hotel in Louisville for the elaborate party. Women would wear costumes and Ava's parents had rented a block of hotel rooms for a couple nights and they insisted she bring Emmie.

She kept her thoughts to herself, but weren't these people supposed to be taking care of some poor dying relative? How could they be stopping to plan an elaborate celebration? Emmie carefully worded the question to Ava. She looked puzzled and shrugged her shoulders. It was Gabe who answered with an annoyed look at Emmie. He blurted out that Al thought Ava's mom needed a reason to celebrate because she had been working so hard to take care of her sick uncle. With a pointed look in her direction he said, "You've been through a lot too. We could all use a reason to celebrate." He tried to add an easy smile but something in his eyes looked anxious.

Ava nodded and agreed, accepting his quick answer. Something about his look told Emmie there was more to the story than just a need for a night of fun but she let it go. She'd be lying if she said she wouldn't enjoy having something like this to look forward to. Emmie hadn't been north of Smith's Grove in years. She would work out the costume one way or another. Goodness knows she still had enough of her mama's old sewing supplies around the house.

Later that night, Silas insisted on driving her home. Emmie supposed it was because he'd grown up in a big city and had an irrational fear of late-night walks. She didn't argue with him this time. Just hugged her friends goodbye and walked to the car. Spotty followed closely behind her, wagging his tail.

"Nope," Silas said, looking at the dog, "you're walking."

"Oh, come on," Emmie laughed. "He'd love it."

Silas sighed and opened the door for her and the dog, muttering something under his breath. She was pretty sure she heard a swear word. The dog settled into the back seat, his face pressed against the window.

Silas always held the door open for her. She realized that she had never seen Ronnie hold the door for her mama. Such a simple gesture but it made her feel like a somebody. The thought struck her out of nowhere. She was sad her Ma had never had that.

"You ever been to a Halloween party?" Silas asked, lighting a cigarette. She liked the easy conversation.

"No, I don't guess I have. Not any with costumes or anything. You?" she wondered.

He shrugged, "A few."

"You're going to this one, right?" she asked.

"You think I'm going to let you go to a party in a hotel with our family alone?" he laughed, "Besides, they want everyone there."

They, who are they? His tone made her feel the same strangeness she'd felt earlier about this impromptu shindig. "Who is everyone? Will your family be there?"

"Yeah. You'll meet the whole McDowell clan." His face looked unsure also.

That made her heart skip. She realized that she knew absolutely nothing about his family.

"I hadn't thought about that. Now, your dad is Ava's uncle... Molly's brother?" she asked, questioning what she thought was true.

Silas nodded, taking a draw from his cigarette. "Michael, Mum is Ann-Claire, me, Patrick, or Trick as you know him, and Jem."

"Jem?" she asked. She'd never heard of another brother.

"Jem," he nodded.

"I didn't know about Jem," Emmie repeated.

He nodded again. "Much younger. Still in school."

School like college or school like really young? Why was he not telling her about his family?

They pulled up to her house and he helped her out of the car then walked her to the door. She was surprised when he walked all the way in and looked around the house.

"Silas? What are you doing?" She couldn't help but laugh.

When it met his inspection he walked back to the front door where she was standing. "I just don't like you all the way out here alone."

She laughed and grabbed his hand. "I'm fine."

"Yeah, I know you think you are. I just wish you'd reconsider," he said.

"Thank you again for my flowers…" It was on the tip of her tongue to bring up again about Mr. Thomas's but she thought better of it. She really wasn't sure what she'd say anyway.

He smiled. His eyes softened. "I'm glad you liked them." He brushed his hand through her hair. They stood there like that for while. It may have been moments or hours. She couldn't tell. Time seemed to play tricks on her in moments like this.

He shook his head and brushed a kiss on her temple. "Emmie I've got a lot of work to do for Uncle Al at the firm. We're wrapping up an important case this Friday and there's a couple of things he needs me to take care of, so…" He shrugged his shoulder like he was having a hard time finding the words. "I'm going to busy the next week or so. I probably won't have much time for…" He didn't finish.

She could assume that sentence could be finished with a "you." He probably wouldn't have much time for her. Emmie nodded, accepting his words. She was surprised to feel a little sting. He seemed to run hot or cold with her and she didn't really know why.

"That's fine," she said because there was nothing else she could say.

He nodded, "Lock up, okay?"

She nodded.

****

The next few days time seemed to tick by slowly. She tutored Max and that provided a much-needed break to the monotony of the home-work-home routine. She was disappointed that Walter didn't meet Max and her in town at the end session like he usually did. She bet he hadn't yet worked out a way to get rid of her apple pie 'shine and didn't have the heart to face her yet.

Ava had called her nearly every night to share some new costume idea. With each phone call her ideas seemed to get a bit more bizarre—last night she said they should dress as their favorite holiday. Ava had actually suggested that she may wear nothing but a gown covered in hearts to dress as St. Valentine's Day. Thank goodness Emmie told her about a few new Halloween patterns that had just arrived at the shop. Ava soon agreed they could brainstorm some alternatives together.

At work the next day Emmie was lucky. A package arrived for Mr. Thomas that he was positively giddy about. He practically skipped to the office and locked himself away in privacy. Emmie peeked her head in to let him know she was headed to lunch. He actually put his arm over a small black box to keep it from her view.

"Emmie, you have worked so hard today." His too easy smile made her wonder what he was up to. "Please feel free to take an extra ten minutes."

Well, that was weird. She knew better than to look a gift horse in the mouth... especially when the gift horse was Mr. Thomas. So, she left as quickly as possible without any other questions.

Emmie walked across College Street and found Ava already sitting on the park bench facing the fountain. She was surprised to see that Ava had a brown bag and two bottles of Coke. She hadn't really expected her to remember the actual food part to their meeting for lunch.

Ava passed Emmie the soda and half a sandwich as soon as she sat down. "Eat up. I know the old coot doesn't give you much time," she gave a look of annoyance as she spoke.

"He actually gave me ten extra minutes. He is elated with some black box that came in the mail," Emmie shrugged.

"What an odd bird." Ava shook her head. "Enough about him. Where are the patterns?" she smiled.

Emmie pulled the envelope out of her purse. There were five illustrations on the front, girls with flapper-style Halloween costumes: witch, bat, pumpkin, spider, ghost.

Ava took the pattern envelope and studied it closely. "Hmm... this will be perfect for you," she said, pointing to the witch, "and this will be perfect for me." She pointed to the pumpkin dress with a full jack-o-lantern skirt and tight bodice.

"When can we start?" she asked with a toothy smile.

Chapter Twenty-seven

Emmie laughed at Ava's impatience. However, the truth was, she actually welcomed the project. It would be good to have something to do with her nights. She found it harder and harder to find sleep these days and it would be a great distraction from everything on her mind.

She swallowed a gulp of her Coke. "I can start as soon as we get the fabric. Do you want the bodice this tight and the skirt to flow out like a ballerina?" Emmie wondered aloud, touching the simple illustration on the cover of the pamphlet envelope.

"Yes, do you like it?" Ava asked excited.

Emmie nodded to answer her question. She gobbled down the rest of her sandwich and finished the soda as she looked over the fabric requirements for the pattern.

"Want to go to the fabric shop and see if they have what we need? I have time, if we make it quick," Emmie said.

The fabric shop was just down College Street. It actually had a whole section devoted to the bold fabrics of autumn and Halloween. Emmie made quick work of picking out what she needed for Ava's costume and headed for the counter.

"Wait, did you get the black and silver for yours?" Ava asked, grabbing her friend's hand.

Emmie pursed her lips. "Oh… well, I think I may have some black that would be perfect back at the house."

"But what about the lace overlay? It's what makes yours beautiful." Ava smiled pointing at the image.

"I'll work something out," she shrugged a shoulder. "I really need to get back to work. Just buy those and I'll pick them up from you later, okay?"

Emmie turned to head out of the store. "Emma Rose," Ava stepped forward and grabbed her friend by the arm, "I have known you since you were three years old and I know when you're lying. Your nose flares... like that." She pointed at her friend and they both smiled. "I'm buying this fabric. My treat... well Dad's treat. But you know he thinks of you as family."

"Ava, it's fine." She put her hand up to stop the conversation. "I know I have some black at home that will work perfectly. Don't worry about me, okay." Her pride made this conversation a tough pill to swallow.

Emmie reached down and touched the burnt orange tulle that would soon become Ava's skirt. "It's going to be lovely. This is your party, I'm just happy to be a part of it. Don't worry about me." She glanced down at Ava's watch. "I'm sorry. I really have to get back." She ran from the fabric shop without waiting for her friends reply.

When Emmie got home that evening there was a large navy box with a red ribbon on her porch. Balancing the box and her purse she unlocked the door. Dropping all of the belongings on the table, she pulled the ends of the ribbon and it fell to the side. She eased the lid off the box to find it was filled with the supplies from the fabric shop, including a soft black silk fabric and full bolt lace overlay material. This was twice as expensive as the fabric for Ava's dress. She was going to kill her. The pattern was at the bottom of the box with a short note pinned to it.

Emmie,

Since I know you won't let me pay you for the sewing, I thought you could accept the cloth for your dress without contest. See, no charity case here. No harm done. Just me paying you for services rendered.

Love, Ava.

Emmie shook her head—she should have known. The cost of this fabric was enough to pay for many weeks worth of groceries. But the gesture was kind and appreciative. Ava was a good friend. She set the lovely black fabric aside and put all of her attention on Ava's pumpkin dress. It was going to be stunning. Emmie wasn't very hungry that evening, so she just snacked on some cheese and crackers while she pinned and pieced Ava's costume together. Too much was on her mind.

Around ten her phone rang.

"Hello," she answered.

"Emmie?" a familiar voice asked.

"Yes."

"Hey. It's me, Silas," he sounded uneasy.

"Hi."

"Sorry. I've been busy. Got good news though. We won that case I was working on. Got the guy off." She heard the flick of his lighter and an intake of breath through the line.

Emmie realized this was the most he had ever talked to her about work. Unfortunately, she knew nothing about law or court trials. She didn't know exactly what to say.

"That's wonderful. Congrats." She hoped that was sufficient.

"Thanks," Silas answered.

Awkward Pause. Then he spoke again.

"Tomorrow is that luncheon after church I told you about. Ya still want to come... with me?"

"Of Course. I'll bring some applesauce. Should I bring anything else?"

"No. That will be great." She could tell he was smiling by his tone. "Well, I've got to go but I'll see you tomorrow, okay?"

"Okay, good night Silas."

"Night."

She noticed her heart was beating faster when they got off the phone but she wasn't exactly sure why. Emmie tried to go back to piecing together Ava's costume but couldn't focus. She blamed it on the fact the dog wouldn't stop whining at some animal outside. But really it was just that her hands and mind didn't seem to be connected. At least she'd be able to see if things were more normal with Silas tomorrow. Whatever normal was.

Now she just needed to hear from Walt. She'd thought of calling him a hundred times. But she just couldn't think what she could possibly say to him. *Hey Walt, Have you unloaded all that apple pie 'shine I made or is it fermenting in your barn?* Probably Not.

She stood and walked to the kitchen to get another glass of tea. She wasn't going to sleep much tonight anyway, at least the added caffeine might help her focus on the costume. As she glanced out the kitchen window she noticed a light in the distance, like a lantern moving up the hill toward the cave.

"Walter," she said to Spotty, "is that who you've been whining about?"

Without another thought she grabbed her shawl and tore into the woods after him, shutting Spotty in the house. She was surprised how quickly he was moving in the distance. Walt generally had a slower gate.

"Walt," she shouted to no avail. He just kept right on moving.

She walked past the barn and made it to the tree, still scorched from Ronnie's wreck. Her heart always dropped when she neared it. She stopped put her hand on the trunk's charred remains and said a quick prayer of peace for his soul and kept walking up the hill.

When she finally made it to the mouth of the cave her entire body froze. It was not Walt she'd followed into the cave.

Chapter Twenty-eight

Emmie's breath caught in her throat. Why would he be here? She ducked behind a large rock near the entrance. Bo Johnson pulled still paste out of a tin and started rubbing it over the nooks and joints of Ole Maizy, Walter's still. She knew him from school. His family owned a huge plot of land down in Riverside. He was one of the Johnsons Walter had mentioned a few days ago.

Bo had always been a nice guy. They were always partnered together for arithmetic and science in school. He was tall and thin with close-shaved hair and a frame of a beard stretching from sideburn to chin. He'd always been such a good guy. For the life of her she couldn't imagine why he'd be stealing Walter's moonshine.

Emmie watched with bated breath as he started up the still, mimicking the motions she'd seen Walter do the first night in the cave. Then he turned his attention to the barrel on the other end of the still. He seemed to be checking things on the spout. When everything seemed to meet his satisfaction he sat down in Walt's chair. Then he pulled a small book out of his back pocket and started reading it.

She couldn't believe it. He was just sitting there, waiting for all of Walt's 'shine to run out into his jar. Emmie had to do something. She knew Bo pretty well but she wasn't sure how he would react to her sneaking up on him. Emmie glanced around in search of something to protect herself if this went awry. She picked up a large rock from the ground and wrapped it tightly in her fist. She took a deep breath...

one... two... three...

"Why Bo Johnson, what in the world are you doing out on my farm this time of night? You like to have scared me to death." She smiled, keeping her hand behind her back.

He jumped up and grabbed the shotgun to his right before he realized who it was.

"Emmie?" He eased his grip on the gun and put it back in its resting place. It didn't escape her notice that he didn't completely let go of it.

He looked down for a second like he was a little embarrassed. "Emmie what are ya doing out here?"

"Well, I was sewing Ava's costume for this silly Halloween party she's got her head wrapped around right now and went to get myself a glass of tea. When I looked out the window I saw a light moving up my hills and I wondered who'd be out here traipsing around my land this time of night. Low and behold if it wasn't you." She pointed with her free hand.

He shook his head and muttered something under his breath. "Emmie I'm sorry if I scared ya. Want me to walk ya back to your house? It's mighty dark out there," he offered, taking a step closer to her.

"No, no I'm fine." She looked around the still again careful to keep her right hand out of his view. "Whatcha doing out here Bo?" she repeated.

He closed the distance between them. "Emmie. You're a smarter girl than your acting like right now. You forget, I sat by you in class for ten years."

If you'd asked her in school if she would ever be afraid of Bo Johnson she would have laughed... but now, as he looked down, her heart pounded out of rhythm. She swallowed hard and gripped her hand tighter on the rock. She didn't want to hit him with it but if he got any closer to her, she would have to.

"What are you doing here? I know this isn't yours," she said, looking up at him, squaring her shoulders for a fight.

"What are you hiding in your hand, Emmie? We're friends," he said, inching closer to her.

Emmie drew her arm back and tried to step away from him. He reached one long arm around her and squeezed her fist until the rock dropped to the ground. She pulled her hand out of his and ran trying to get out of that cave. She heard his footsteps closing in behind her and screamed as he grabbed her around the waist and pulled her back into the light of the cave.

"Emmie. Good Lord girl. Calm down. I ain't gonna hurt ya. Just didn't want ya throwing that rock at me. Now if I let go of ya, do you promise you'll hear me out?" he asked, his voice as kind as she had remembered.

Emmie nodded. What other choice did she have? She stood as still as a mouse.

"Alright," he said, "it ain't what it looks like. Walter will be here any minute and we'll sort this whole thing out."

"He might shoot ya if he see you stealing his 'shine, Bo. You know that, right?" she warned him.

Bo's voice boomed with laughter. "You ain't gotta worry about that, Emmie."

"Emmie?" They heard Walter's voice before they saw him. Unlike Bo, he didn't travel these hills with a foolish light.

"What the hell is Emmie doing up here?" he shouted as he rounded the corner.

Walter's footsteps crunched on the freshly fallen leaves that littered the entrance. He came through the mouth of the cave and walked straight over to her. He pointed a crooked finger in her direction. "You may not be my child but I got about a half a mind to take you over my knee. What are you thinking being out here? Your lucky Bo didn't shoot ya with that shotgun."

"I'd never shoot Emmie," Bo said, wiping his hands on his blue jeans. This whole discussion was making him uncomfortable. "But she was gonna hit me upside the head with this rock." He grinned handing Walter the rock he'd forced out of her hand earlier.

Emmie glared over in his direction then turned to Walter. "I was just taking up for you, ya know. I thought he was up here stealing your moonshine."

"So you was just gonna attack him with this little rock? Ain't you got a lick of sense girl? First ya take all that…" he started but didn't finish. He just pulled out his pipe, sat in his chair and shook his head, leaving her actions and his thoughts unspoken.

"Well, what's he doing up here then?" she asked, pointing at Bo.

"How does she know about this, Walt?" Bo asked.

Walter looked back and forth between the two of them and laughed. "I don't owe no answers to neither one of ya kids." Bo and Emmie shared looks of annoyance. "But since you was gonna bust him open with a rock for me, I guess I'll tell ya this." He looked at Emmie. "Me and Bo's grandpa got a deal. Remember how I told ya that Revenuer Cliff Harris's barn got burned down for being a Revenuer?"

Emmie nodded.

"Well, Cliff blamed Bo's grandpappy. Your friend's dad and his fancy team of lawyers got him off. Bo's pap wants to have a little get together with his family and friends for a celebration. And, of course, they are needing a little 'shine. Being as he's had to mind his Ps and Qs lately with the heat of the case and all, his family ain't got no mash to distill."

"Walter. You speak too freely to her," Bo warned.

"Kid, you are on her land... taking 'shine from my still. You don't make the rules here." Walter stood and dared Bo to go on.

"Like I was saying with the trial and all, they ain't been in operation and need some goods quick. I had something I needed to take care of and Bart Johnson had the right friends to help me do that," Walt said with an arched eyebrow. Emmie knew she was missing a piece of this story but hadn't put it all together yet.

"So you're giving him your mash and letting him use the still?" Emmie asked, trying to be sure she understood.

"Yep. But it ain't charity," Bo said. "My pap's helping him too. We gave him the right connection. That's something that don't come cheap."

Walter nodded. "That's right." Then after a pause he added, "That's as much as either of you two needs to know about this. Except you," he pointed at Bo, "you don't know nothing."

"What's that supposed to mean?" Bo asked.

"I mean, you don't know nothing about seeing her tonight. Me and you... we just met up here and had a boring night distilling this mash. No Emmie, are we clear? I want to be sure this is plain as day. I've known your pap all my life but if I hear word that you told him anything about Emmie being up here or had known about any of this mess...

you're gonna need more than that shotgun to keep you safe," he said. Emmie was surprised to hear him sound so ruthless.

Bo thought about it for a minute. "Emmie I don't know how you got mixed up in this but you ain't got to worry about me telling nobody," he said, looking down embarrassed again.

"Bo you were better than a life of this too. You were smart. You could go to jail. Why are you doing this?" she asked curiously.

Walter looked like he might tell them both to be quiet but he didn't. He just chewed on his pipe and looked annoyed.

"Emmie, it ain't even about the drink or the money, it's about the tradition. This trade's been passed down from my pap's greatgrandfather... probably even before that." He thought then looked right at her again. "No government or 18th amendment is gonna stop us." He spoke with such passion that she felt bad for questioning him. "We do it for us. It's a part of our heritage that we won't let go just because congress makes some law. This tradition has been in our family all these years. Now, times are tough... if we can make a few bucks off it we will. Our recipe is the best in the hills."

"Second best," Walter said with a smile.

"Hmm," Bo huffed, refusing to fully take the older man's bait.

Emmie rubbed her face and took in her surroundings: barns burning, car crashes, tradition, court cases, old friends, and old men. This was so much bigger than she was. She suddenly just wanted out of that cave. She felt claustrophobic, like the walls were closing in around her.

Emmie shrugged her shoulder and sighed, "I'm sorry. I didn't know... I just..." But she didn't know how to finish.

"Emmie girl, just go back to ya house. Bo, walk her back. I'll keep an eye on things up here," Walter ordered.

Bo shuffled toward the mouth of the cave, stopped and arched an eyebrow at Emmie, waiting to see if she would join him. Emmie walked over to Walter, swallowed hard and whispered, "I know I just keep messing up. I hope you know I'm just tryin' to help."

Walter laughed and pulled the pipe out of his mouth. "I know girl. Get down to your house. Let Bo walk ya, he's a good boy. Nothing to fear." His eyes sparkled. What was he playing at? Emmie turned and fell into step with Bo.

"I'm sorry about that rock. I just didn't know if you were going to do," she said.

"Nah… I shouldn't have been so stupid as to carry that lantern up the hill. Just didn't know where I was going exactly. You aren't gonna call the police or nobody are ya?" he asked, helping her over a fallen sapling.

Emmie laughed. "Lord no, don't worry about that." He really had no idea how much Walter meant to her or how deep she'd already dug herself into this moonshine mess.

As they rounded the corner Bo glanced over at the charred tree. "Is that where it happened?"

He didn't have to say what. Everyone here knew Ronnie had died in a fiery crash on her farm.

"Yeah," she said.

"I'm sorry about that. It's awful about you being out here all alone. Guess that's why Walt's taken you under his wing though," Bo thought aloud.

Emmie hadn't thought of that but it might be true. They were quiet most of the way back to her house. He stopped as they neared her porch. "I guess since I'm running your water through that still it'd only be right to invite ya to the celebration. Walter will be there, you could probably go with him and Mae. Nobody'd question it, they'd probably be glad to see ya. You ain't been at church since Ronnie passed. Every-one's been wondering how you're holding up."

Emmie hadn't expected this turn of events. "Okay, well… sure," she shrugged. "I just might come."

She had to be polite. She wasn't exactly sure that she would go to the party but surely she had to pretend to consider the invitation, right?

"Good. Hope you can come," he smiled.

She turned and unlocked the door and waved through the window. Spotty propped up beside her barking at Bo as he walked away. That night she slept a little easier with Walter and Bo on the farm. She didn't feel so alone. Emmie still felt bad about messing up Walter's moonshine and almost messing up whatever was really going on in that cave tonight. But it felt good to not be alone.

By the time she closed her eyes it was nearly two in the morning and she had to make eight o'clock Mass. Her stomach flipped at the thought of seeing Silas tomorrow, so she tried to keep her mind on other things, like if Bo's granddad didn't burn down that barn, who did? Were there more moonshiners in the county than Walter and Bo's pap? She had no idea… but she was sure of one thing—she didn't really want to find out.

Chapter Twenty-nine

Four hours of sleep did not look good on her. Her eyes were puffy and red. She couldn't get Bo out of her mind but it wasn't the same way she couldn't get Silas out of her mind. Bo's family as moonshiners had thrown her for a loop. Their family seemed so normal, they were smart with a strong farm, respected in the community, and well-known, but they made moonshine. They'd even attracted enough attention that a revenuer had blamed his pap for burning down his barn. She had awoken all night thinking about this, like her body rested but her mind never let go of the new information she'd learned.

Surprisingly enough, she didn't feel that tired though. Her nerves were up with the thought of seeing Silas for the first time in days. Emmie put on her best dress, the same drop-waist frock from Chicago that she had worn the day she met Silas. Being he was a guy, he probably wouldn't even notice. Looking outside the small kitchen window she noticed the gray skies had opened up and it had started to rain.

Maybe she should add a car to the list of things that she needed to be saving money for, but would never be able to afford. That thought actually made her laugh out loud. Even if she had a car, she had no idea how to drive. Ronnie always told her there was no need for her to learn because she could depend on him to take her places until she married. He didn't think it was right for a woman to drive around alone. Eventually, she had just given up the fight—choose your battle was an important thing to remember with Ronnie.

She walked around the stairs and pilfered through a small chest in the living room until she found an old black umbrella. Walking in the rain was something that Emmie enjoyed, however, she'd spent an hour and half this morning trying to look nice: pinning, powdering, primping. The rain was sure to make her makeup smear and leave her ankle-deep in mud.

Emmie reached to the top of the cabinet and pulled out a large dark brown picnic basket. She'd come across the umbrella and basket a few days ago when she was cleaning. She had been spending so much time away lately that she had barely noticed how the place was beginning to fall apart around her.

Besides, a day spent on her hands and knees scrubbing the floors and washing the windows meant she couldn't think about how she had messed up Walt's income with some silly apple pie moonshine idea. Or that Silas was too busy with his job to phone her. Well, that had been the theory anyway. Her mind still wandered back to those things from time to time.

Pilfering around in the drawers, she found some of the blue gingham fabric that was left from decorating the moonshine jars. Decorating moonshine jars—her face flushed at the memory. What a dumb idea. She wrapped the fabric around the jars to keep them from knocking against each other on her walk to church. Balancing the umbrella on her shoulder and tucking the basket handle into her elbow, Emmie stepped out into the weather. Spotty settled into step with her.

The rhythmic sound of the rain drumming on the umbrella was peaceful. Rain always made her feel more spiritual. She couldn't put her finger on the why exactly. It was just the balance she guessed. People gave the sun all the credit for plants growing, sustaining life, and happiness. She chose to find her solace in the rain.

The ground was already soft. She walked down the drive, near the road that would lead her to town. Emmie tried to keep most of her weight on her toes but could still feel her heels sinking deeper into the earth. The loud hum of a car was closing in on her. She was surprised when it stopped about ten feet from her. Trick hopped out of the passenger side and waved his arms for her to hurry. She picked up pace, he took her umbrella and pushed her into the car before sliding into the backseat. When the dog acted like he may try to nose his way into the car Silas looked back at Emmie and spoke.

"You don't expect me to give the dog a lift to church do you?" A smile played at the corner of his lips.

"No. Go back to the porch, boy," she said out the window. He took a step away from the car but didn't move all the way back to the house until they had pulled onto the street.

"What were you doing?" Silas asked, shifting the car into gear.

"Umm… walking to church," she answered.

"In the rain?" He shook his head. "Were you in a hurry and couldn't wait for the car?"

"I didn't know you were coming to get me… And, I don't melt in the water," she smiled.

"You're sweet enough to. Don't all things made of sugar melt?" he mocked.

She snorted, "That's about the sorriest line I've ever heard, Silas McDowell."

"Ohh," Trick laughed from the backseat, "a girl just put you in your place, brother."

"Shut up, Trick," Silas barked but then his crooked grin appeared and gave away his amusement.

"Alright, no more lines… unless they are original. Let's just say from now on if I ask you to go somewhere, assume I'm going to pick you up, okay?"

"Alright," she nodded. "And thank you."

****

Saint Joseph Catholic Church was as beautiful as she remembered. It was built in the late 1800s by German and Italian immigrants that moved to the area. Its handcrafted brick walls reached up taller than any of the small houses that surrounded it. Elaborate gothic style stained glass windows displayed popular stories from the bible. Even those in town that couldn't read or understand the language of the Mass could still learn just by looking at the stories the windows told. Two elaborate wooden doors were propped open welcoming those from the street. By the time they arrived at the church, the organist had already begun playing. The eerie calm of the hymn bursting through the organ pipes filled the air. With every breath you took, the music went straight from your lungs to your soul.

Emmie had grown up going to Ronnie's church sporadically. Sometimes in the sermon the preacher would mention the local Catholics. Saying they were just folks that "liked their wine" and "used the church collection to buy new golden things to hang on their altar." It was the general belief among most of the folks in town that Catholics believed in the same God and Jesus but that's pretty much where all the similarities stopped.

Emmie remembered repeating this to her mother once. She'd looked at her with a stern eye and said, "Emma Rose. Who are we to judge how people want to worship? Maybe they just want to make things be as pretty as possible for God. You know how we put on our best clothes? Maybe that's all there trying to do with their building. It is not our job to judge. You'd be best to remember that."

Mama didn't get angry often but when she was disappointed, her words were wrapped in meaning. It was a conversation Emmie had never forgotten. From that day on when she had gone to church with Ava, she'd only looked for the beauty in the building. She found it everywhere—in the long wooden pews, in the elaborate columns that reached to an arched ceiling, but mostly she found it in the way the church was stone-silent all through Mass other than the music or the priest. It was like everyone there was so caught up in the experience they didn't have time to think about anything else. It never ceased to amaze her.

Silas was no different than all of the other church patrons. He walked in and genuflected, bringing his knee all the way to the ground and bowed his head in reverence before entering the pew. She wanted to mimic his movements but was afraid of doing it wrong. So she kept her head down in what she hoped looked like a sign of respect and then scooted across the bench next to him. As soon the three of them were in place and had their belongings situated, he and Trick knelt on the ground. Arms rested on the pew in front of them, hands folded together, heads bent in prayer. He and Trick seemed to move in unison almost like synchronized swimmers.

But when she looked at their faces, she realized they were doing more than mindlessly going through the motions. They looked so honest, so pure. Trick's mouth was actually moving as he whispered some silent prayer. Silas was still but she could tell by his expression that his brain was working. She wondered what he might be praying for. Was he asking for something or maybe it was a prayer of thanksgiving? She would never know. Suddenly, it seemed like the moment was too private to watch.

She looked down and pushed her umbrella under the pew before deciding to join them on the kneeling bench. She guessed that she needed to do some praying of her own. Emmie closed her eyes and she brought her hands together. Before she whispered the first word, she felt a warm hand wrap around her right arm and squeeze it gently. Emmie peeked open her eyes to see Silas smiling over at her. He looked so pleased. He rubbed her arm and his eyes bore into hers, speaking without words. Then he folded his hands back together and continued his quiet meditation.

Chapter Thirty

The rain caused the luncheon to be moved from the parish lawn to a nearby restaurant downtown. The place was closed on Sundays but being that the owner was a member of the church he was more than happy to open it up. There weren't any tables large enough for them to all sit together. Ava and Gabe had joined another young couple that Emmie vaguely recognized from the store. They were a few years older than her. She was pretty sure that Ava had gone to school with them at St. Joe. Ava waved Emmie over to say a quick hello.

"Thanks for my fabric. But I told you not to do that." Emmie hugged her friend.

"Pish Posh." Ava waved her hands. "I can't look all hoity-toity and have you in some hand-me-down costume. Besides, I knew you'd never let me pay you money, so this way it's fair. Have you had a chance to start on them yet?"

"Yep. I started on yours first. I have most of it cut and pieced together, if you want to stop by I could get a couple of measurements before I start sewing," Emmie said.

Ava clapped her hands together and the girls made plans to get together later in the week for a fitting. If Ava was this excited over a simple costume, Emmie couldn't imagine how she would react when she found her wedding dress. She glanced over at Gabe and idly wondered if he had picked up the ring yet. He was in an easy conversation with Silas. It crossed to her mind to ask Silas if he knew when Gabe planned to propose. But then she remembered she had promised Gabe her silence. Emmie sighed and turned back to Ava who was going on about how beautiful the black silk was and how pretty it would be against her skin. Emmie smiled and tried to look happy. She really could use a good party, they all could.

"Are you dressing up?" Ava asked Silas.

"No way," he laughed.

"Oh, you and Gabe are a pair of wet blankets. I cannot get him to either." She elbowed Gabe.

"Well, we better find a seat," Silas said, grabbing Emmie's elbow to lead her away from the table.

The place had filled up quickly. Nearly every available table was taken. Families had spread out their picnic blankets in every space for kids to pile onto the floor. It was warm, busy and loud—such a contrast from the environment at the church. Emmie took her basket up to the row of tables to hold the food. She added a couple of jars of applesauce to each side and put a serving spoon out with each.

"Got us a seat over here," Trick called from a small square table in the back where he, Silas, and another young man were seated.

When she reached the table her breath caught in her throat for a moment, then she composed herself and sat. Sitting opposite her was the tall blond man that had let them into the speakeasy in Smith's Grove. She swallowed hard and nodded a polite hello to him.

Her mind raced with questions. How should she act? Was she supposed to act like she knew him? Her mouth felt dry. She was such a fool. Why had it not it occurred to her that she may see someone from the joint out in public.

"Emmie, this is Robert Drake. I believe you know his father, Sheriff Tim Drake." Silas pointed to the short dark-haired man sitting with his family in the corner.

Emmie swallowed hard trying to get enough saliva in her mouth to form a word. "I do," she nodded. "I do know Sheriff Drake. It's nice to meet you, Robert." She held her hand out over the table. He smiled and his eyes looked like they may be laughing at her discomfort. Robert glanced over at Silas but was met was a look of indifference, so he kept his amusement to himself.

Trick had the same natural talent as Ava. He struck up some conversation about the World Series, trying to ease an awkward moment. Something about the Giants vs. Senators in game seven and a new record. Thankfully, baseball was something that she knew almost nothing about. It would not be obvious if she bowed out of the conversation.

Silas scooted his chair closer to hers. "Ya alright?" he whispered.

"I'm fine, really." She gave him a smile that she hoped looked confident and easy. She could do fake faces. She'd had to give a lot of them in her life. When your step-dad was a drunk and you didn't even know your real dad, you learned to give fake faces of indifference or happiness. Silas seemed to buy it.

"Just didn't think about seeing folks out. But it's fine," she whispered. "So, you said his dad's the Sheriff?"

Silas sighed. You could always count on Emmie for a loaded question. There was so much more to that question than the words she asked. He chose to avoid the loaded part and just go for straight-line honesty, "Yep, that's what I said."

She stared right at him, blinking her eyes. God, he should take her in when he's questioning people. She communicated more with each blink than he did with a mouth full of words. Where was she going with all of this?

"Let's go get food before it's all gone," Silas said, interrupting the World Series discussion.

Silas grabbed her hand and led her to the makeshift buffet. It was odd holding hands in public. Not a bad odd, just odd. People noticed because Silas was a stranger in a small town and they were curious. If he noticed, he didn't let on. But then again, he wouldn't let on anyway. It wasn't his style. He didn't really seem to care about what folks thought.

While they waited in line she stood on her toes behind him and whispered, "I have some more questions... about the sheriff."

He nodded never looking back. "I thought you would." Then he helped himself to a couple spoonfuls of beans and a sliver of cornbread while grinning up at her. She caught his meaning and laughed in spite of herself.

When they returned to the table the conversation turned back to sports. Emmie had completely tuned them out to watch a couple of kids on the floor play a game of jacks. She laughed as one little girl continually beat an older boy. He didn't like it and pouted away before they could finish the last match.

"You did a good job," she smiled down at the child.

"Thanks." The little girl smiled back showing she was missing at least three teeth.

"You changed your mind on my offer of school, yet?" Silas asked. She hadn't noticed he was watching the jacks' game too.

She shook her head. "I already told you. I want to try this myself. You were right though."

His eyes widened, "I was? What about?"

"There is no timeline. Just because it doesn't happen now, doesn't mean it won't. I'm going to figure this out." she said. Nothing like a little rain and a good service to help clear your head. Well, that and watching Bo talk to passionately about his family's moonshine tradition. She wanted to speak with passion about something. The only thing she felt that strongly about was teaching. When she worked with Max, she felt like she was doing something important, something that mattered. Just like Bo felt when he was talking about his family's tradition.

Robert interrupted their conversation, "So, what about that Harris case against Mr. Johnson? You were working with Johnson, right? I heard he got off."

"Yeah, we represented Johnson. He was acquitted of all charges."

Silas shrugged. Emmie knew he wasn't going to elaborate.

"Well, I still say that Johnson was a scapegoat for him. He was afraid to put the blame on the real fellow. Johnson's just an old man, easy target. Cliff Harris is a..." Robert started then looked Emmie and chose his words carefully, "...coward for throwing the blame at him."

Silas said nothing just shrugged noncommittally again. But something about his eyes told Emmie that he agreed with Robert.

Cliff Harris, she had just heard that name. It was with Bo and Walter last night. Silas was representing Bo's pap? Was this the case he'd been spending all of this time on lately?

"The barn trial," Emmie said aloud. All three of the guys turned and looked at her. So she added, "Sorry, the barn that burned, right... that's what you're talking about?"

Robert nodded, "I'm surprised you know that. Most women around here don't keep up with the 'shine wars."

Emmie chewed her lip trying to think quickly. "Oh, I think I just overheard someone talking about it at the shop the other day." She felt guilty for the lie as soon as it came out of her mouth. She didn't want them to know how she'd heard it. No doubt they would be curious why Bo and Walter would talk to her about that sort of thing.

Silas frowned and faltered for a moment before picking up the conversation. He didn't believe her lie.

****

Trick caught a ride home with Ava and Gabe. It was weird that Emmie seemed to spend more time with Silas than Ava now. So much had changed in her life in the last few months. She guessed it was just as well considering Ava would be a married woman soon. Things change.

"I've still got my questions, you know," she said on the drive back to her house.

Silas nodded. She had expected him to tease her for asking so many questions but he didn't. He seemed to be as lost in thought.

"I may not be able to give you all the answers," he said cryptically.

She nodded unsure exactly what that meant or why he looked so serious now.

"You should probably know, I've got a few questions of my own," he said.

That caught her off guard.

I may not be able to give you all the answers either, she thought to herself.

He spoke again as he pulled into her drive, "Maybe I should come in and we can talk? Or would you rather do this another time?"

Emmie grabbed her picnic basket and umbrella. "Now is as good of time as any, I suppose."

Chapter Thirty-one

Her stomach somersaulted while she fiddled with the key to unlock the door. She walked in and put her wet umbrella on the hook by the door. Emmie unloaded the applesauce in the kitchen and put on a pot of coffee. The four hours of sleep she'd had the night before… and the grim expression on Silas's face made her think they were each going to need some caffeine. He pulled out one of the small kitchen chairs and sat down. His long legs folded double, barely fitting under the kitchen table.

"We can go in the living room, it would be more comfortable," she suggested.

"It's up to you. I'm fine in here though." He put his elbows on the table and rubbed his face like he was trying to get the courage to speak. He looked so torn. What was going on in his mind?

"So, who goes first?" she asked with a smile trying to lighten the mood.

"Ladies first," he said.

"The sheriff's son that I met today, he works at the speak. Is that normal? I mean is that intentional?" She dove in headfirst—beating around the bush wasn't her strong suit.

He thought for a minute. Trying to decide how to answer. "Yes." He was surprised at the honesty in his reply. At lunch today he expected just to tell her a lie. Just sell her on the story that Robert was just some young rebellious kid working at the joint behind his father's back.

She sat in silence waiting for him to continue explaining. When he didn't she opened her mouth and started to ask, "Why is…"

Silas cut her off. "Ah ah, my turn. You've already gone." For the first time since he entered the house, he smiled.

Well, she cut right to the chase, he would too. He didn't like that she had known about the moonshine wars between the bootleggers and revenuers. He had an uneasy feeling about her knowledge. The girl he thought she was, wouldn't have known that. She was Ronnie Talbot's stepdaughter after all... any knowledge had to make him suspicious. What else did she know?

"How do you know about Cliff Harris's barn and the trial?"

"I already told you..." she began.

The sound of his hand smacking the table made her jump out of her seat. She visibly flinched away from him. "Do not lie to me like you did at the lunch. I want the truth."

Damn, he'd scared her. He didn't mean to do that. Silas took a deep breath.

"I'm sorry, Emmie." He stood and turned, walking to the window. He rubbed his face again like he might rub the shadow of a beard he had right off his chin. This is why he knew it was a bad idea to mix business and pleasure, too much emotion tied up in it to do a good job with either.

He felt her small hand on his arm. When he looked down she was shaking her head with one hand on her mouth. For that instant she looked older than her years.

"Look, I'm sorry that I lied to you. I don't really know how to say the truth. I don't want to get people in trouble," she answered honestly and then continued. "But don't intimidate me, Silas. I will not be scared of you or anyone else. I've lived too many years afraid of Ronnie's next drunken move. For as long as I can remember it was like that. I won't have it now."

"I know, I know. I'm sorry," he opened his mouth but then closed it. "I shouldn't have talked to you like that, like you were one of the guys." He wanted to reach out and hug her but didn't for fear she may jump again.

She nodded and grabbed his arm. "Let's sit back down."

Once they were positioned for conversation again at the table, she started talking. "I'm sorry. I shouldn't have lied to you. I'm going to give you as much of the truth as I can, okay? You'll have to just trust me with the parts I can't say."

He nodded. That's all he could ask for right now because it's all he could offer her.

"I heard it from a friend that used to work with Ronnie." She swallowed hard and picked at her fingernails for a while before she finished. "Silas, I'm pretty sure Ronnie was doing more than just drinking 'shine."

She looked up at him to see how he processed that information. If he was surprised, he kept it hidden well. "I think he may have been selling it."

"I still don't understand why this mystery person would tell you about Cliff's barn being burned down," he said.

"Well, I told that person that I found some of the 'shine. I guess they just wanted me to know it was not a safe business." Emmie had justified that this was totally true. She was just focusing on the first time he mentioned about Cliff's barn rather than last night. She couldn't quite think of how to tell him any piece of information from last night. Hanging out at a still with Bo and Walter wasn't going to go over well.

He did not keep the surprise off his face this time. His eyes were wide.

"What did you do with the moonshine you found?" he asked. He had searched this house top to bottom and not found any moonshine two weeks ago. What had she done?

"Ah ah," she repeated his phrase, "One question at a time, remember?"

He looked like he wanted to argue but then crossed his arms conceding.

"Ask away," he said.

"Why would you intentionally want the sheriff's family at the speak? It makes me question our law enforcement," she wondered.

"You are a smart girl Emmie," he answered, which is probably why she asked all of these questions. All of the other girls he'd taken to speaks in Chicago wouldn't have put any of this together. They would have been just so happy to be out at a secret place. Everything else would have passed right on by. He guessed that's what he found intriguing about Emmie, but it was also what complicated things.

"Thank you but that does not answer my question." She smiled.

"Okay, okay. Don't you think we would need some law on our side to keep a place like that open? I think I've already told you a dollar will go a long way in this town," he answered honestly. She did remember him saying that now that he pointed it out.

"So, is Sheriff Drake a bad guy then? You know, because you've bought him off?" She looked genuinely confused.

"One… that is another question but I am going to let this slide and answer it anyway because I behaved badly earlier. Two… no, he is not a bad guy." Silas shrugged. "Am I a bad guy for taking you to a place that serves alcohol when we both know it's against the law? Some would say yes, some would say no. Good…bad… Most people are just people falling somewhere in between, Emmie. I guess most of us try to do more good than bad. But no, he's not bad."

She nodded thinking through what he'd said.

"Now my turn," Silas began. "Explain to me what you did with this moonshine of Ronnie's that you found."

"Oh… good verb choice there. I have to tell a lot if you say explain. Sort of sounded like a teacher there," she teased him.

"I've had a lot of practice… a lot of years of school." He smiled pleased with himself.

"Actually, Ava found the 'shine a few weeks ago when I asked her to get something from the pantry. We each tried a sip, just out of curiosity. But there was this friend of Ronnie's," she started to falter. She wanted to tell him the whole truth: finding Walt in the cave, making the paste, asking him to buy it, the dumb apple pie moonshine idea, and following Bo through the woods. She wanted to tell him every last detail but couldn't bring herself to do it. She didn't want to lose him over this or get Walt in trouble. So she told him as much of the truth as she could. That's all she'd promised anyway, right? She took a deep breath before continuing.

"He was just this guy that used to be around. So, I told him he could have it. I know I should have just poured it out but I couldn't." She looked down ashamed. "I wanted some of the money and thought maybe it would help me dig my way outta this hole I'm in." She finished and looked up at him.

His mouth was actually open in surprise.

"Please, please don't think less of me," she actually said aloud.

He closed his mouth and composed himself. "Emmie do you have any idea how dangerous that was? Never, ever, go confront anyone else about selling moonshine. You think this partner of Ronnie's owes you anything? Em, these guys are ruthless out there. Burning down Cliff's barn is not the worst thing they have done."

He walked over and pulled her up from the chair and wrapped his arms around her. He had no idea she felt this desperate for money. He'd met the moonshiners in this town. Most were three-tooth rednecks with no heart.

She slipped her hands inside his suit coat, wrapped her arms tightly around his waist and buried her face into his brown vest. Emmie breathed him in. He smelled so good—fresh and oddly like leather too. It made no sense but he did. She was half afraid he was going to walk right out the door when she told him about the 'shine but he didn't. Her brain was arguing there was more of the truth to tell. She chose to push the rest of the truth away for now.

Silas picked her up like she was as light as a feather. He sat her on the counter so they could be eye level. He meant to just kiss her once on the forehead. But one kiss turned to two, three to four. Her forehead, her cheeks, her nose, her mouth. His hands snaked into her hair pulling pins until her hair fell down around her shoulders. She was beautiful. He put his hands gently on each side of her face. "Promise me you will not talk to that man again. You asked me about good and bad. No one involved in these moonshine feuds is good. The thought of you being mixed up... I can't..." He shook his head and closed his eyes.

"You really needn't worry about this man I promise." She laughed at the thought of him being so scared for her to talk to Walt or even Bo. Both were good people.

He pulled back from her and tensed. "This is nothing to laugh at Emmie. This man is dangerous. I really need to know who you gave this moonshine of Ronnie's to. Who is he?" He cursed himself for asking but he had to know. This man could have this money. Or at the very least that moonshine was probably the goods he had already paid for, it was his moonshine she'd given to some stranger. More importantly, this man was involving Emmie in some business he didn't want her to know about, much less caught in the middle.

"He's harmless. Trust me." She pushed her unruly waves behind her ears then reached out to touch his face.

Silas stepped away from her. His brows wrinkled. He reached into his vest and pulled out a cigarette and lit it, pacing the length of the counter.

"Emmie I can't just trust you on this. I need to know." He made every effort to keep his voice calm, hushed even. He would not scare her again.

Her heart raced. She couldn't, there is no way she could tell him. Walter was family. The dog must have returned because he started pawing at the front door. She ignored him and swallowed hard. "Silas, I can't."

"It's not that you can't, it's that you won't," he snapped.

"No, you don't understand," she pleaded, hopping down from the counter.

"No, Emmie you don't understand. This man is using you, some naive little girl desperate for money. This man is using you just like Mr. Thomas is using you," he said, walking toward the door.

"Please, don't leave angry." She reached for his arm again. He pulled away and opened the door.

"You really won't tell me his name. Don't you see I'm just trying to help you?" He made one last attempt.

"I can't. It's not what you think," she repeated.

He looked hurt first, then angry. He walked out and started to close the door behind him. He had to leave before he lost it. He didn't know what to think about her protecting this other guy. Which bootlegger was it? He mentally started going down the list of those he knew in this area. He would find him and when he did...

She pulled the door open before it snapped all the way close. Spotty ran inside. She stepped around him quickly. "Silas, come back. Let's talk about this."

But he kept right on going without another word. Never looking back.

Chapter Thirty-two

That night Emmie couldn't sleep—or the next night—or the next. There was too much on her mind. She hadn't seen Walt since the night she'd followed Bo into the cave. She hadn't heard from Silas since their fight on Sunday afternoon. She wasn't sure exactly which direction to step with either of these issues. So, she had done nothing but spend the last few days stewing over how to fix things.

Luckily, the isolation had given her more than enough time to work on their Halloween costumes. Although, things were so screwed-up with Silas she wasn't entirely sure she wanted to spend four hours in a car with him on the way to Louisville. The only positive that had come from this week was Ava's reaction to her costume. It was nearly finished. She just needed to take in the bodice and hem the skirt. She'd even gotten most of the fabric cut for her dress. Ava was thrilled with the progress on both, wondering why in the world Emmie would want to work with children when she had such a natural talent for fashion, one of the highest compliments Ava could offer.

Emmie poured her third cup of coffee and drained the cup as quickly as possible, in hopes it would give her an instant energy boost. Unfortunately, it didn't seem to be working this morning. She put a few extra dabs of powder under her eyes in an attempt to hide the dark circles forming there then headed into town.

When she entered the store, she noticed Will looked almost as tired as she did. "Good morning, Will," she called, putting her purse in the drawer behind the counter.

"Morning," he answered, barely looking up from the money he was counting.

"Good Morning, Emma dear," Mr. Thomas sang from his office. She hadn't realized he was in there. "It's nice to hear you call my brother by his first name," he added snidely.

Of course she called him by his first name, she had known Will since they were in the third grade. His family had moved into town and taken over the shop his brother now owned. But even back then, Mr. Thomas had been old enough to work at the store. He had always been Mr. Thomas and Will had always been Will. It was a tough habit to change.

She just ignored his jab, having too much going on in her mind right now to be drawn into his little game. "Good Morning, Mr. Thomas." Okay, so maybe she didn't totally ignore the jab. Emmie just threw him a little passive-aggressive punch of her own.

Mr. Thomas said nothing but turned and walked to the back storage room, busying himself with who knows what. She and Will worked in silence for a while. It wasn't exactly uncomfortable but not friendly either; which was odd because they had always gotten along fine. Will was always the smiley kind of boy. Lately she hadn't even seen him grin. Without saying a word Will walked into the backroom, carrying that same small black box Mr. Thomas had received in the mail. What in the world was that thing?

"Emma?" a familiar voice pulled her from her thoughts.

She looked up to find Bo Johnson smiling back at her. In the light of day she could see he wasn't quite as lanky as he used to be. No doubt toting barrels of 'shine had added to his girth.

"Good Afternoon, Bo. What can I do for ya?" Emmie put her fabric and thread back in the sewing basket and stood to meet Bo's stare.

"Well, I ran into Walter this morning. We was getting things ready for the…" he looked around to be sure they were alone, "for my pap's celebration and he said he didn't know if you were coming. I was coming into town anyway, so I told him I'd check with ya."

"Oh, I'm sorry Bo. To tell you the truth I didn't realize it was so soon," she answered honestly. Well, partially honest, she had actually forgotten all about it.

"Yep, it's tonight. Think you can make it? We're gonna have plenty of food. My uncle is gonna smoke a pig," he answered.

Emmie laughed out loud, "Excuse me?"

He smiled, his hazel eyes dancing with humor. "Not like smoke." He mimed a cigarette. "He's gonna smoke a pig... like the cooker? He makes really good barbecue." He looked down like he was embarrassed.

Emmie hadn't been out for fun since the speakeasy a few weeks ago. She hadn't seen any of those folks for so long, maybe she should go. She knew Bo and Walter went to Ronnie's old church, so there was bound to be plenty of people there she knew.

That would be a long walk though. "Is Walter going?"

Bo nodded. "He said to tell ya he could pick you up, if you want to go." He paused and looked down again. "Or I wouldn't mind to pick you up."

"No, no need to go to any trouble. Walter lives right next door." Emmie thought for a moment. What had she planned to do tonight, work on their dresses? She still had nearly two weeks to get those finished. Didn't she deserve a little time out? It would be good to be with Walter and Mae.

"Yeah. I'll be glad to come. Thanks for the invite. Can I bring something?" she asked.

He smiled from ear to ear. "Nope. Glad you're coming."

"See ya tonight, Bo," she said, digging out the supplies she needed from her sewing basket.

"See ya, Emmie." He turned to head out then spun back around on his heel. "And Em, this is a barn party. So, don't feel like ya need to dress fancy. I know you been hanging around them Del Grande's... it ain't gonna be like that."

Emmie smiled. She nearly asked if she could bring Ava with her but she knew better. She got the feeling this was a private gathering and Ava would rather be tarred and feathered than go to a party at a barn.

****

When Walter showed up just after seven in his truck, she was disappointed at first to see that he was alone. Spotty chased the car until it reached the end of the drive and moved faster than he could keep up.

"Where's Mae and Max?" Emmie asked.

Walter laughing and chewed on his pipe before he answered, "You think Mae's gonna let Max go to a barn party at the Johnson's... celebrating the fact that ain't none of the Johnson's going to jail?"

"Oh," Emmie thought aloud, "I guess I hadn't put all that together." She started to feel a little out of place. What was she stepping into? Emmie bit her lower lip as she thought.

"Don't fret about it, Emmie. Just gonna be some folks playing music and some good food. We ain't gotta stay long. Just felt like I needed to show my support to him. Mr. Johnson's been a friend," Walter said as they made their way to the Johnson's land.

Walter pulled his truck into the flat area about fifty feet from the barn. They were actually in an older barn. Walter pointed out their newer one off in the distance.

"How close are we to the river?" Emmie asked. Except for the glow of the lights from the barn and the stars in the sky it was so pitch black she couldn't see the river but she could hear water rushing in the distance.

"It's just right there. If there was a fuller moon tonight, you'd see it," Walt answered, pointing to his right.

As they neared the party she could hear music coming from the barn. Banjos, guitars, and a jug band were set up near the back. From the looks on the smiling faces they'd hit the 'shine early. There was a group of teenagers dancing at the front of the barn.

For a barn, it was pretty nice. It was certainly not like the small run-down shelter left on her farm. The Johnson family had swept and raked the dirt floor, leaving only soft earth in its place. Every shelf and table was filled with candles and lanterns. None of them matched but the warmth of the light made the area seem inviting. The barn was tall, double story at least. Some of the shingles from the roof were missing— it was like the party opened right up into the heavens. A sliver of moonlight and stars shined over them. A few rows of picnic tables were set up along the sides where most of the older folks had parked for the evening. There were also a few chairs scattered here and there but most folks were standing. Several people were grouped off, talking and laughing. Emmie recognized several people from Ronnie's church and school.

She even recognized a few of them as Ronnie's friends. Walter and Mr. Johnson of course, but then there were two others. She didn't know one by name but she'd seen him around the house. He was a short, balding, pudgy man with a scraggly brown beard. He'd always given her the creeps. One of his eyes was black and swollen shut. He was sitting next to a pretty good friend of Ronnie's, Sam Young. He'd even stopped by once to check on her and get some tools Ronnie had borrowed from him. Sam smiled and waved a polite hello then turned and said something to the bearded man with a black eye.

Emmie waved and glanced around. Some of the men were drinking from brown bags, she assumed that was Walter's 'shine. Just as she turned to ask him, she noticed he was no longer by her side, but halfway to the picnic benches with a wide grin on his face. Bart Johnson stood and put his hand out for Walter. The two shook hands then Walter took a seat to Mr. Johnson's left. Everyone laughed as Mr. Johnson said something. Walter refilled his pipe and smiled, forming deep creases around the corner of his eyes when he laughed. This was the most laid back Emmie had ever seen him. He looked up and made eye contact with Emmie. She could tell his eyes were asking if she was alright. She nodded. He motioned with his thumb for her to join the younger folks and smiled. She nodded again and made her way deeper into the barn.

Bo wasn't lying about the dress code. Everything was casual and comfortable. Walter fit right in with most of the men in his bibbed overalls. Emmie had worn one of her mama's old hemmed-up dresses. It was soft worn cotton with a tiny pink flower pattern. If she'd worn one of Ava's Chicago dresses, she would have been laughed right out of this place. The air had a chill and she wished she had worn her wool stockings rather than push down socks. She gave the room another scan. She hadn't talked to these people in months… well years for some of them. She didn't know who to talk to and decided to start over at the food table. Everything was set up like a big buffet. The barbeque smelled divine as she helped herself to some and took a corn cake too.

"It's as good as it smells," Bo said, coming up beside her.

"I sure hope so. Everything is nice out here. You got music and eve-rything." She balanced her plate in one hand and pointed to the band with the other.

Bo smiled. "Yeah, it's a pretty big celebration." He spooned a huge helping of barbeque and all the sides he could squeeze onto his plate.

"Want to sit with me and my sister?" he asked, leading them over to a couple chairs on the opposite side.

"Lead the way," she said, falling into step next to him.

Emmie was surprised how much his younger sister Millie had grown. She was pretty, earthy pretty not flapper pretty. Her straight blond hair hung long, just past her shoulders. Her blue eyes widened and she smiled as she saw Bo and Emmie nearing.

"Emmie, we're so glad you came." She stood and gave her a hug. "It's been a long time since we saw you. Everyone's been worried about you." Millie's voice was soft and quiet.

"It's good to see you too. You look lovely," Emmie said.

As they ate, they fell into an easy conversation. It was nice here. Emmie could breathe. She had space to think and no secrets to hide. A few young people gathered around their chairs. Some eating, some sipping from paper bags, some just talking and tapping their toes to the music. One of the girls pulled out a flask. Emmie was pretty sure it was one of Bo's cousins but their family was so big she couldn't tell where one Johnson stopped and another family started.

"Wanna try it?" Bo asked, holding it out to her.

"Umm… no thanks," she said.

"Come on, Ma made it with your water." He wiggled his eyebrows again. "It's not that strong, promise."

"Bo, since when is moonshine not that strong?" she laughed.

"This is mainly peach juice… like a cider. Mama calls it Georgia's peach 'shine." He smiled.

Emmie felt her pulse picked up. Georgia's peach 'shine. She'd had that at the Smith's Grove speakeasy. It had been what had given her the idea to turn Walter's 'shine into apple pie 'shine—this was all connected.

The Johnson's were selling moonshine to the speakeasy... Silas had represented Bart Johnson in the case against Cliff Harris. Emmie took a good look around at the many faces she recognized—a few were strangers. She looked at each of them closer. One of the men in the band, the one playing the banjo. It was Sheriff Drake.

"Emmie, it's fine. Mr. Drake don't mind about the 'shine. He keeps us safe from those crazy ole bastards like Cliff Harris. Remember that tradition I told you about? Well, Mr. Drake gets it, he understands our heritage." Bo would have no way to know the real reason that Emmie's heart pounded out of her chest. She was right earlier. This place wasn't about keeping secrets inside—it was about them all coming out in the open.

The Sheriff and his son were here. Bo's pap made moonshine, and by the looks of his house and their new barn, they were making decent money off it. All the pieces were starting to fit together. Curiosity overwhelmed her. She turned and faced Bo and looked at his flask. It was on the tip of her tongue to ask him if his family sold their 'shine to a speakeasy but she decided to hold on to her secrets. Emmie didn't want him wondering how she knew about the joint. So, she went with plan B—act like the girl he expected her to be.

"You promise it's not too strong? I don't want to make a fool of myself and spit it out everywhere," she said.

Bo unscrewed the cap and took a sip. He swallowed it down without the smallest wince and smacked his lips to let her know how good it was. He shrugged his shoulders and held the flask out to her. "Like cider that warms your throat. And if you need to spit," he glanced around and winked, "nobody's watching."

Emmie smiled then turned her attention to the flask. She closed her eyes and took a swig. She sighed and licked the residue from her lips. That was it, the same 'shine. When she opened her eyes she noticed Bo had leaned in, smiling at her reaction. Something behind him caught her attention. Her heart stopped. Emmie opened her mouth to utter a warning but she was too late.

Bo was caught off guard or he may have been able to defend himself against the attack.

"Silas," Emmie shouted, kicking her way out of the chair. "Stop!"

Chapter Thirty-three

Silas picked Bo up over the back of his chair and shoved him against one of the supporting posts in the barn.

"Silas," Emmie repeated, "what are you doing? Stop!"

Silas reared back his fist and punched Bo square in the jaw. At first Bo looked confused but that quickly faded to anger. He picked up his feet in an attempt to kick Silas off him but wasn't exactly successful. Silas took a step back but never let go of Bo's shirt.

Emmie stared at the pair with her hand clasped over her mouth. They were in a full-fledged brawl. Why in the world were they fighting? She couldn't believe Silas would jump straight to hitting. Wouldn't he say something first if it was just jealousy? She didn't understand what was going on, but she did know she had to stop it. Emmie glanced around for help. Most people hadn't even noticed the fight. Only those in their immediate vicinity had circled around them. She knew it wouldn't take long for others to catch on but she was afraid for Silas when they did. This party was full of Bo's family. They weren't going to take too kindly to the sight of him getting beat up by a stranger.

Millie took off toward the picnic tables. Smart girl, she was likely going for her family. Family. Emmie knew Silas wouldn't come here alone. Pushing through the small crowd Emmie saw Trick and Gabe. She let out a breath in relief. They could break this up. They stopped when they reached the inside of the circle. She couldn't believe it. They were just watching. Still, silent, arms relaxed at their sides, they watched.

"Gabe, Trick." She looked at each one. "Stop him. They're hurting each other."

Gabe grabbed her arm and turned his attention back to the fight. Emmie couldn't believe it. They weren't going to break it up. This was ridiculous. Bo and Silas were shouting obscenities at each other but no one could really understand either of them. She felt nauseous watching them trade licks. They were both hurt and bleeding. But Silas had the upper hand now. She couldn't take it anymore.

She pulled away from Gabe and pushed herself toward the fight. Emmie shouldn't have been surprised when she got hit. After all, that's what happens when you get in the middle of a fight. It felt like her cheek was split open. Surely, the pain was bound to be worse than it actually was, right? Letting go of her cheek she stretched her arms wide and put one hand on each of their chests.

"Stop it," she panted.

Emmie felt them moving toward each other. She pushed as hard as she could on their chests but her weight was split in opposite directions. They barely moved an inch. She turned to face Silas. He lifted a hand and gingerly touched her cheek. He glared at her then turned his eyes to Bo.

"What's your damn problem, Yankee?" Bo shouted, wiping blood from his mouth.

"You," Silas said.

"You think you can just come onto my family's land and hurt me? I don't know what you're used to up north but that ain't how shit works down here," Bo said.

"Hurt you?" Silas grinned, "No, I wanted to hurt you when I threw your ass against the wall." Silas swallowed hard. "But Hillbilly, I could kill you for leaving that mark on her face."

Silas grabbed Emmie with one arm and pulled her behind him. With the other arm he produced a gun from nowhere and held it point-blank at Bo. His chest was rising and falling in a steady rhythm but it was the only part of him that seemed to move. His arm, stick straight. His gaze focused.

Emmie was frozen. Her brain said grab the gun, grab the gun, but she couldn't get her arms to move. Even if she wanted to, she wasn't sure she could move from Silas's grip. That's when she heard it. The rhythmic sound she'd been waiting for since this argument started—the double clicks of a shotgun. She turned around and found Bo's pap, Mr. Johnson, with a double-barreled shotgun pointed straight at Silas's back.

He wasn't close but with that weapon, he didn't have to be. Even she could hit a target with a shotgun.

"Now, easy there boy. I appreciate all ya done for me but I can't let you be putting holes in my grandson. Ya best be putting that pistol down," the old man said. Emmie noticed as he spoke he only had about half the teeth God had given him. His voice was easy and calm but his eyes were wild. She knew he would pull the trigger, if he had to.

But before she could finish the thought, Trick stepped up behind the old man. "And I can't let you be putting holes in my brother," he said coldly. Emmie didn't have to guess. She could tell by the arch in the old man's back that Trick had a gun at his back.

Finally her body came into motion again. She stepped in close to Silas and gently put her hand on his outstretched arm. "Stop this. This is all out of hand. Bo is my friend. Whatever you think you saw, you didn't."

Silas laughed. It came out as a cold, unhappy sort of sound. "It's him isn't it?"

"What?" she asked confused.

Silas leaned over and whispered quiet enough that others couldn't hear but he never took his eyes off Bo, "He's the bootlegger you've been protecting from me."

That's what this was about. It wasn't just jealousy about her sitting here with Bo. He thought Bo was the one she gave the moonshine to. He was so mad when he left her house the other night and now he thought Bo was the man she was keeping secret.

"No," she whispered quickly, "not him. Wrong guy. Stop this."

He believed her. She could tell because his eyes changed. He released the hammer on the revolver slowly and pulled the gun back to his side. Emmie glanced back to see Mr. Johnson had lowered the shotgun. Trick moved over to stand near his brother.

"Stay out of my way," Silas spit at Bo and then added, "and stay away from her."

"She's a pretty smart girl. Never needed nobody to do her talking before; probably doesn't need you to start now," Bo said.

Emmie rolled her eyes at the pair of them and let out a sigh. Silas turned to take a step toward Bo. She pushed against his chest with everything she had. "We need to go, now." Her voice left no room for argument.

Clearly, Gabe agreed because he touched his friends elbow and nodded toward the entrance of the barn. Emmie realized for the first time since the start of the confrontation that everyone was watching. Even the music had stopped. The sheriff had come nearer to the fight but hadn't pushed his way to the center.

"Thanks for the help, Sheriff," she said as they walked past him. She was disgusted that he hadn't stepped in. Grown men had pulled guns on one another and he'd just stood there with his stupid banjo.

She turned her sights on the exit. Walter was standing there like a guard. His face was set in a grim line. Silas had a hold of her arm and was leading her out. Walter had no intention of letting her pass. Oh God. Walter. If he acted too protective, Silas might figure it out. She didn't know if Silas knew the moonshiners in this town but it wasn't worth the risk. What if he pulled that gun on Walter? Would she be able to stop him? Would the Johnsons intervene? She wasn't sure.

Emmie shook her head no at him. She mouthed, "I'm Fine." He crossed his arms over his chest. She turned her serious expression to a plea. "Please. Let. Me. Go," she mouthed. She saw Walter sigh. He didn't like this. He rubbed his whiskers and then nodded once. He had to trust her. Walter didn't know what she was playing but she was a smart girl.

"Trick, drive. Emmie, in the back. Now," Silas commanded as they reached the car. When she got settled into the back, she looked out the window and noticed Walter was making his way to his truck. She was relieved to see he hadn't chased them down.

Emmie closed her eyes and rested her head against the seat. The moisture gathering behind her eyelids threatened to leak out. She did her best to keep it at bay but that only made her throat swell. She felt something soft and cool against her cheek. It stung a little, she sucked in her breath and popped open her eyes. Silas was leaning over her pressing a handkerchief to her wound.

"I'm sorry you are hurt," he said. His voice was still gruff and clipped but honest.

Emmie didn't know what to say to him, so she said nothing. She grabbed the cloth from him, pressed it firmly to her cheek and closed her eyes. Maybe when she opened them again, this would all just be a dream.

Chapter Thirty-four

Emmie's body swayed with the rhythm of the car. She opened her eyes and stared up at the roof. No, not a dream. Occasionally the dirt path would thrust her into Silas's shoulder. He visibly scooted away from her. Good, she didn't want to touch him anyway.

The car was silent until they reached the road at the end of the farm. "That sure was a fun party. Thanks for bringing us along, Silas," Trick said. Gabe laughed. Silas said nothing he just pulled a cigarette out of his vest pocket and lit it, hiding a smirk.

This was not funny. How could they joke about this? Emmie swallowed and wet her lips. She found her voice and spoke up, "Actually, it was a fun party. People were eating, dancing, visiting… Then some jerks showed up and caused a big dramatic scene."

Gabe and Silas stopped laughing and were stone silent. A moment of awkward silence filled the car. Silas nodded and looked down. He clenched and unclenched his jaw a few times and rubbed his forehead before he spoke.

"We all saw you having a good time, Emmie." His voice was cold. "What were you doing there?" he asked. But he knew and just wanted her to own up to it. He needed to hear the words from her lips. Whoever the bootlegger was that told her about the Harris vs. Johnson trial had invited her to the party.

"What was I doing there?" She avoided his question. "I went to school and church with those people. Those are my people," she shouted. "What were you doing there besides causing good folks trouble?"

"You want to do this now? You want to shout at me now, in front of my brother and my friend? Is this what you want?" he said coolly.

How dare he turn this to her. She saw red. "Oh, you want to act like I'm the one causing a scene? Honey, you're the one that just showed your ass in that barn back there."

Silas laughed and touched his pants. "I showed my ass… in the barn?"

Trick and Gabe lost it in the front seat, making rude comments about her choice of words. She didn't find any of it funny, in fact, it just made her angrier. "Oh, shut up all of you. You probably weren't even invited. You all think this town is no fun, so you just aimlessly drive around looking for folks to pick on."

Silas turned toward her and put a hand on her knee. She tried to move away from him but there was nowhere to go. "Okay, I'm sorry," he smiled down at her. She could tell he was trying to use his smile to worm his way out of this mess but it wasn't going to work. Not tonight.

"I was there because I was invited," Silas answered her earlier question.

"Why would they want a Yank like you at their celebration?" she spit.

"Are we name-calling now?" He arched an eyebrow. "At least you could be original. That redneck boy has already used that one."

She sighed. He was right. That was the first time in her life she'd ever called anyone that. She never understood why Yankee was a derogatory word in the south. But she couldn't let it go of her anger. It consumed her.

"Maybe I should have said bastard or S.O.B.—do either of those names work better for ya? If you like, I may be able to think of some more." She lifted her eyebrow.

Silas rubbed his face and turned to look out the window before speaking again. He was doing his best to stay calm.

"I was his attorney, Emmie. I got him off, scot-free. That damn celebration was because of me. It was because of my hard work."

Emmie couldn't believe that she hadn't already put that together. Of course that's why he was there. She pinched the bridge of her nose and looked down.

"Now, I'll ask again and I want the truth," he said. "Why were you there?"

Because the other night when I was visiting with Bo and Walter in the cave, distilling moonshine by the way, they invited me. She'd like to see the look on his face if she did tell him the truth. But the consequence of that wouldn't be worth it. He'd probably have Gabe turn the car around and lord knows what they would do to Walt.

"Bo invited me. I saw him in the store. He said his family hadn't seen me in a while, they were worried about how I was doing and invited me for dinner. I didn't know I had to run all social obligations by you," she said.

"I've had about enough of your sass, Emmie," he said firmly then continued. She rolled her eyes and looked out the window, turning away from him.

He grabbed her chin and pulled her face back toward his. "This Bo, how do you know him?"

She sighed and threw her hands up. "I'm weary of telling you this. I've already said school, church. I've known him a long time. In case you haven't noticed this town's not that big. Folks know each other."

He leaned into her, needed to see her face as she answered the next question. "You swear to me he's not the man you gave the moonshine to? The man you're keeping from me?"

"I swear to God. I didn't give him the moonshine I found." It felt good to be honest.

Silas sighed and rubbed his jaw and thought for a second before asking his next question. "Was the man there tonight?"

"Why do you get to ask all of the questions, huh? I've got a couple of my own." She bit her lip. There were a lot of people at that party but she didn't want to answer that question. It'd be just like Silas to check names off a list. Admitting that the person was at the party was a good as giving him a list to run through.

Silas tilted his head to the side and looked annoyed. Finally he put his hands up and conceded. "Fine. What's your question Emmie?"

She smiled feeling a brief satisfaction. "When you walked in, I was tasting some of the Johnson's peach moonshine."

"From the asshole's flask," Silas nodded calmly, "I saw. Go on."

Emmie pursed her lips and blinked a few times to let him know she was irritated before continuing.

"Jealousy looks good on no one, Silas," she said then went on. "Bo said his mama made that 'shine."

"And…" he said, wanting her to get to the question.

"It tasted just like the moonshine I had at the speak in Smith's Grove. The Johnson family supplies the moonshine for the speakeasy, don't they?" she asked.

"Yes, they make the 'shine for the speak and the pig, why do you want to know?" he asked.

"The pig?" Her eyes were wide.

Silas rubbed his jaw. Why the hell did he say that? "Yes, the pig. That's all you need to know about that. Why do you care?"

She shrugged, "Just curious." For the first time in the whole car ride, she smiled. It made him uneasy.

"You've heard what curiosity does to cats, right?" he asked dryly.

"Are you threatening me, Silas?" she asked.

"No, not me." He squinted his eyes at her as if to say that's crazy. "Them." He pointed back in the direction of the Johnson's house.

"They were pretty nice folks before you pulled out a gun on their grandson," she said. "I'd have to say you started it."

Silas thought about that for a moment and shrugged his shoulders. Then he looked at her seriously. "Maybe that's true. But believe me on this, you don't want to be sniffing around their secrets. Trust me."

Emmie frowned. With a knitted brow she asked, "Did they really burn down the barn?"

"I am not talking to you about this," he answered.

"Your lack of an answer makes me think they did," she said with wide eyes.

He grinned, "Just like your lack of answer makes me think your bootlegger was at that party tonight."

Gabe interrupted their conversation, "Any idea why an old man with a white beard would be following us?"

Oh God. She had to come up with something. "That's my neighbor. He watches out for me sometimes. I could tell he didn't like me leaving with you guys." She said the first thing that came to her mind.

Silas turned around and looked at the man through the back window. "For a poor girl living out here all alone, you sure do have a lot of men sniffing around trying to take care of you."

Emmie frowned, "He and Mae are like my surrogate grandparents. He just wants to be sure you take me home safely."

Gabe made the turn into her drive. Walter slowed down behind them. Emmie turned and waved for him to go on. She smiled to say, "I'm alright." He frowned and turned to head back to his house. She appreciated that he cared but she didn't want them to become curious about him.

Silas seemed to be convinced she was protecting the bootlegger because she loved him. He was right. Only, he wasn't thinking of the right kind of love. Sometimes, he saw things too black and white and didn't even realize it. There were all kinds of love. She loved Walter like family. That's why she couldn't sell him out. If Silas ever opened his eyes, he might figure it out. So, she had to keep him away from Walter.

Silas helped Emmie step down out of the car. He walked her up to the porch.

"Are you sure you won't stay at Ava's? Or I could stay here with you... I mean... it's been a rough night," Silas said.

"I'm fine." She shook her head. "It won't be me they will come after." Her face looked concerned for him.

Silas rubbed his jaw. "Don't worry about that. They won't come after me; they need us too much. I'll make it right."

Emmie nodded. They stood there on the stairs in silence again for a moment.

"When I walked up and saw you there in the barn, you looked so happy. " His face fell. "I'm sorry I embarrassed you." He leaned in and kissed her cheek where it was starting to bruise. "I'm sorry you got hurt. But you're wrong. Those are not your people." Silas shook his head. "They are not like you."

Not knowing what to say she left it alone. "I'm sorry I cursed at you."

He laughed then fell serious again. "Emmie, please let me help you with this problem you're dealing with. I can see your thinking about things all the time. Asking questions about the pig and the speak... I know it's got to be connected to that moonshine you found. I just need to you fill in the missing pieces. Tell me who you gave it to."

"I'm sorry I can't." She shrugged. "I wish I'd gone to you first. But now he has it. I can't ask him for it back. I think it's part his anyway." After tonight, I'm even surer that I can't tell you. If you ever treated him like you did Bo..." The words she wanted to say caught in her throat.

Silas cursed. It was his moonshine, not Ronnie's, not this bootlegger's. And attached to it was the money that was standing between him and Chicago. He had to get this fixed. "Damn it, Emmie. Let me help you."

"I can't," she said, feeling like they were repeating the same argument they'd just had days ago.

"Emmie, please. You don't understand..." He put his hands on each side of her face, begging.

"No, you don't understand..." she said softly.

He took a step back and ran his hands through his hair in stiff motions. "I can't do this. I can't be with you... if you don't trust me..."

"I just can't risk it. I'll work all this out though. Just let it go, please," she begged.

Silas shrugged and repeated the phrase she'd said to him just second ago, "I can't."

He walked away and left her standing on the porch. The boys sat in the car with their headlights shining on the door until she made it in. Gabe shouted, "Lock up," out the window as the car pulled away.

Chapter Thirty-five

Walter called her that night to be sure she made it home okay... and that she was alone. He didn't ask too many questions but she could tell by his tone he was uneasy. The next few days passed painfully slow. Too much time to think and only her dog to talk to. She threw herself into making the costumes. Ava's was finished. It was stunning. Ava had asked her to create a headpiece with a black fabric candle to go with the full pumpkin skirt. Emmie thought that may be a bit much, but that was Ava. So, she did what she was asked from leftover material she'd used to make the black bodice.

She'd stayed up until the wee hours of the morning working on her own costume. It was difficult to pin your own body, so she'd invited Ava over yesterday as a stand-in. Of course their bodies were totally different. She was mostly just guessing, but it was looking pretty. Ava convinced her to make a tiny witch-themed fascinator. Her dress was basic—brown, with black lace. She intentionally made it look like a regular drop-waisted dress, veering a little off the pattern. If she had black silk and lace, she wasn't going to waste it on a dress she would wear only one night. She put a little silver ribbon accents around the neckline and hem. But she just used a whipstitch, something that could easily be removed later without doing too much damage to the dress. With her hat and the small broom she'd crafted from a branch and some old straw, folks would get the drift she was a witch. And if they didn't, she didn't really care. She was just using the dresses and easy conversation about the party as a distraction.

Emmie had woken early, despite only a few hours of sleep the night before. She drank her last swallow of coffee, scratched Spotty's ears, and turned to head out the door. He followed her outside and to the store, just like he always did. His face was smiling and his tongue rolled out of his mouth. When she reached the store, she pointed to the bench just outside. Spotty took his usual place under it while he waited for her. Perhaps this is who she was to become… an old maid… a lady surrounded only by her pets… a dog lady.

When she entered the store, she noticed Will looked worse for wear. She tried to engage him in conversation but he avoided every attempt. Sometimes he just blatantly ignored her. Emmie had absolutely no idea what was going on. She felt she was physically repelling people now.

"Will?" She made his name a question.

He didn't answer just looked up at her waiting for her to continue to speak.

"Not that it's any of my business but is everything alright?" she asked.

He shrugged his shoulders in reply and went back to working.

An awkward silence ate up some time in-between a couple customers. Will let out what must be the third yawn since he got there that morning. This last one was loud. She heard his back pop as he stretched his shoulders.

"If you want to go take an early lunch break, I can handle this," she offered.

He sighed and put his hands on the counter thinking it over.

"You really wouldn't mind?" he asked.

She shook her head. "Not at all."

"Thanks Emmie. I'll be back in twenty minutes, I promise." And he walked out the room and into the side parlor she used to use for sewing. Emmie was surprised he didn't head upstairs to his apartment. He dropped right down on the small sofa and was snoring in about five minutes.

Nearly an hour passed but she didn't have the heart to wake him. Anyone that tired needed to sleep.

****

"Emma? Where is Will?" Mr. Thomas asked in a clipped voice, his eyes searching the store. She smiled and pointed to the side room. Peering in there he could just see Will's long legs draped over the side of the sofa and hear the faintest rumble of a snore.

"He was so exhausted. I told him I could take care of things for a bit. It has really not been that busy. I'm all caught up, so I've just been unpacking these dishes," she explained. But he wasn't listening. As he moved past her into the parlor he spit, "That wasn't your decision to make, Emma."

"Get up," Mr. Thomas shouted.

Will awoke startled, taking in his surroundings for a moment.

"What the hell were you thinking? I pay to you work, not lie around here and sleep like some lazy dog," Mr. Thomas shouted.

Emmie wasn't sure if she should intervene or not. Maybe they'd had some sort of quarrel she didn't know about it.

"Lazy?" Will said incredulously. "Lazy?" he repeated a little louder. "You really have the balls to call me lazy? You sign us up for this bullshit but I'm the only one I see out all night long."

Emmie tried not to listen to the family fight. It was none of her business. She moved further away from the parlor and began putting the dishes on a shelf. "You promised me we'd be making good money. We'd be doing what was right and just. But I ain't seen a dime and it don't feel right and just, out there stalking folks."

"Will, you know this is for the best. And there will be money," Mr. Thomas whispered. "We've almost got it."

"We? We? Paul, we haven't almost got anything," Will whispered. "It was my ass camped out all night at the shoe store, not yours. Then you expect me to be here first thing in the morning all bright-eyed and bushy-tailed. I can't do it anymore." Will took off his white linen work apron and threw it on the ground.

"Will, think about your actions," Mr. Thomas said, sounding more like a father than a brother.

Will laughed. "You think I haven't been thinking about my actions?" He leaned in a whispered to his brother just barely loud enough so Emmie could still hear, "I don't think it was you that got chased away by the shotgun-toting sheriff at two o'clock this morning, was it? Think about that, brother."

Emmie dropped the plate she was putting on the shelf—the sheriff.

Will turned and stormed upstairs to his room, his loud feet pounding. The light fixtures shook on the ceiling above them as he charged into his room. Emmie walked to the back room to find the broom and dustpan to sweep up the broken glass. She hoped they hadn't noticed she overheard their fight.

When she walked back into the store, she found Mr. Thomas standing over the mess she'd made.

"I'm sorry about that. I'll pay for it," she apologized. "Sometimes I'm clumsy." She tried to add an easy smile but he didn't smile back.

"Emmie. I'll ask you to use discretion with any of that conversation that you may have overheard. It's important business we're up to." He grabbed her arms and bent down a little so they were eye level. "Business that would make you proud." His smile looked off. She didn't know what to say or do, but just nodded and turned to start cleaning up the mess.

The rest of the morning her mind was abuzz trying to process the fight she'd overheard. Will had been chased by a shotgun-toting sheriff. A sick feeling in her stomach told her it was Drake.

Sheriff Drake was the one who came to tell her about Ronnie. It was from his lips that she learned about his crash. He'd even walked with her to see smoldering remains of the car. He seemed like such a nice man that day. Now, she knew he protected the moonshiners. He was the kind of man that let grown men pull guns on each other while he stood by and watched. Her feelings were all mixed up. What could Will and Mr. Thomas be into that would make Sheriff Drake chase him?

****

"Emma, if you want to take your lunch, I'll watch the store for a bit." Mr. Thomas had been all pleasantries since his argument with Will this morning, walking around like a peacock with his tail feathers out. Why in the world would he be so happy that she'd overheard his conversation?

"I think I'll just step outside for a bit. I could use the air." Emmie was glad that he had offered to let her have lunch today. She wasn't sure she'd get one since Will had stormed off. Most of the time, if Will was away, she ate at the store counter or not at all.

Emmie looked under the bench for Spotty but he was nowhere to be found. He'd probably gone to sniff trash bins, hoping for a handout. Goodness knows he wasn't going to get it from Mr. Thomas. She aimlessly walked around downtown until she found herself in the center of the square on a weathered black iron bench. She took in her surroundings: Mr. Thomas's Shop, DeCarmilla Law Firm, the restaurant for the potluck where she'd learned about the sheriff. And that's when her eyes spotted it—Dillard Brother's Shoes. Will said he'd been outside of the shoe store last night. And there it was, nestled right in-between the restaurant and the law firm. Just across the block from the store she worked at everyday. Shops. Secrets. Lies. It was like she didn't even know where she lived anymore. Somehow she'd worked herself right into the middle of it.

She stood and walked toward the shoe store, unsure exactly what she was looking for. Nothing looked abnormal to her here. She pretended to be peering into the windows. When she reached the edge of the building she found a small narrow alley that separated the law firm from the shoe store. Her heels clicked loudly on the brick path beneath her feet. The sound echoed off the buildings. She kept a close eye on the exterior of the shoe store. Was she looking for a door maybe? Nothing seemed abnormal. When she reached the back of the store everything looked normal there too. It was just some men carrying crates through a brown door into their storeroom. She was probably just being paranoid. Maybe she had misunderstood what Will had said or maybe it was another shoe store. She tried to recall the locations of other shoe stores in town.

But just when she was getting ready to turn around, someone rounding the corner caught her eye. He was short, about her height, with tan skin. It was his eyes that really caught her attention. They were the most stunning shade of warm chocolate. Piercing. She knew them at once. It was the same eye she'd seen peering back at them through the peephole in Smith's Grove. He was the man from the speakeasy. He tipped his hat to her and walked back to talk to the men unloading boxes. The young fellow she'd just passed spoke to the others, the tall middle-aged man looked up at her. He waved and walked over to her.

"Can I help ya miss?" His voice was not unkind. She was sure she had no reason to be nervous but her heartbeat pounded in her ears.

"Oh, sorry, I just got turned around. The entrance is this way," Emmie smiled and then spun on her heels. She tried to act nonchalant as she walked back down the brick path. The man's footsteps clicked loudly behind her. He was following her. She picked up her pace nearing the end of the alley. Ten more feet and she would back into the crowded comfort of the town square. She wasn't afraid exactly, just uneasy. For once, she wished Spotty was close on her heels.

As her foot inched out into the sunlight of the square once again, a dark shadow appeared in front of her. She was blocked. Emmie screamed and jumped back into the alley.

Chapter Thirty-six

"You will walk with me." His familiar fingers bit into her arm as he turned her body and then led her back down the alley.

"Lord have mercy, Silas, you liked to have given me a heart attack," she laughed.

"Thanks, James. I've got this," Silas said, walking past the man who had followed her down the alley.

"What have you got? Silas, I have to head back to the shop. I've only got a few minutes of lunch left." she continued.

He said nothing just kept right on leading her to the end of the alley. He stopped when they reached the back of the buildings. Then spun around on his heel and faced her. Emmie took a step back until her back rested against the brick wall of the law firm.

"What are you doing?" he asked with an arched eyebrow. Clearly he was still angry with her.

"Enjoying my lunch break with a little walk downtown. I just needed some air," she sassed him, feigning innocence. Emmie didn't appreciate his tone or the fact he hadn't called in days.

"Really, in this alley, you're getting fresh air?" he asked sarcastically.

She nodded, batting her eyes.

He glanced over at the guys unloading boxes. Silas leaned in closer and rested one arm against the wall beside her. To the men it may have looked like they were in some sort of lovers embrace but his eyes suggested differently.

"Emmie. I don't care how doe-eyed you are trying to appear right now. I know you were not just walking down this alley for fresh air. Do you know why I am here and not up there?" He pointed up to an open window of one of the offices of the law firm.

She shook her head and did her best to look disinterested in whatever he was about to say.

"Because I got a call from the shoe store saying some crazy young lady was staring in the shop windows and snooping around the back alley," he informed her.

"Pish... that cannot be true," she laughed, "I was only down here for a few minutes and I most certainly did not look crazy. Besides, there wouldn't have been time for someone to call you."

She looked up at him but his eyes were serious. Then she realized something strange about what he'd just told her.

"Why would the shoe store call you? Why not the police?" she asked.

This time he did smile but it didn't meet his eyes. "Are you ready to tell me who the mystery bootlegger is that you've been giving moonshine to and having late night parties with?"

She rolled her eyes and clamped her mouth shut in a firm line.

"That's what I thought. I'll answer your question when you've answered mine," he said.

She sighed, frustrated, "Really mature, Silas. Are we ten years old?"

This time he didn't answer.

"I'm going to ask you again and I want to know the truth. Why were you snooping around back here?" he repeated.

She had to keep the truth from him about Walter—he was like family—but Mr. Thomas was not. Emmie glanced uneasily over at the men who had now stopped unloading and were smoking next to the delivery truck. She could see them periodically looking over at her.

"Okay." She closed her eyes in silent resolve. "I will explain why I'm here but I really do need to get back to work. Can we talk tonight?"

Silas knew he had to make a choice. He was tired of this arguing. She was her and he was him. He had to decide to keep his guard up or let it go. He moved his hand from its resting place on the wall and rubbed his jaw. Emmie noticed that he did that a lot when he was working something out in his mind.

"Yeah," he nodded. "Tonight is good I guess."

"Okay." She nodded again and started to walk past him. "I promise. I'll tell ya what made me come down here today."

He caught her hand in his, lacing their fingers together. He didn't say anything about the gesture but fell into step alongside her.

After a few steps he said, "I still don't like that you won't tell me the name."

"I know. And I wish I could. Maybe when this is all through, I will. Not the name probably but I'll be able to explain it better," she shrugged.

"Emmie, it needs to be ended for you now." He stopped when they reached the center of the square, near the fountain. "This isn't a game. You have to stop." His voice was soft, pleading.

"I know..." she started. "That's what..." she stumbled over Walter's name, "he said too." That's what he'd told her the day she gave him the apple pie 'shine.

"You know that if you would tell me, I would take care of whatever it is you feel like you need to finish." He paused thinking of what to say next. "I can do things Emmie. I can take care of things, but I have to know what's going on."

Her heart shouted, "Tell him." She knew he wasn't lying. Unloading that apple pie 'shine, getting the money. With his connections at the speakeasy and the blind pig, he could probably have it done in ten minutes. Maybe she could get all the moonshine back from Walt and let Silas just take care of it. But she couldn't take the risk of selling out Walt.

"I appreciate that. But it is my problem to fix," she said softly.

He nodded accepting her answer but added, "I don't like this."

"So, are we still on for tonight? I'll explain everything about my leisure walk through the alley," she smiled.

"Yes, I'll have to meet you at Ava's okay? I have to work late—it will probably be at least seven or eight," he said as they neared Mr. Thomas's store. Emmie agreed.

"Back to work for me," she said, making her feet move to the door.

"He treating you okay?" Silas nodded through the door toward Mr. Thomas.

She nodded. "It's fine, but I really am about ten minutes late. And trust me, he'll notice. He docked my pay by forty-five minutes the day I had to take the flowers back to you." Emmie rolled her eyes as she looked back at the store.

Silas stood there and thought for a minute. "You won't let me fix the moonshine problem but I can take care of this. Will you let me?" he asked.

Emmie shrugged and nodded. How in the world was he going to talk Mr. Thomas out of docking her pay? Mr. Thomas didn't even like him. She started to tell him as much but she didn't have the chance. Without saying another word, Silas walked ahead of her into the store. Emmie scrunched her eyebrows together confused. She followed in behind him, walked to the counter, and put her purse away.

Mr. Thomas looked torn. He glanced a few times at Emmie then Silas. His lips puckered together like he'd just earned first place in a lemon-sucking contest. After a passing look of disgust at Emmie, he decided to turn his attention to Silas.

Emmie made her way back over to the dishes she'd began unboxing this morning and picked up where she had left off.

"Mr. McDowell, I thought I made it clear that you were going to purchase your goods elsewhere." Mr. Thomas said as he walked behind the counter. He might be mouthy but he wanted some space between himself and Silas.

"Oh Paul, I think you'll find my money is as good as anyone else's." Silas moved around the store easily. He grabbed tobacco, some penny candy, and a pack of playing cards. What was he doing?

Then he walked to the counter grinning like the cat that swallowed the canary. She recognized that grin, it was devilish. Mr. Thomas stood and looked at him for a moment. For a second Emmie thought he might refuse Silas service. But at last he rang up the items and gave Silas his total. His voice was angry and clipped. Emmie did her best not to pay attention to the interaction or she may explode with laughter. This was the most absurd exchange she had ever seen.

When Mr. Thomas got out a brown bag and started to package the goods Silas put his hand on the top and smashed it close. "Oh, you can just keep your bag, Paul. I don't need it. See this," he held up the tobacco, 'it's for me. I can just keeping right here in my pocket." He opened his coat and slid the small pouch into the pocket of his vest. He was wearing the strangest suspenders she'd ever seen. Emmie could see the faintest tan line of leather straps around his shoulders on the outside of his vest. Mr. Thomas looked annoyed.

"And these," he held up the candy sticks, "these are for my sweet girl." He nodded in Emmie's direction. Silas turned and closed the few feet between them, "I like to tell her she's made of sugar... so sweet she'll melt in the rain." He winked, leaned in, and planted a loud, showy kiss on her lips. Emmie dropped the plate she was holding. Mr. Thomas nearly lost it.

When Silas stepped away from her he noticed that she looked like she was about to die—either from embarrassment or amusement. He hoped she was amused.

"Guess I better throw in a few dollars for that plate." He tossed a few more bills on the table.

"But don't worry, Paul. I didn't leave you out. These are for you. He slid the playing cards across the table and patted them a couple of times. A gift from me to you," he said with a crooked smile.

"Why ever would I want these cards, Silas?" Mr. Thomas spit at him as he turned to walk away.

"Oh, I don't know. If you play your cards right, maybe next time you prey on a desperate young girl, she'll pick you... Daddy," Silas glared at him. Daring him to say anything else.

Emmie's mouth fell open. She didn't even bother to close it as he walked past her, squeezed her hand, whispered quickly and quietly in her ear, "Trust me Em, he's not thinking about the fact you were ten minutes late from lunch."

Without another glance, Silas turned and left the shop. She looked up at Mr. Thomas, unsure what to say. Emmie honestly didn't know how she felt about that little show. Part of her was cheering. Okay, a huge part of her was cheering... but another part, the more sensible part, was afraid he'd crossed some invisible line.

Mr. Thomas did not look up from the cards for a long time. He gripped the counter until his knuckles turned white. He opened his mouth to speak to her but then just shook his head. Muttering something to himself, he turned and walked into the office slamming the door behind him.

Chapter Thirty-seven

M r. Thomas didn't come out of the office for the rest of the afternoon, which was really unusual. Apparently, he hadn't yet shaken off the Silas Show. Although Emmie wanted to enjoy every moment of the confrontation that had transpired, she felt a bit bad for him in spite of herself.

"Mr. Thomas, I'm heading out for the day," she called gathering her belongings.

No response. She was met with only the sound of shuffling papers from inside the office to let her know he was alive in there.

Emmie quietly walked over to the door that was pulled closed and knocked gently. "Are you okay in there?" She tried to keep her voice soft and kind like she was talking to a wounded animal.

"Emma, I am very busy." His tone short, his voice off. When most men got angry their voice got deeper, growly, gruff. But not Mr. Thomas, it got higher, scratchier, like nails on a chalkboard.

It was apparently going to take him some time to get over this, which was understandable. Silas had utterly humiliated him. She hoped things were better by tomorrow. Emmie really didn't want to sit through another day like today. Between Will's fight this morning and Silas's in the afternoon, that store was a toxic place to be.

"Miss Emmie?" a quiet voice called from behind her as she walked on down the street. She glanced around to see Max shuffling up to her. Spotty was diligently walking at his side. The dog always had loved Max. She hadn't even realized either of them were sitting on the bench outside of the shop.

"Oh Max! I am so sorry. I forgot all about our session this afternoon. It's been a long day," she explained.

"Well, if you are busy, we can just skip it today. It's fine." He walked back to the bench to collect his books.

He looked so disappointed. As he turned back to her she noticed an ugly purple bruise under his right eye.

"Max, what on earth happened to your eye?" She grabbed his chin gently and pulled his face up for a closer inspection.

His face flushed crimson and he bit his lower lip. It was obvious he didn't want to tell her.

"Did someone do this to you?" Emmie felt her temper flair. She'd heard Walt's son-in-law was a horrible father but she was pretty sure he was out of the picture and had been for years. Who on earth would have done this?

Max shook his head no in a quick jerky motion. His mouth was set in a heavy frown. It was a younger version of one she'd seen on Walter when she left the barn the other night.

"Max you will tell me who did this to you. Or you are gonna tell your grandparents. You do not keep these things a secret." Her voice left no room for argument.

Max sighed and pulled away from her. "It's just embarrassing, alright?"

He walked back over and sat on the bench staring straight ahead. Emmie knelt down next to him, so they were on level ground. The dog walked over and plopped down at their feet. Max reached his good arm down and rubbed Spotty's belly.

"I'm not going to laugh. You wouldn't believe all the embarrassing things I've done lately," she said.

Her mind flashed back through the events of the last few weeks: the apple pie 'shine, and her investigation attempts in the alley today. Both of those things were done completely in vain. That moonshine was still hidden somewhere on Walter's farm. She had learned absolutely nothing from her nosey walk around the shoe store. Well, other than men were stocking the storeroom of a shoe store and that wasn't exactly newsworthy. The only thing interesting about that was the guy from Smith's Grove was there. It was weird that that guy delivered shoes and worked at the restaurant/speakeasy. Seemed like an odd job combination to her. But the strangest thing was that for some reason they felt compelled to call Silas. The whole combination was off but her brain could not get it all to click together.

"Okay, I trust ya not to laugh," Max finally said, pulling her out of her daydreaming. He looked down at the dog and started talking.

"Today, I got so excited when Cole asked me to play ball. I ain't never had a single town kid ask me to play baseball. Most folks don't want me on their team." He held up his bent arm that he struggled to move, his wrist falling limper than it should. It wasn't that he couldn't move it, it was just more difficult. He put his hand back down and finished talking. "We met behind the theater after lunch. Cole loaned me his glove and said we needed to warm up. That means throwing the ball back and forth, Miss Emmie," he told her.

Emmie nodded, encouraging him to continue.

As he started to speak his little bottom lip began to tremble. "I was so happy, Miss Emmie. I felt just like them boys... no one was really staring at me or nothing. It was like they didn't even care about my slow arm. But the first pitch he threw..." His voice cracked and he pointed a sharp motion to his eye with his good hand.

"Most the kids were laughing, everybody but Cole, anyway. He probably would have but he just felt bad because he was the one that did it." Max looked down as a single tear escaped his eye and he quickly brushed it away. "I'm so dumb. I don't know what I was thinking that I could be like them."

"Oh Max." She pulled him up into her arms and patted his head. "Sounds like you have had one of those days. I promise you in two weeks no one will even remember that ballgame and that shiner will be all healed up. See look that this. I'm clumsy too. I bet you didn't even notice it, right?" She brushed her hair back from her face and pointed to the fading bruise on her cheek.

He squinted his eyes and leaned in for a closer look. When he pulled back his eyes were wide. "You was clumsy too, Miss Emmie?" he asked.

"Yep," she smiled and added, "you want me to run inside the store and get you some ice?"

Max shook his head no. She could tell he wanted this part of the conversation to be over, so she tried to move on.

"You know, sounds like we've both had rough days. I think you need this more than I do." She pulled the candy stick from Silas out of her purse and gave it to Max. His little face showed a hint of a smile. He made quick work of unwrapping it. His movements were off balance but he managed quite well.

"Maybe we should just do something fun this afternoon, hmm?" she asked.

"Like what? Don't you think learning to read is fun?" He looked at her confused. He really did enjoy this. This was the highlight of his day.

"Of course. But you don't need books to read." She took his books from him and started walking. He stood and followed her. "What's that say?" She pointed to a sign on the door.

Max looked at her confused for a moment. Then spent some time working over the letters and sounds. "H-e-l-p, Help Want?"

"And add the last part to want."

"Help Want-ed," he shouted, touching the sign.

Max and Emmie continued this game all the way down Main Street until they reached a fencerow that surrounded a farm sitting adjacent to Walter's land. Max ran up the row a bit in search of a sign to read that he'd spotted in the distance.

By the time Emmie reached him he was looking back at her with growing satisfaction. "I already know this one. It's easy." He hooked his thumbs under his overalls just the way Papaw Walt did when he was talking. Emmie smiled at the comparison.

"Well, out with it," she prompted.

"Pigs For Sale." He huffed for emphasis. He was so proud. That was the good thing about kids. Their world could be crashing around them for one second and they would be happy as a lark the next.

"You know, pig is about the easiest word to read. P-I-G," Max started rambling.

Emmie was listening to him talk when all of the sudden the pieces fell into place. All of the gears matched up allowing the secret to spill out. That was it. Pig. It had been in front of her the whole time.

She could see Walt's house in the distance. It was a small white-washed farmhouse just off the main road. "Max," she cut him off. I'm going to walk you all the way to your house today. Think Walt and Mae will mind if I stop by for a bit?"

When they reached the house Mae barely got out a hello before having a fit about Max's black eye. Her reaction was not that different than Emmie's had been. She dampened a cold washrag and made him sit at the kitchen table with it pressed firmly to his face.

"Sounds like his pride was hurt more than his face," Walt said to Mae. "But don't worry, we'll practice. Those boys will ask you again."

Seeing them both revolve around Max like he was their sun was sweet. Emmie had that once. Her mama would have been upset for her if she'd seen this bruise on her face. People felt sorry for Max sometimes but he got more love than most kids.

"Emmie, dear, I am sorry." Mae walked over and gave Emmie a very grandmotherly hug. She was an inch or so shorter than Emmie. Mae was one of the few people that Emmie could actually see the top of her head. She had two thick grey braided coils that wound in one large bun around her head. Her back was beginning to crook. Her hug was soft. She smelled like a grandma... something between detergent, powder, and cookies. Emmie smiled and hugged Mae back.

"I ain't seen enough of ya lately," Mae nodded. She touched Emmie's cheek. Luckily, Mae's eyes weren't as good as they used to be or she would have noticed the fading yellow bruise. "You're looking a little bit thin." Then she clapped her hands together and smiled. "But don't worry Emmie. I just put on a fresh pot of coffee and a cobbler's cooling on the oven. "You like apples, right?" she asked.

"She sure does," Walt answered dryly. But his eyes were sparked with humor.

Emmie ignored his comment and answered for herself, "I'd love some cobbler. Can I help you?"

"No, child. Just go sit down and rest. Ya been working at Thomas's store today?" she asked. Emmie nodded. Mae went on, "This will be a nice way for me to say thank you for what ya been doing for my boy."

Emmie followed Walt into the small sitting area in the front of the house. Walt sat in an old handmade rocking chair and fired up his pipe. Emmie sat across from him on a small sofa. It was threadbare and covered with mismatched pillows. She put one in her lap and started picking at the loose threads.

Walter just sat there doing more chewing on the end of his pipe than actually smoking it. His eyes never left her. She felt like he may stare a hole right through her forehead. She heard the click of Spotty's toenails on the weathered wooden floor. He had apparently begged his way in the house. He sighed, plopped down at her feet, and let out a long sigh. Even he could feel the tension in the air.

"I'm sorry about the other night," she said, looking down at the pillow.

"I guess I don't really need to know all of it. Just that you're okay." He took his pipe out his mouth and inspected something on the side.

"I'm fine," she answered, keeping her eyes down.

Walter gave a humph sound. She wasn't exactly sure what that noise was supposed to mean.

"Them boys that caused trouble." His eyes looked uneasy. "They kin to your friend, Ava?"

Emmie swallowed and nodded. Walter chewed on his pipe again and frowned. "I suppose they had their reasons for what they did?"

Emmie nodded again. She didn't know what to say. She didn't want to tell him how much they knew about the moonshine.

"They are Ava's cousins and boyfriend." Emmie swallowed hard. The lie caught in her throat but she pushed it out anyway, "I think they thought Bo was getting fresh. He offered me a drink. That must have been what started it."

Walter looked down his nose at her. She knew he didn't completely believe her.

"And you think that warrants a gun?" he asked, trying to keep the judgment from his voice.

She shook her head no. "He overreacted when I got hit. He wouldn't shoot anybody though. He's not a bad person."

Walter huffed again, louder this time. "You keep telling yourself that, girl." He paused for a second and then added, "But it's your life. I just don't want you too messed up with them. Lie with snakes and you might get bit."

Emmie's hands shook as she pulled a thread out of the pillow. Walter really didn't like Silas. She wasn't sure how she felt about that. What would happen when things finally came out in the open? She pushed all of that out of her mind. That wasn't a problem she could fix today. The blind pig—that's what she'd come here to talk about and she was ready for the conversation to move on. She just wasn't sure how to move it forward.

"Well, spit it out girl. I can tell by all your fidgeting that you're itching to tell me something," he said through clenched teeth holding his pipe in his mouth.

"I know what to do what that apple pie," she rocked forward, keeping her voice quiet.

Walt said nothing but arched a thick gray eyebrow. He was listening and not shutting her down yet, so that was a good sign.

Chapter Thirty-eight

"There is a *blind pig* here in town. It would be the perfect place to unload the apple pie! I think I've even figured out where it is—somewhere in the shoe store." She folded her arms proud of herself.

Walter actually smiled. "Somewhere in the shoe store is a blind pig, should we call a vet?"

"Don't play dumb with me you know exactly what I'm talking about," she said.

He sighed, "I know about the pig." He took a puff from his pipe drawing out an annoying silent moment for Emmie. "You sure do think too much. I'm pretty sure I remember telling you the day I picked up that apple pie 'shine that I didn't want you worrying any more with this."

"I couldn't just leave you with the mess I made of your moonshine. So let's make a plan. Should I take a jar or two down there? How does that work?"

Walter shook his head at her amused. "You think you're just gonna walk down to that shoe store and they're gonna buy your apple pie?"

"Okay, so tell me what to do," she said, sitting up shifting her weight forward. The dog thought they were leaving and he stood and paced the length of the couch. It was like he was waiting for an order.

"I tell ya what you're gonna do, the same thing I told ya to do weeks ago, nothing. I've got this taken care of," he snapped.

"How?" she asked, ignoring his attitude.

"Alright, Miss Nosey. Why do you think I let Bo use my still?" he asked.

Emmie thought for a minute then a light bulb went off. "You said his pap, Mr. Johnson, was doing something for you too. Are you selling the 'shine to him?" she asked.

"No, it don't work like that. Wish it was just that easy," he answered.

"Okay," Emmie thought aloud, "well, he would have the connection anyway, being that they sell that Georgia's peach 'shine to the speak and pig. That's what you needed, isn't it? The connection to the joints in town?"

Walter nodded then his face looked grim, "The connection… and permission."

"Permission?" she asked.

"Bart and I have been friends a long time. But I don't think he would have taken too kindly to me cutting in on his business. The same kinds of people that drink peach 'shine are the ones that drink apple 'shine. His supply was getting a little low with the case and all… He needed a favor and I needed to unload some 'shine. Win-win for both of us. But if things hadn't been like they were… with him needing something from me, I would have never tried to sell that moonshine to his customer. The outcome wouldn't have been worth the cash," Walter said honestly. He considered holding back the truth, but Emmie was so curious, if he didn't tell her the truth he was afraid what kind of mess she might get herself into trying to find the answers.

Emmie chewed her bottom lip and stood to pace the room while she thought this over. Silas alluded to the fact the Johnson's had skeletons in their closet last night and now Walter looked half afraid of them. "Walter do you think they are the kind of people that would burn down the Cliff's barn because he was nosing in their moonshine business? He's a revenuer, right?"

Walter thought before he spoke, "I don't think Bart did it, if that's what you're asking. But he's got a lot of friends and I don't think he would stop nobody from doing it either. Understand?"

Emmie nodded.

"Why don't you just ask that snaky lawyer ya been hanging around? He'd probably know the truth being as he represented Bart and all," Walter said with a grin.

"He's not a snaky lawyer," she defended him. Walter made another humph. "Well, at least we got rid of the apple pie, right?" She smiled down at Walter.

"Don't get your hopes up yet, Emmie. The pig is a hard place to break into even with a connection. Every moonshiner in five counties is fighting for the rights to the few pigs and speaks that we got around here. Bart Johnson may have been able to get me the connection but he doesn't make the decision. Some other fella does that. I met him at the barn party the other night. I left him with a few sample jars of our stuff. They're gonna try it out this week, see how it sells and get back to me. Imagine it'll do pretty well since they're low on the peach stuff."

His face went serious. "I'm not sure I want to know how you figured out the Johnsons was selling flavored moonshine to the speak and pig, do I?"

"Probably not," she answered honestly.

He didn't push her any further. "I made it clear to that man. And we ain't carrying on with this forever. If they wanted the goods, it was a one-time sale. I ain't got access to no more, you got that girl?" He pointed his finger out at her.

"Clear. I'll not be making any more apple pie 'shine." She put her hands up and shook her head.

"That's right!" He took a slow puff and leaned back to relax in his chair before adding, "Ya did good though girl. At first I could tell that man James didn't even want to listen to me. I was just another old man with a jar o' white lightning." He chewed his pipe before he continued. "Then they saw that I was actually a crazy old man that had decorated his jars of 'shine with gingham fabric. It caught their attention." He smiled mischievously and winked. "Apparently not many of us old bootleggers do that sort of thing."

He laughed. She wasn't sure if he was laughing with her or at her. But either way, she didn't care. She had a good feeling about those sample jars that Walt had given away. The blind pig would want them. Then they would sell off all that moonshine and she wouldn't have this cross to bear anymore. Maybe today was looking up after all.

****

It was dusk by the time that Emmie left Walter and Mae's house. The sun hung over the hills in the distance. It was casting a soft reddish glow on the horizon as Emmie walked toward Ava's house. The nights were beginning to get cool; Emmie wished she had grabbed a wrap before she left home this morning. As she passed her house Spotty turned to run up her drive.

"Not yet, boy. We're going to Ava's tonight. Come on," she called to the dog. He looked like he wanted to protest and actually turned his face back to the house. "Alright, you go on home. I'll be back shortly." Emmie turned and headed up the road.

She let out a long sigh that she felt like she had been holding for over a month. She didn't know how much money she would get if the blind pig decided to buy all the apple pie off Walt's hands but she guessed it was a good amount. After all, Walt said moonshiners in five counties were trying to break into the speaks and pigs, it must offer a good cash flow. Maybe she'd even done something good for Walt. If she gave him that apple pie recipe, he could probably do it. It might even boost his income. Emmie smiled to herself in satisfaction.

She heard Spotty panting behind her, knowing he'd never let her walk to Ava's alone. She scratched his ear as they walked. "If only I knew for sure how those sample jars Walt had given the pig were working out. I sure would love to be a fly on the wall there tonight," she said to the dog. He looked up at her like he was really listening. His head tipped over to the side, like he was thinking with her. That's when it hit her.

"Fly on the wall... well, not a fly... but just maybe..." she told the dog. Then she picked up speed.

When she reached Ava's front porch, she was slightly out of breath. She paused for a minute on the step to compose herself before she knocked on the door. Spotty found his favorite spot under the front swing and curled into a ball. He was smart enough to know that no amount of begging was going to give him entrance to Ava's house.

"It'll be fine." She talked herself into the conversation she was getting ready to have with Silas. She brushed her hands together; as if wiping away the negative thoughts and walked toward the door.

The door swung open immediately. Trick came tearing out of the house like it was on fire, running over Emmie in the process.

"Oh God, Emmie. Are you alive down there?" he asked. He had knocked her to the ground. Trick always had time for a joke, no matter his hurry. Apparently, Gabe didn't. He had leapt over the pair of them unable to stop moving once he'd seen Trick and Emmie go down.

Gabe reached back in one motion and swung Emmie up from the ground and shouted at Trick, "Come on."

"What's wrong?" Emmie shouted after them. They were already halfway to the car, but the housekeeper and Ava hadn't come out yet; it must not be an actual fire.

"Umm. Something at the office came up. Tell Ava we are gonna be late," Gabe shouted, slamming the door to the car and starting it all in one motion.

Trick waved bye quickly. Despite his earlier joke, even his face looked stone-sober as they pulled away from the house.

Emmie looked down and brushed the dirt off her dress then headed into the house. In their hurry to leave the boys had left it wide open.

"What in the world was all that about?" Ava asked, walking down the stairs. "I looked out the bedroom window and saw you on the ground and then Trick and Gabe flew to the car." Ava's voice was slow and calm.

Emmie shook her head. "I honestly have no idea. Gabe just said they'd be home late. They looked serious though. You think everything is okay?"

Ava just shrugged her shoulders, "It'll be fine. I'm sure."

The phone rang. Ava walked over to answer it then turned and held the phone out toward Emmie. "It's Silas, for you." Ava found this much more intriguing than the events of the last two minutes. Kindling romances… they made her giddy and excited. People running out of the house like it was on fire to unknown drama. That was just another day. Emmie admired her eccentric nature.

"Hello," Emmie answered.

"I'm sorry, Emmie. Something has come up. I've got to work at the office late. Maybe tomorrow night would be better," Silas apologized.

"It's fine. But really, I should probably tell you why I came down there today—" Emmie started but he cut her off with a swear.

"I said I'm coming," Silas shouted at someone else. Emmie pulled the phone back from her ear. "I'll talk to you in the morning, okay?"

He hung up without waiting for a reply from her. She tried to call him back but got no answer. Something had bothered her since she had figured out that the blind pig was somewhere near the shoe store. Why had Will been hanging out there? Even more than that why would Mr. Thomas have said they almost *had it*? Money? She didn't know but she had a sick feeling that was something she needed to tell Silas.

Emmie decided to cut right to the chase. She turned toward her friend. She took a deep breath and then blurted out, "Ava, do you know what a blind pig is?"

Ava smiled so big it showed all of her teeth. She slowly nodded her head.

"I will explain to you the whole story later but I think there is one on the square," Emmie said.

Ava looked sideways at her friend and thought for a second before she spoke, which was very un-Ava like. "There is, why?"

Emmie ignored her question and asked one of her own, "Do you know how to get into it? I mean after going to the speak in the Grove the other night I am sure it is not the sort of place you can walk into. I'm sure there are passwords and stuff, right?"

"Emma, dear, I love where this conversation is headed." Ava touched her hand to her cheek like she was trying to contain her excitement, willing Emmie to continue. "Yes there are passwords."

"Can you take me there?" Emmie whispered, taking a step closer to her friend.

Ava thought about it for a minute then clapped her hands together in front of her body. "Let's do it!"

Chapter Thirty-nine

Ava said it was best they go dressed just as they were. It was odd because an evening out with Ava usually equaled at least twelve strands of additional pearls. Emmie remembered Silas talking once about blind pigs. He had told her the ones around here were rougher than speakeasies. She assumed that's why Ava had decided to dress down. Well, as dressed down as she ever was. Today she was in a yellow embroidered flapper dress that draped just past her knees. Her shoes even matched—always composed, always coordinated.

As they walked to the car Spotty tried to follow them. "Go on back home, boy. I'll see you there later." The dog whined, not liking to be left out. "Go on," she repeated. He didn't leave the house right away. He chased them down the road for a bit before he turned to cut through the fields that would lead him home.

On the drive there Emmie looked down at her plain, baby blue dress she had made last summer and realized it came up short. If she'd known she was going out, she would have brought something better. That was probably for the best anyway. Fly on the wall, right. She was there to blend in not stand out.

"So Emmie, did Silas finally tell you about the pig?" Ava asked, speeding up a bit as she pulled onto the open road. When she drove, the car always jerked as she shifted gears. Emmie wouldn't complain though… she couldn't drive period. She just braced her hand on the doorframe.

"Not exactly," Emmie answered discreetly.

"Come on, Emmie. Be on the level with me. You've been too quiet lately," Ava begged, lurching the car forward again. Emmie's knuckles were white as she gripped the doorframe a little tighter.

Emmie recounted the events of the day: the argument between Will and Mr. Thomas, the shotgun-toting sheriff, and how Silas had stopped her in the alley. Ava interrupted her in the middle of the "Silas Show-down" part of the story saying that Mr. Thomas was the biggest, smelli-est, wet blanket. Emmie was sure that was the most accurate and hilarious description of the man she'd ever heard.

When they pulled into the parking spot behind the law firm Emmie noticed that Silas's car was still there. Ava caught her staring over at it.

"You know he's carrying a torch for you, right?" Ava added serious-ly.

Emmie shook her head and shrugged, "Some of that may have just been for show. He doesn't like Mr. Thomas."

"You are as blind as this pig we are getting ready to go into. Speak-ing of which... you should know this is going to be different than the last speak. We should probably stick close together."

Emmie listened earnestly to her friend's directions and helpful hints at how to blend in. Most of it involved Emmie standing there and smiling while Ava did the talking.

"Wait," Emmie whispered as Ava headed down the alley. "Don't you think I should try to tell Silas really quick about Mr. Thomas's interest in the... you know." She pointed toward the shoe store/blind pig.

Ava looked longingly down the alley then turned toward her friend. "You're right, but let's hurry."

The girls scurried up to the front of the law firm. The doors were locked. After a few minutes of loud banging, no lights came on and one came to the door. Emmie was thoroughly confused.

"Do you think maybe they are upstairs?" Emmie asked.

"Umm..." Ava looked up. "I don't see any lights on. Probably not sitting up there in the dark."

"But his car is here," Emmie rationalized.

Ava said shortly, "Let's go."

She hooked her arm in Emmie's elbow and dragged her into the al-ley.

"He said he would be at the office," Emmie said, unable to let it go.

Ava didn't answer. She kept walking, picking up pace until they reached the back of the building. She then led Emmie over to a large brown door. She opened it quickly and closed it behind them. Emmie had expected to be in the storage room of the shoe store but they were in a staircase. It was narrow, steep and long. Wooden stairs stretched up to the second floor of the building. At the top, she could see another door with a huge handle and a golden door knock.

Ava took the stairs two at a time. With her short skirt and long legs, this was an easy stretch for her. Not so much for Emmie but she did her best to keep up.

"Okay, remember, smiley happy Emmie. Care free, Emmie," Ava said with wide eyes.

Emmie smiled.

"Relax your eyes," Ava said.

Emmie tried.

"Don't fidget with your hands," Ava added.

Emmie stilled her hands at her side.

"Can you show less teeth, it may look more natural," Ava said.

"Knock on the door, Ava," Emmie whisper shouted.

"Gee, alright, alright." Ava turned and knocked once.

A peephole opened. It was similar to the speakeasy.

Ava said, "Down with the 18th."

When the door opened, Emmie recognized the man working there as one of the men from the alley. She couldn't tell if he recognized her or not. He pulled them into the small hallway and then snapped the door closed behind them.

"Ava, you brought a friend," he said in a familiar tone.

Emmie tried to keep her smile light and happy but really she was wondering how often Ava had been there to be on such easy terms with this man.

"Yeah, she needed a night out. She's been fighting with her boyfriend. I thought you wouldn't mind, right?" Ava smiled and grabbed his arm casually.

He was young enough to be easily entranced by her charm. She didn't even have to try.

"Sure, Ava." Then he turned his gaze to Emmie. "We always welcome pretty little dolls that have been fighting with their beaus. "

Then he led them to a narrow door at the end of the hall. He opened it up for them and motioned for them to go on inside. And there it was... the blind pig.

Emmie wasn't quite sure what she expected but this was different.

One. It was really, really crowded. Like shoulder-to-shoulder, hard to breathe crowded.

Two. It wasn't much. The walls were stark white with chipping plaster. There were only a few seats and tables. And those that were there didn't match, just odds and ends.

Three. There were all sorts of people there. Folks in suits, folks in overalls. There was no filter. She and Ava were two of maybe six girls in the whole place.

Four. The bar area was the only nice area in the place. It was a brick wall with about five stools pushed up to a heavy wooden bar. The bartender looked almost identical to the one in Smith's Grove. He wore a long white apron and was quickly moving down the length of the bar pouring drinks for people.

But the last one was probably the most surprising thing she found...

Five. Silas was sitting at the table near the back of the room with Gabe, Trick and three men she didn't recognize.

Emmie grabbed Ava's hand and pulled her as quickly as possible across the room to the bar. Fly on the wall, Emmie repeated to herself.

"What are you doing?" Ava asked, pulling away from her friend. "Let's go over and say hello. Didn't you have something important to tell him about Mr. Thomas?"

"No, no please. We will in a minute because he has some serious explaining to do." Emmie paused keeping her anger under control. "I just want to see something before he knows I'm here," Emmie said.

"What on earth do you want to see?" Ava asked.

Emmie didn't have time to explain all about the apple pie moonshine. She didn't really want to yet. She wanted to wait until just the right moment.

"I'll tell you all about it later, promise. I'm looking for..." Emmie stopped in her tracks. Sitting behind the bar was a jar of amber colored moonshine with a blue gingham wrapped lid. It was hers. It was the 'shine she made. Emmie was surprised how proud she felt to see that the jar was nearly empty. When she peeked behind the bar, she saw a bin with another one of her jars that was completely empty.

Emmie pulled Ava down to the end of the bar where the jar of apple pie 'shine was.

"What'll it be?" asked the bartender, wiping his hands on the long white apron.

Ava opened her mouth to speak but it was Emmie who spoke first, abandoning their earlier agreement.

"Two of those please," Emmie said, pointing to the gingham wrapped jar.

The man poured, Emmie paid, and Ava looked confused at the whole interaction.

Emmie took a quick glance around the bar and noticed two or three other folks were drinking her 'shine. It was obviously darker than the clear white lightning but lighter than bourbon, so it was fairly easy to spot. The people drinking seemed to be enjoying it. Fly on the wall mission, almost a success. She looked at her glass and tipped it back taking a little sip.

It was just like she remembered. Good, smooth. It was as sweet as apple cider with the warmth of moonshine. The pig had to buy the rest. Emmie glanced at Ava. Her friend was looking at her like she had grown another head.

"What?" Emmie asked confused.

"Emmie, what is going on?" Ava asked.

She smiled. "Just give it a sip and tell me what you think."

Ava looked at the glass for a moment and then tipped it back, swallowed hard, and nodded. Emmie leaned in waiting for judgment. "Wow, that is really good. It's like a warm apple pie." She took another sip.

Emmie smiled, proud.

"What have I missed...? Why are you smiling like that?" Ava asked, looking around.

"I'm smiling because..." Emmie whispered, "I made it."

Chapter Forty

Ava rolled her eyes. "Oh, Emmie. Really, tell me what all of this is about."

"No, Ava. It's the truth." She nodded her head pointing at the jar on the edge of the bar. "I did that with the moonshine we found in the pantry. I swear."

Ava cocked her head to the side, waiting for Emmie to say "Just teasing" or "Gotcha" but she didn't. Ava stretched her arm across the bar and picked up the jar for closer inspection. The bartender gave her a look, obviously questioning her decision to touch the liquor but said nothing.

She turned the jar over in her hand and then rubbed her fingers against the fabric-covered lid. Ava looked up and stared at her friend composing her thoughts. Her eyes were wide, her mouth set in a straight line. She was genuinely shocked. Emmie had expected Ava to laugh or ask her a million questions but she didn't. She bit her lower lip and continued inspecting the jar. All at once Ava's gaze moved back to the table where the guys were seated.

Emmie turned and followed Ava's eyes across the length of the long narrow room. It was easy to spot what had captured her attention. Clearly, the boys were in some sort of intense discussion. All attention seemed to be focused on the man in the center. He grinned and said something pointing at Silas. They weren't speaking loud enough to hear but you could tell by the reaction of the others at the table it wasn't good. All at once Silas reached across the table and grabbed the guy by the back of the neck. Bringing his hand down in one quick motion, he slammed the man's face against the table. The thump echoed off the walls. The entire place stilled at the sound. Slowly and disoriented, the guy pulled his head back up. Trick and Gabe stood almost in unison looking around the place. The other two guys they were seated with picked the guy up and led him through a door behind the side of the bar. Silas followed close on their heels. Trick followed his brother, while Gabe continued to check the surroundings.

The rest of the blind pig customers went back to their business like nothing had happened. But Emmie couldn't drag her eyes away from the door they had just entered. That man—she knew him. Not well but she knew him; she'd even seen him at the barn party the other night, sitting at the table near Bart Johnson. He had also come to her house just after Ronnie had died. He said that Ronnie had borrowed some tools to work on the truck. He told Emmie he was sorry to bother her but his car was broken and he really needed those tools back. Why in the world would Silas be fighting with that guy?

Emmie spun around on her stool to ask Ava. However, Ava's eyes were still fixed in the distance. She lifted her hand in a bashful wave and shrugged her shoulder like she was saying, "Sorry."

Emmie turned around to see Gabe closing the distance between them. Pushing people out of the way in the process.

"What the hell are you doing here? I thought I made it clear you were never to come here alone," Gabe shouted as he walked up to them.

"Emmie's had a rough day. We won't stay long, promise." Ava smiled up at him. Her smile almost always worked on him. His expression softened only his eyes showed he was still annoyed. She reached up grabbed his tie and pulled him down for a quick kiss.

As he pulled away she said, "And technically. I'm not alone. I mean, you're here, right." Her eyes were full of humor.

"Don't push me." He grabbed her chin. "And don't leave until I can walk you down. I've got something I need to take care of here first." Then he turned his eyes to Emmie. "You know, I have to tell him you are here... and he's going to be pissed off."

She didn't need to be told who *he* was. "I know, he probably won't be happy."

"Sweetheart," he laughed without humor, "there's no probably about it."

Gabe turned and headed for the door the boys had disappeared through earlier. Emmie's stomach turned. Maybe she should just go.

Folks were drinking her 'shine and enjoying it. The night was young and the bartender had already gone through two jars. That had to be good news. Emmie was sure they would buy the rest of the apple pie 'shine from Walt. Fly-on-the-wall mission was complete. She had seen what she came here for... and honestly, she'd seen more than she came for.

"Ava what in the world were they doing with that man... Sam Young, I think that's his name?" Emmie asked.

"What makes you think I would have any idea? Do you know him?" Ava asked.

Emmie shook her head, "Not really. One of Ronnie's friends..." But she never got to finish her sentence.

The ground below her was gone. She kicked her feet but felt nothing. All at once the world shifted and she was flipped upside down. Emmie still couldn't see who had grabbed her. But her face was planted into the back of a dark brown suit coat. She continued kicking her feet and beating this man with her hands. A strong arm clamped down across her legs to keep them still. That's when she smelled the familiar aftershave and leather. She knew who this kidnapper was and what was coming. Emmie stopped fighting and peeked her head around to his torso to see Ava grinning and waving. She held up her drink and mouthed, "Good Luck." A lot of help she was.

"Silas," she said calmly. Well, as calmly as you can speak when someone is carrying you like a sack of potatoes.

He said nothing. He just continued walking through the pig. People moved out of his way and gave Emmie little more than a passing glance.

"This is very caveman like Silas, don't you think?" Emmie asked, smacking his back with her palm. When she tried to give one more kick for good measure she was met with a swift smack to her bum.

"Put me down, Silas. You made your point, okay? You don't want me in there," Emmie shouted.

They left the pig through the same narrow door she had entered. He shouted at the young guy who was sitting in a barstool next to the stairwell door that admitted the customers.

"Get your ass over here and open this door," he said, walking to a large wooden door on the opposite side of the hall.

"Yes, sir." The guy flew off the stool and pulled a ring full of keys out of his pocket, taking his time to find the right one.

Really, he is not even going to question the fact he is carrying a girl out of the joint, Emmie thought. This is absolutely ridiculous.

Finally the guy unlocked the door and held it open. Then he spoke to Emmie as Silas carried her past him. "Ya should have mentioned that Mr. McDowell was the beau you've been fighting with."

"Shane," Silas spoke the boy's name.

"Yes, sir," he said, standing in the doorway.

"Take one step back." Shane did as Silas instructed. Then he kicked the door shut leaving the boy alone in the hall.

Silas flipped Emmie off his shoulder and onto an old worn-out couch that sat along the wall.

"If you need me I'll just be out here, sir," Shane shouted from the hall. Not a smart one that kid.

Emmie pushed her blue dress down, stood, and put her hand on her hip, bracing herself for the upcoming confrontation. She met his glare with one of her own. Her heart was pounding out of her chest but she refused to let it show.

"Emma, why in the hell are you here?" Silas shouted.

"Well, I'm in here," Emmie emphasized the word here by spreading her arms out, "because some Neanderthal threw me over his shoulder and carried me in here."

"Don't you get sassy with me, Emma," he said, pointing at her. "Now is not the time."

It didn't slip by her that he called her by her given name. His glare was ice. His face was stone. It was only upon closer inspection that she noticed his face was cut just over his eyebrow. It was freshly scabbed over. You could see the red blood along the outer edge. The cut hadn't been there this afternoon. What on earth was going on tonight?

He turned his back to her and rubbed his jaw, pacing the length of the couch. She stepped away from the sofa and walked up behind him.

"I didn't know you would be here because you said you were work-ing late at the office," she spit. "This sure doesn't look like any office to me."

"Damn it, Emmie," he said, walking toward her. "This isn't about me. We are talking about you. What the fuck are you doing here?"

She took a step backward and felt her knees buckle when she reached the couch. She sighed and looked away from him. "I just…" Emmie swallowed hard, "I just wondered if this really was a blind pig." The lie caught in her throat. It felt wrong. It burned in her mouth like her first taste of moonshine. She swallowed hard and continued. "I asked Ava to bring me."

He looked down at her with his hand rubbing over his mouth like he was trying to decide what to say next.

"Emmie that place," he pointed across the hall. "that place is a shit hole. Nothing good comes from in there." He scrunched his eyes. "It's full of drunkards, bums, and liars. I don't want you in a place like that. You don't know what goes on in there…" he started.

"I saw you…" she nodded her head. "I saw what you did to that man. Sam Young, I saw what you did to him."

A quiet moment passed between them, each too overwhelmed to know what to say next.

"Did he do this to you?" she reached up and gently touched the cut.

He was surprised that her eyes didn't look afraid at what she had seen; they looked curious and sad. He flinched away from her touch.

"So you do know him," Silas spit. "It's him isn't it?"

"What?" Emmie looked confused.

"It is him—Sam Young is the man who used to work with your father," he said.

"Yeah, I don't know how much they worked together but he was one of Ronnie's buddies," she said, her eyebrow arched with question.

"Don't play dumb with me, Emmie. Sam sent someone in here a few weeks ago selling some of your stepdad's 'shine. I saw him at that barn party and he is the man you gave those jars of 'shine to. He's the one you have been keeping a secret from me… admit it… tell me the truth," Silas yelled.

Chapter Forty-one

"What?" she asked, confused. How could Sam have been selling Ronnie's 'shine?

"What kind of moonshine did he bring in?" she asked quietly.

"What kind of moonshine? Emmie, don't you try and play innocent with me. You know what moonshine is... white lightning, 'shine, unaged bourbon... moonshine," he said.

Silas continued ranting, pacing, slamming, but she was no longer paying him any attention. How would that man have Ronnie's 'shine? In all their conversations, Walter had never once mentioned anyone else involved in their bootlegging. She suddenly felt like she didn't know half of the things she thought she did. Would Walter keep this from her? For a passing moment she wondered if maybe Walt had given the jars she'd found to Sam. But that couldn't be. She'd turned all of their moonshine into the apple pie.

Emmie walked over and sat on the sofa and stared down at the ground trying to piece it all together. She had to call him. She glanced around the room in search of a phone.

"Emmie, Emmie." She felt his hands around her shoulders shaking her out of her thoughts.

For the first time she left her thoughts and focused on him. "What the hell is going on in there?" He tapped her forehead. "Were you even listening to me?"

She shook her head no, honestly. "I'm sorry. It's just... I'm confused. How much of Ronnie's 'shine did he have?"

Silas stopped moving. He knelt down in front of her, putting his hands on her knees. Then he brought his hands together and gazed up at her like he was trying to read her mind. He looked like he did at church. Kneeling, praying, maybe some remorse.

For the first time he realized she knew more than he thought. More than just the identity of some hillbilly bootlegger.

"Emmie, be straight with me." His hands clasped together tighter like he was holding them down. She could see his veins on his neck popping out as his jaw clenched.

"Were you helping Ronnie with the bootlegging?" he asked point blank. The lack of emotion or inflection in his voice was more frightening than the little fit he'd had earlier.

"No," she answered honestly. "When he was alive, I didn't even know."

Silas nodded, accepting her information as the truth. "Did you know he owed people product or money?"

"No." She shook her head. Her eyes wide, "Who did he owe?"

He ignored her question. "That man in there," he pointed his finger toward the pig, "you are telling me he is not the man you gave your stepfather's 'shine to?"

"No." She swallowed. "He's not. I've only seen him a few times. He and Ronnie would talk at church or social functions. Just in passing. I don't think they were real close or anything. A few days after Ronnie's funeral Sam showed up at my door. He said Ronnie had borrowed his tools to work on the truck before he passed. I let him into the barn and he got them out. I never saw him again, well... until the Johnson's barn party the other night. And that was it, I swear."

Silas was quiet, processing the information. He nodded. "Did he take the tools?"

"Yeah. I mean. I think so. I was running late for work but he didn't come back again, so I guess he got what he needed." As soon as the words left her mouth she knew.

"You think he was stealing Ronnie's moonshine?" she asked.

Silas shrugged, "Maybe stealing, maybe taking something he was promised."

That hit her hard. She knew Ronnie was a drunk but he wasn't dumb. Was he out making promises to people that he didn't keep? Silas could tell her wheels were spinning.

"So, how long have you known?" he asked, still speaking in calm indifference.

Emmie swallowed hard. These were the parts she hadn't spoken to anyone. Could she trust him? She felt her hands start to tremble. He must have too. He grabbed her forearms firmly and ran his hands down the length of her arm without speaking. When he got to her hands he brought them together and covered them with his, kissing her fingertips softly. This was certainly a new way to use his hands in an interrogation. He stared down at them for a moment then brought his eyes back up to her. They were piercing, serious, alive.

"I need you, Emmie." His voice caught in his throat. He swallowed and shook his head. That came out different than he meant. He looked up at her out of curiosity. How would she take that?

Her eyes were wide with surprise.

"I need your help with all of this. I don't understand where you fit in." He laughed without humor. He was on the balance of control here. "Because obviously you do. Or you wouldn't fucking be here." He let go of her hands and rubbed his face. He stood and stretched his legs. "I've got to know, Emmie."

She licked her lips and nodded staring up at him.

"Okay." She nodded again like she was convincing herself that she could say the words… that she could trust him.

"It was the night Ava's family came back. We were talking about Ronnie, the moonshine we'd once found as kids. It was… in the barn." She cursed herself for never questioning Sam being in the barn. "And it got me thinking. I started to wonder why Ronnie was gone all hours of the night. Why our money always came in spurts. I had to know. So, for the next few days I roamed our property looking for a still, more out of curiosity than a desire to be involved. Each time I thought about giving up the hunt for it, I'd pass the scorched remains of that tree again where he crashed and just keep on looking. It took a little over a week but I found it." She took a deep breath. This was getting to the tricky part of the story.

"But…" she sighed, "Ronnie may have been dead, but the still wasn't."

He arched his brow then motioned for her to continue.

Emmie stood and wiped her hands on the skirt of her dress and walked the length of the room. She didn't stop until she was on the opposite side staring at some old water-damaged oil painting. Silas closed the distance between them in a few steps. He put his arm around her waist and slowly turned her around. He wanted to be looking at her face when she told the rest of the story. He knew whatever was coming was crucial.

She took a step and leaned her back against the wall. One arm covered her stomach the other her mouth.

"I want to tell you. I'm just afraid." Her eyes searched his.

"Emmie, do you honestly think I would hurt you?" He brushed her temple with his fingertips. "The things you have been keeping from me are driving me crazy. But, I would never hurt you. You," he paused. He had not expected or wanted the conversation to turn to this. "You mean more to me than..." he shrugged, unable to finish the sentence. He didn't really have the words to say. She meant more to him than he wanted to admit to himself much less say it out loud.

She nodded because the words failed her. She hoped he knew she felt the same way.

He ran his hands over his eyes to compose himself. "But Em, it doesn't change the fact that I have to know."

"It's not me I'm afraid for. It's him. I don't want to drag him into all of this... I don't want you to hurt him," she explained.

Silas's nostrils flared and his look turned to stone. Was she in love with this man? He fought a wave of jealousy. He had to keep it under control.

"But..." she continued, "I trust you. It sounds like this may be deeper than he knew. If someone finds out I gave him moonshine... he may be in trouble too. Maybe you can help him... we can fix this together?"

Not likely. Silas kept his thoughts to himself.

"So when I got to the cave the still was up and going and he was there. I was scared at first because I didn't know who I'd find at the still." She intentionally left out his name. She could come back to that point later.

"You walked right up to a still... Emmie, you're lucky he didn't shoot you," he said.

Emmie laughed. "Well, I'd be lying if I said my knees weren't knocking. But he wouldn't shoot me."

Silas flexed the muscles of his jaw. He and Emmie were way too familiar for his liking.

"And he was on my land. So, that's what I told him. If he was gonna be making 'shine on my land. I was going to need some money." She felt so embarrassed telling this part.

His mouth actually dropped open and he was dumbstruck. "My God, Emmie! Are you an idiot?"

Emmie smiled at his expression. Some sick part of her loved his reaction. It felt good to tell someone. "I guess. And he was putting this goop on the pipes. But it wasn't any good. It was so thin it just kept sliding right down the sides. Bless his heart. I was trying to talk my way into helping him. Silas, you know it wasn't the 'shine I wanted to make... I just needed the money. And I am so tired of workin' for Mr. Thomas and I want so desperately to go to school.

"I saw that little sack of flour in the corner. I'm used to baking and I know about making a good batter. What he had was way too thin to keep the steam from escaping those pipes. So I mixed up a thicker batch. He told me he would pay me a dollar a week to make him paste."

Now, Silas was sure he was going to kill this guy. Any man who would agree to bring some naive girl like Emmie into his bootlegging scheme deserved to be shot.

"So, you've been making paste?" Silas asked, keeping judgment from his voice.

"Well, I did. I was really good at it too. I beat the fire out of an old tea kettle and experimented on..." she started but cut herself off when she saw his face. He didn't look as excited about her experiments as she was. "I guess that's beside the point. Ava and I found all those jars in the house and I showed them to him. Then there wasn't any reason for him to keep up the process. He said it would take him months or more to sell all that."

Silas paused thinking. "You think he could have given the jars to Sam?"

"I know he didn't." Her heart caught in her chest. She dreaded telling him this next part almost as much as she didn't want to tell him about Walt.

"How do you know?" he asked, confused.

The door flew open to reveal a somewhat disheveled Trick in the doorway. "Silas we need you. He's ready," he said, panting.

"Trick, I'll be there in a minute," he said, never looking away from Emmie.

"Silas, seriously brother," he pleaded. "She's going to have to wait."

It wasn't often that Trick spoke up to Silas. He knew that he needed to go but also knew whatever Emmie was getting ready to share was important.

He looked at his brother then back at her. Her breathing was fast and her hands were trembling.

"I'll go back in there with you. It's easier for me just to show you than to say it anyway," she said, stepping around him.

Silas had no idea what she was going to show him. But he knew she was scared. He grabbed her hand and together they walked back into the pig.

Chapter Forty-two

When they walked past the door where he wanted Silas to go Trick shouted, "Come on, Silas."

Silas glared at his brother and held up a finger telling him to wait a minute. He had to see this before he went back into that room. This whole ordeal was all related and somehow Emmie was the missing piece. As they reached the narrow aisle between the bar and row of tables he pushed her in front of him, never letting go of her arm. She had to lead since he had no idea where they were going... and this was his family's pig. That irony was not lost on him. As they drew nearer to Ava, Emmie noticed the young man, Shane, had taken her seat. He and Ava were in the midst of some conversation. It was apparently hilarious because they were laughing so hard her face was red.

"Ava, where's my drink?" Emmie asked.

She was surprised when Shane was the one to answer. "Oh, this was yours? I'm sorry sweetheart. I wasn't thinking and I just drank the whole thing. I'll get you another."

Ava glanced from Silas to Emmie a few times before speaking. She stood up to her full height, leaned down, and whispered in her friend's ear, "Emmie, honey you don't want to do this. Not now." When she pulled back she was looking right at Silas.

"I appreciate the advice but I've got to." Emmie reached down and picked up Ava's leftover drink and handed it to Silas.

He looked at her confused. "Emmie?"

"Just drink," she said, pushing the glass up to his mouth.

Because he didn't have time for the argument he humored her. He took a quick swig from the glass. It was pretty good shine. It had the spices of apple pie and the warmth of moonshine. But something about it was familiar.

Emmie opened her mouth to speak but Ava stopped her. "Silas, don't lose your mind over this."

Silas was getting pissed off. He didn't have a clue what they were flapping their jaws about and he had things to do. Emmie reached across the bar and pulled a jar off the shelf. The bartender came over with an outstretched arm to take it away from her then pulled back when he spotted Silas in the group. Silas nodded and raised his hand to dismiss him. He left them alone.

Emmie took in her audience, held the jar to her chest, and led Silas to the opposite end of the bar. When she stopped he pulled her through the door she'd seen the guys disappear through earlier. She expected to be in a side room but found herself in a tiny hallway with two doors on either side. She pulled the jar away from her chest and handed it to him.

Swallowing hard she said, "Okay... here goes. I know that he didn't give the jars to Sam because you said those were just plain ole moonshine. And with all of the moonshine that I found, I..." She stopped talking. Why was this so hard to say?

Silas looked down at the jar. When he inspected it closely he could tell it was one of Ronnie's jars. All of Ronnie's lids had a small X scratched into them. As he pushed back the fabric on this one, he could see it—wait the fabric. He'd seen that fabric before... and the familiarity of the spices. The applesauce. His mind flashed back to her kitchen and the stacks of canned applesauce jars. All decorated with scraps of gingham fabric just like this. Then at the church picnic... Those jars had been wrapped in blue gingham just like this.

He tightened his grip on the container. He turned and threw the jar, smashing it against one of the doors. Amber liquid oozed down the side. Silas turned and looked at her. His breathing was heavy. "What the fuck were you thinking, Emmie?"

Her eyes welled up and she felt her throat tightening. "It's just, he told me that he didn't have anyway to sell the 'shine—that it was hard to break into being a distributor for the blind pigs. I wanted to help him get rid of it. I needed the money. I had that peach 'shine at the speak you took me to and thought... I can do that. I just wanted to help him get rid of it quick. I didn't really think it through. I made that out of all of the jars I gave him," she spit the words out of her mouth like they were burning her insides.

The door Silas had smashed the jar against opened, revealing a stark white room. A couple of men were sitting at a metal table. In the center Emmie could see Sam Young barely holding his head up. Gabe appeared in the doorway looking at the shards of glass on the floor.

"Everything okay?" he asked. Silas didn't answer him.

"You're damn right you didn't think it through. For Christ's sake Emmie. See that…" he said, pointing at Sam, "That's what happens to men who screw up in this business. You think it wouldn't happen to a woman?" He ran his hands over his face.

He just shook his head at her… like he was disgusted. "Silas, it's just…"

"I cannot do this right now. You gave me the information I needed. Now if you'll excuse me, I've got some other shit to take care of." His cheeks flamed with fire as emotion settled there.

Silas walked into the room. Gabe closed the door behind him. However, before he had snapped it all the way shut he gave Emmie a look of pity. He didn't know what was going on, but being on the wrong side of Silas's mood was enough to make him feel sorry for her.

"You okay?" he asked quietly.

She nodded. He snapped the door closed.

Alone in the hall, the reality of the situation closed in around her. Silence rang in Emmie's ears. It was hard to breathe. She slid down the wall until she came to rest on the floor, knees pulled into her chest. With her head in her hands she could feel moisture from the tears that had finally spilled over her cheeks. After taking a few minutes to collect herself, Emmie stood and brushed off her skirt. She didn't want to walk home yet but needed to make a call. She tried the door across from the room the guys were in. She was surprised to find it was open. It was a small closet that was being used as an office, barely enough room for a desk and a chair. Thankfully there was a telephone on the table. She picked up the receiver and called Walter.

She knew it was late to be calling. They would all be in bed.

"Hello." Walt's voice was heavy with sleep and annoyed.

"Walt," she whispered into the phone.

"What's the matter, Emmie?" He sounded panicked.

"I need to see you."

"Girl, you got any idea any idea what time it is?" he fussed.

"Yes, I wouldn't call if it wasn't important. We can wait till the morning if you want but it needs to be early. Can you come over to my house first thing?"

"Of course. What's going on?" he asked.

"I'll tell you the whole thing tomorrow but let me ask this really quick. Do you know Sam Young?"

"Emmie, what have you done?" Walter asked, stone serious.

"Just answer me, hurry. I don't know how much time I've got," she whispered.

"He's no good. Don't trust him. Get away from him," Walter shouted.

"Have you given him any of your 'shine? Or would Ronnie have?" she asked.

"Lord knows I haven't. I don't think Ronnie would have either," Walter sighed loudly. "I do think Ronnie was messed up with him though. I think he may have owed him some money. You need me girl? Are you mixed-up in something tonight?"

"No. I can take care of it. I'll see you first thing in the morning though, okay? I got some things to talk to you about."

"Alright… you're givin' me an ulcer, you know that girl?" he said sharply.

"I know but it's almost over. I'm sorry but I'm gonna work this out," she promised and hoped that she could. Lately working things out had just turned into major messes on her part.

Walter said something but she didn't hear him. The door opened slowly to reveal a man she had seen earlier in the alley. They'd called him James. "I gotta go," she shouted and slammed the phone down on its cradle.

"What the hell are you doing in here?" the tall middle-aged man asked.

She put up her hands like he was holding her at gunpoint. From the look on his face, he just may do that.

Thank goodness Trick came into the room. "Emmie?" he questioned.

"You know this lady?" James asked.

"James, she's fine." His voice slow and easy, "Just had too much to drink probably." Trick looked at her pointedly.

Emmie relaxed her posture and smiled up at James. She mimicked the lazy look she'd noticed on a few of the women out in the pig. She stumbled walking up to Trick and he caught her.

"I'll take care of her." Trick swept her off her feet like a groom carrying his bride. She grabbed his hair playfully and smiled up at him.

"Ssssstrong handsome man ssavess the day," she slurred convincingly.

"Sounds like she needs to be taken home," James said.

Trick smiled and wiggled his eyebrows, "That's something I'll be glad to do." Trick played the part but she could tell he was tense.

He carried her out of the office, shut the door and set her down. "Well, aren't you just a ball of trouble tonight?"

She looked up at him. He knew everything. How could he know so quickly? She could only guess some of it came out in their discussion in that room with Sam. She wondered how that was going. Emmie peeked over at the door, still wet with the splattered moonshine.

"They're done... for now anyway," Trick answered her unspoken question.

"Are they still in there?" she asked.

"Nah... They've taken him to rest for a bit before they finish. You know I cannot tell you anymore," he said. "It's late Emmie. It's been a long day. Want me to drive you home?"

Emmie thought for a moment. She nodded. Nothing else could be solved tonight.

"You'll be damned if you do." Silas emerged from the room.

He had taken off his coat and was wearing only his vest. She now saw the full view of the tan leather strips that she had only seen part of at the store. The worn leather crossed over his arms and closed around his back. But she was wrong. They weren't a part of the vest or some new fangled suspender. It was a holster holding a gun at each side. Silas pulled the cigarette out of his mouth and exhaled.

"She's coming home with us."

Chapter Forty-three

The walk to the car seemed to last an eternity. The whole entourage left in silence. Between the five of them they had three cars waiting in the parking lot. The men separated, each heading for their own car. Ava followed Gabe. Emmie stopped in her tracks. She really, really wanted to follow Ava... or heck, even Trick. She was not looking forward to this awkward ride home. As if he was reading her thoughts, Silas put his hand on the small of her back and led her to the passenger side of his car. He opened the door for her like everything was fine, just a normal night out among friends.

They drove in an uncomfortable silence for a while. She had to speak. This problem wasn't going to go away.

Emmie scooted closer and turned to face him. He had to notice but he didn't push her back to the other side of the car. She took that as a good sign. "I am sorry that I hurt you. I shouldn't have kept the truth from you. But I was afraid. Well, to tell you the truth, I was afraid of this." She held her arms out and shrugged at the uncomfortable air of tension that surrounded them.

He pulled the car off the main road and turned down the dirt path that would lead her home. Did he have a change of heart about where she would stay tonight; didn't he say he wanted her to go to Ava's? She decided to hold that question and wait for him to explain.

Silas stopped the car at the end of her drive. They were left sitting in a dark field with only the glow of his cigarette to light their features.

He turned and faced her. His eyes looked tired. "What were you afraid of?"

"That if you found out I know about moonshine... that I'd made the apple pie 'shine," she shrugged her shoulder, "I wouldn't have a chance with you anymore. I mean look at you—you've been to school, you're a lawyer, you live in a big city, you're funny, kind, smart and...

handsome. But most of all, you believed in me. You were the only person other than my mama that ever said I was good enough to go to college. And I knew, if you found out I was helping… him… you would look at me, like I was just another redneck. Just another hillbilly selling 'shine for a dollar." Her face flooded with embarrassment. Thank goodness he couldn't see it.

"You would always say that I was a good girl but I'm not… I'm just a girl. I guess I never stood much of a chance anyway. I just couldn't let you drive away without saying all that… So, there, I said it. Out loud."

She'd said it. If she was destined to feel some kind of lonely her whole life, like her ma did, then at least she knew she had put it all out on the table.

It seemed like an eternity passed. He said nothing and it drove her crazy. He finished his cigarette staring off toward her house in the distance. "You're wrong. You are a good girl, you just got yourself all mixed up in some bad business."

Emmie nodded, glad he understood that. Something in his voice let her know he didn't believe she'd hurt him on purpose. "You've got me all wrong, Emmie girl. You've asked me a lot of questions." He swallowed hard. "But you've never asked me the right ones."

His riddles confused her. Silas started up the car and pulled all the way up to her house. He got out, opened her door, and together they walked up the porch.

Emmie was convinced he was sending her packing. "Thanks for the drive home," she said, fumbling with the key. He took it from her and opened the door.

"I'm not driving you home. We're getting your stuff. You are not staying here. This is a problem goes deeper than either of us thought. Now that I know you are involved, even at a minor level, I am not leaving you in this house by yourself. Go pack a bag," he said.

"No one really knows I'm involved other than you. I think I'll be okay. Besides I've got Spotty and a shotgun," she said.

"Emmie, how do you load a shotgun?" he asked.

"You put the bullets in, snap it closed and pull the trigger." She smiled.

"Where are your bullets?" he asked.

"Umm… that's a good question," she answered, putting a finger to her mouth to think about it.

"Besides I'm pretty sure you wouldn't shoot a fly. And that dog," he pointed to Spotty who was lounging on the mat at the front door, "is a worthless guard dog. Trust me. Pack your bags."

Emmie frowned that he had talked about her dog like that. But she decided not to fight it. Choose your battles. She went to Ronnie's old room grabbed a suitcase and hauled it upstairs. "I really think I would be fine," she shouted down. "Other than you and your family, he, my moonshiner friend, is the only one who knows about me being involved. I trust him."

"Yes, I know you do. But being as I don't know who he is, I don't trust him. So, you'll be coming with me," he said.

Emmie decided to let it go. When she came back downstairs Silas was waiting with an outstretched arm for her bag.

"Oh, wait, since we are being honest, here…" She ran over to the pantry and pulled out the two jars of moonshine that she had put away. "That's the last of it. No more 'shine. My bootlegging days are done. Well, if you can get the pig to buy the rest of it that is."

Silas looked at the fabric and shook his head. "Who decorates moonshine?"

"You eat first with your eyes. If it hadn't been for the pretty package it would have never made it into your blind pig," she answered.

His eyes hardened again. "We'll be talking more about that later. Wait here, I'm going to take this to the car."

Silas literally ran out, dumped the bag, and walked back into the house.

"Now, come with me." He grabbed her hand and led her back into Ronnie's room. The dog beat him there. Emmie wondered where he could be taking her. This was her house. Silas bent down and touched the wooden floors. The dog stood inches from his outstretched hand, barking at Silas. This was the same spot the dog had gone crazy over the last night Silas was here.

He pushed the dog away from him. Spotty walked over and stood next to Emmie, never taking his eyes off him. Running his fingers along the joints until he felt one give, Silas popped the floorboard up and pulled out the box.

"See," he smiled without humor, "you're a good girl. Too good to even see how to ask me the right questions. How do I know where that is, Emmie?" He turned and took a step away from her. "Why do I care so much about your stepdad's moonshine and where it ends up? Why do I really want to know who you've been working with? Ask me the right questions, Emmie," he shouted, his voice cracking.

"It's not just you that's been keeping secrets, Emmie girl." He walked away rubbing his jaw like he could tear the skin from his face.

She stared down at the box. "How did you... why?" She had a hard time deciding which question to ask first.

"I searched your house. When you were out there that day, crying on your Mama's grave, I was in here going through your things, which is why your pathetic guard dog has been barking at me... at this room. He's trying to tell you what kind of person I am. Is that the kind of man you want? Is that kind, funny, or handsome?" He shook his head like he was disgusted.

"Why would you do that?" She looked horrified.

"I was looking for the moonshine or money," he answered levelly.

"Why?" she asked.

He pointed at her and nodded his head. "That's it. That's the question you needed to ask. Why do I care so much? See that's why I cannot trust you about this other guy. You're judgment is off. You see the world through lenses of good. You think I'm the good guy here. But, I'm not."

"Why?" she repeated, laying the box on the table and walking over to him. "Why were you looking for moonshine or money at my house?"

Silas pulled out another cigarette and lit it. "Ronnie was selling to the pig. James, I think you met him," he gave her a pointed look that said he knew she'd been in his office, "fronted your step-father a large sum of money for 'shine. We never saw any payback or moonshine for months. When Pop sent me down here, he said I couldn't come back to Chicago until I helped Uncle Al with that Johnson case and I found our money or moonshine. I was on my way to see Ronnie the night he died. That's when things got more complicated."

"It wasn't a car crash was it?" she asked.

"No," he shook his head looking down at the ground.

"It wasn't you, please tell me it wasn't you." She put her hand over her mouth.

"Oh, God no, Emmie… I mean, I'm not going to lie to you, I was mad enough too. I don't like cheats but it wasn't me. Gabe, Trick, Sheriff Drake, and I found him. He was already gone."

"So why the fire lie? Why can't we investigate it? He may have owed you something but he deserved better than a fiery lie," she said.

He smiled but his eyes were sad. "See, there's my smart girl. That's a good question. The answer will tell ya about me. I didn't want it to mess up our investigation. I wanted to find that money and get home as quick as possible. I didn't want the police around here messing things up. Figured if this guy was lying and cheating people out of 'shine and cash, like he did us, he got what was coming to him. We were doing our own investigation. I thought we could bring justice better than any court."

Emmie closed her eyes and covered her face as she sat at the table. She actually cried. She'd always suspected Ronnie may have been killed but to have it confirmed and to hear Silas tell her these things about himself, it broke her heart. She had been used as a pawn in an investigation.

She didn't want to leave with him but now that she knew the truth about everything she was afraid to stay, also. Emmie looked out the window to the car.

"If you want me to call Gabe or Ava or somebody else to come get you, I'll understand," he said.

She wanted to take him up on the offer but that would have been petty. "No, its fine. We've both been liars. Let's just get out of here." She shook her head to clear it, ready to move on and get some sleep. "Spotty's coming with us. I'm not leaving him here." Silas nodded and patted his leg. Emmie was surprised when the dog followed him to the car.

The drive back to Ava's was awful. Her heart was broken and she felt like an idiot. She drummed her fingers on the box impatiently. When they finally pulled into the house she reached in the back and grabbed her bag. When he tried to help her she shot daggers out of her eyes at him, daring him to touch it.

She went to the mudroom that led to the pool and grabbed an armful of several white towels. She carried them out to the front porch and made a pallet for Spotty. He'd been trying to tell her all this time that something was wrong and she didn't see it. He licked her arm as she patted the towels. She scratched his ears and he rolled back his lips in what looked like a smile.

Emmie went back through the large entry and carried her suitcase upstairs. Out of habit she went to open the door to Ava's bedroom but she heard her laughing and talking to someone else. Of course, Gabe was there. It was probably better that she was alone anyway. She went to the first guest room and opened the door to find Trick lying in the bed.

"Oh, gosh. Trick." She held her suitcase up over her eyes. "I'm sorry. I thought it was empty."

He laughed. "Emmie it's fine."

She turned her back to him and spoke, "Is Silas in the other guest room?"

"Mmm hum," he answered.

"Goodnight," she called, closing the door.

"Night, Emmie," he said, rolling back over on his side.

So that left Vince's room for her. But she couldn't bring herself to sleep in there. Instead, she went to his chest and searched, pulling out a few afghans and a quilt. She slipped into her nightgown and padded down the long hall until she reached the sleeping porch. It had started to rain, so it was damp and cool out here. And the rhythmic sound on the roof overhead was soothing. She propped up on one of the small twin beds, folded back the covers and tucked herself in. She wrapped an afghan around her shoulders and pulled out the box Silas had found in her house. She couldn't imagine what on earth it was that would be hidden under the floors.

She slid off the lid. Her mouth fell open in shock. Inside was the largest roll of cash she had ever seen in her life.

Chapter Forty-four

Seven hundred twenty-seven dollars. She counted the cash three times and had gotten the same number each time. Why did she have seven hundred twenty-seven dollars in a box in her house? She looked down at the box again and noticed a small envelope with her name on it. She tore it open.

Emma Rose,

Since your mother passed your stepfather has returned your envelopes unopened, so I didn't get to help out much these last few years. He said he'd give you this one when you were ready for it though. I've heard through the grapevine that you want to go to college to be a teacher. I hope this money helps with that dream. I hear you are a lot like your ma, so if that's true, I know you can do it. I know $1000 doesn't make up for the fact that I missed your childhood but I hope it helps you better your life. I know that's what she wanted for you.

Love,

M.V.D.

Emmie was surprised to find another letter scrawled on the back.

Emmie,

If you're reading this letter, things are probably not going good. I'm sorry I had to use some of your cash from your father. I wasn't always able to make ends meet, so I just borrow a little from time to time. I do try and replace it though. I know I ain't been the best stepfather but I did more than that guy who sent ya the money. I hope you'll think a little of me that at least I'm not using your money to pay off my debts. They're getting a little hefty right now and folks might come around looking for some cash. So I wanted to hide this for ya in case that happened. So... hope you never find this letter, but if ya do... Use the money good.

Ronnie

P.S. I know your Mama really never talked to ya about your real dad. There's some pictures of them in a box in the barn, near the rafters. Your mama thought I didn't know she kept them but I did. Thought you may be curious someday.

Emmie's mouth fell open as she read the letters once, twice, one thousand times. Her father's letter was dated three years ago, on her eighteenth birthday, but Ronnie's wasn't dated. She laughed when she reread his. It sounded just like his voice. Tears sprang to her eyes. She could hear him saying those words in her mind. He could have used that money to pay off his debts or a big portion of it anyway but he didn't want to steal from her. Her heart swelled that her last memory of him was not of him shouting at her about making coffee... it was this. He cared for her as best as he knew how. That's all she could ask of him. It may sound weird but a part of her felt more at peace with Ronnie's death seeing this letter.

Her real father's letter is what bothered her most. She knew nothing about her dad. She had assumed he'd died some horrible death and that's why her mom had never discussed it with her. She felt so conflicted. How could her mama take a secret like this to her grave? She was going to have to spend a lot more time stewing over that one. A lot more time when her eyes weren't quite so heavy. She carefully folded the letters and placed them in the box.

Then she sorted the bills and rolled the cash up neatly and put it back in the box on top of the letters. She lay down and pulled the covers up around her neck, closed her eyes, and waited for sleep to claim her.

But it didn't. Her brain kept running through everything that had happened. The box. Her mama. Her two dads. The money. $727. Her eyes popped back open. Emmie threw back the covers, reached down, grabbed the cash, and ran to Silas's bedroom. She threw open the door and he jerked straight up out of bed.

"Shit, Emmie, you scared me," he said, putting down the book he was reading.

She frowned. "I didn't take you for a reader."

"Thanks," he said, laughing.

"No, I didn't mean... never mind," she said.

She walked over to his bed trying hard to keep her eyes focused on his face. She pulled the afghan closer around her shoulders and laid the cash on the bed.

"Emmie, what's this?" he asked confused.

"You're still lying to me," she said, looking at him at eye level.

"What do you mean, lying to you?"

"You found that box," she said.

"Yeah." He tried to follow.

"And you didn't take the my money." She smiled.

"Of course I didn't take your money. It had your name on it," he said sheepishly.

"Oh, come on, Silas. If you were as bad as you acted like at my house you would have taken that money and headed back to Chicago." She hoped she was right.

He shook his head trying to decide what to say. "I did have it in my pocket you know. I made it all the way to the door. Then I turned around and put it back." He shrugged his shoulders and shook his head.

"See, you didn't take it," she repeated pointedly.

"Emmie, I know what you're doing. You can not talk me into a good guy," he said.

"I'm not trying to talk you into a good guy. I just," she tipped her head and thought before she spoke, "I don't think you were just using me as a means to an end to all this. Tell me honestly, was I your pawn in this game?"

"No." He shook his head. "I guess not."

"So, you admit it then. You did have some feelings for me?" she asked.

He shook his head and opened his mouth to speak, "I don't know Emmie. Just give it a rest for tonight, okay?"

She nodded. Picked up the money and turned back to him. "Are you really so eager to go home to Chicago?"

He closed his eyes and laughed without humor, "More than you know."

"Then you can take it. I'll pay off whatever Ronnie's debt was to you and you can head home in good graces. It's nothing to me anyway. It came from a man I don't even know." She left the money on his bed, turned, and walked out the door.

Emmie had no more than pulled the quilts around her when she heard bare feet padding out onto the wooden floor of the screened in porch.

"Why are you sleeping out here?" he asked, turning the corner.

"All the rooms are full but Vince's. I'd rather be out here anyway. I like listening to the rain." She propped herself up in the bed and got her first good look at him.

He'd put his brown pants back on but his feet were bare. There was something oddly intimate about that. She gazed up his body to his chest. The only man she had ever seen without a shirt was Ronnie. Silas's body was totally different. Firm. Tight. Gorgeous. She quickly looked down at the quilt and started pulling at a loose thread.

She felt the bed sink as he sat down. She scooted her legs over to give him some space. He put his hands on hers to still her fidgeting. Her gaze went up his arms. It was like this man was cut from stone. He was like the marble statues she'd seen in art history books.

She felt her face flush.

"Emmie, look at me." She pulled her eyes up to his.

His blue gaze was piercing. He swallowed. She saw all of the muscles in his neck flex and relax, "You asked 'did I care' about you. It's not that I did care about you... it's that I still do."

Her heart leapt. He'd admitted it. He wasn't only using her, she knew it.

"But I am who I am. I'm not sure it's right to drag you into my world. Maybe in another world if I wasn't me and you weren't you," he started.

"Silas, what are you saying. We've both made mistakes. But we've got no secrets left to keep. Don't you see that? It's all out, we're free." She smiled honestly.

"You're still keeping one secret," he reminded her, "the identity of the mysterious he."

"Can you promise me you won't hurt him? If I let you meet him with me tomorrow?"

"I don't like making promises," Silas said, looking down at her.

"If you want to meet him, you will," she said.

"I promise you I will keep an open mind," he said in compromise. The truth is he was already going to be able to figure out who she was working with tomorrow when he talked to the guy who ran the pig. James had met the guy to get the 'shine. He would have no problem telling Silas who it was. But, if he had a choice, he would rather hear the truth from Emmie's mouth.

"Okay, you can come with me tomorrow," she said. "I'm showing you that I trust you. So don't ruin it." She punched his arm playfully.

"Ouch." He rubbed. For the first time all night he was himself. "Violence is never the answer."

She arched her brow at him thinking back to the events of the last week but was too tired to rehash any more of the details. Emmie shivered.

"Emmie, it's really cold. I think it's a bad idea to sleep out here," he said, rubbing his arms.

She lay down and pulled the covers up closer to her ears. "It really is toasty under here," she teased.

He looked annoyed for a second, then devilish. "Well, if you say so."

He jerked back her covers and slid in next to her. "Silas McDowell!" she screamed and rolled backward in the tiny bed. He snaked an arm out and wrapped it around her waist to keep her from falling. Once she was safe on the bed she expected him to move it but he didn't. His touch was so easy, so familiar. She kept trying to relax her body.

Silas propped up on one elbow and looked down at her. "You were wrong you know." He shrugged, "You're the smart and beautiful one. I shouldn't have had a chance with you. That's what I kept telling myself, 'She is too good for this, Silas.' But I couldn't ever seem to stay away." He leaned in and kissed her forehead. "I'm sorry I hurt you. Please forgive me. I promise from here on out, I'll tell you as much as I can. And no more lies. If we are going to work at this that's what I promise."

"I thought you didn't like promises?" she asked.

"Emmie girl, I plan to make lots of promises to you." He smiled.

Silas wrapped his leg around hers bringing her closer. He ran his hands up the length of her body, taking in every curve, dip, and patch of soft skin. She pushed forward onto her elbows and brought her mouth to his. He kissed her until her lips were swollen and plumped. Then he moved to her ears and neck brushing his lips over every inch of skin. Her hands moved further down his chest and she pulled him in for another long slow kiss. He pulled away from her before things got too far gone.

"I'm going to sleep out here with you, if that's okay?" he asked.

She nodded biting her lower lip. Her brain was reeling and exhausted. She rolled over onto her side to give him more room. Then she felt his legs press into the back of hers. She felt her body tense.

"Relax. We're just sleeping. No fast moves, trust me," he said, wrapping his arm around her stomach.

She grabbed his arm and held it tightly. "I trust you."

Chapter Forty-five

The birds sang early the next morning. It sure had been a long night. Her leg was asleep, she jerked trying to kick it awake, and someone cursed.

"Damn Emmie, it's me." His voice was groggy and grouchy. "I thought I was the fighting Irish in this bed. But you, you're giving me a run for my money."

"Oh, Silas. I'm sorry... you okay?" She turned around and faced him. He was beautifully disheveled. She reached up and toyed with his hair and then ran her fingers the length of his jaw.

"I'm fine." His face spread in a wide grin staring up at her.

"Why are you smiling like that?" she asked.

"I just remembered last night when you let me kiss..." he started.

"Silas," she looked around laughing, "don't talk about it. It's too embarrassing." She pulled the covers up around her face.

He dug her out of them laughing. "You asked why I was smiling? And we promised honesty from here on out."

He leaned up and kissed her forehead. "Good morning sweetheart."

She smiled. She was so beautiful. Her ebony hair covered every inch of the pillow and when she leaned forward to kiss him it hung several inches past her shoulders.

"I like this long. Why do you keep it all pinned up?" he asked, running his fingers through her hair.

She shrugged, "It's what's in style I guess."

"I like it like this," he said, giving her a mysterious grin.

Silas sat up and pulled her into his lap facing him. He leaned back on his arms, drinking in the sight of her against the rising sunlight.

"It's a new day," he said.

"Yes," she agreed.

"Sometimes I wish we could just meet all over again. Start fresh you know? So we didn't have the complications of the past couple of months in between us," he said, looking right up at her. "We could do that you know. Pretend like we're meeting for the first time right now."

"No." She shook her head.

"No?" he questioned.

"I like the Silas I know. Besides, I'm pretty sure if I met you in my nightgown like this," she pointed at their close position, "I wouldn't have been the kind of good girl you liked." She crinkled her nose and shook her head.

"Oh, well that's true." He nodded in thoughtful consideration. "I like it best when I meet my girls at the pool... in their underwear... wet see-through underwear." His eyes were wide with humor.

Her mouth fell open and she dove for him. He lifted his arms, prepared for her attack, and caught her before bringing her back down to the bed.

"What the hell is going on out here?" Gabe said from the hall. "Oh, shit Silas, shit. Sorry Emmie." He grabbed a quilt off a nearby chair and threw it over them.

"Get out," Silas shouted.

"It's just... Emmie's had a call. The housekeeper just came to Ava's room. He's called twice. Some man and he's upset."

"Oh no." Emmie's heart sank. How could she be so thoughtless? "He's probably worried sick. I was supposed to meet him first thing this morning." Emmie threw back the covers forgetting all modesty and started to get out of bed, heading into the hall.

Silas visibly tensed. He stood and pulled his shirt on all in one motion. He grabbed the quilt and pulled it tight against her shoulders before she reached the hall.

"I'll meet you downstairs in ten minutes," he said.

"Make it five," she called, closing the door to Vince's bedroom to change clothes.

When she came downstairs Gabe and Silas were waiting for her by the door.

"No," she shook her head. "This wasn't the deal."

"We made no deal," Silas barked.

"You promised," she said.

"I promised to keep an open mind. And I will. Gabe is not going to close my mind. I don't know this man. Gabe is coming," he said.

Emmie walked up to Silas and ran her hands along his chest then threw open the sides of his coat. She pointed right at the guns. "No, I don't want you to wear those."

"Okay, we will compromise." He reached in and pulled one of the guns out and laid it on the table. "I'll only wear one. Let's go." And with that he turned and walked out the door.

"Fine but I promise you that if either one of you pull a gun on him, I will jump in front of it. So keep that in mind, Tough Guys." She gave them each a pointed look before flying down the stairs and to the car.

They drove in silence. Emmie wasn't surprised to find Walt's truck already at her house. She was surprised to see the lock had been shot off her front door. He was watching from the doorway as they pulled closer to the house. His thumbs were hooked in the straps of his overalls and his pipe was dangling out of his mouth.

Silas couldn't have looked more shocked if she had slapped him in the face. "Is that Walter? Is that the man you have been protecting?"

Emmie glared over at him unsure how to judge his reaction, so she went with defensive. "Yes, that is Walter. Why are you so shocked?"

"But… why didn't you tell me he was an old man?" he asked.

"You never asked the right question." She threw his words back at him with a smile. "Why would it matter if he was old?"

Silas didn't answer but Gabe chuckled in the back seat.

"Never mind. Let's just get this over with," Silas said as he turned off the car.

Emmie tore out of the door without waiting for Silas or Gabe to open it for her. When Walt saw her coming she took a step in her direction. "Ya alright, girl?" he asked, never taking his eyes from Silas or Gabe.

"Yes," she nodded her head. "What happened to my door?"

"Sorry. When you didn't answer, I panicked and got my shotgun. I thought maybe you were hurt in there." He looked sheepish.

She smiled. "It's fine. It's just a lock. No big deal. We need your help though."

"We?" he questioned.

"Walt, this is Silas and Gabe. Silas and Gabe, this is Walter. Let's go in and sit down," she said, making quick introductions.

"We've met." Silas smiled as they sat at the kitchen table. Emmie put on a pot of coffee and joined them.

"You have?" She looked from Walt to Silas confused.

He may have been a fool to be jealous of this old man but he still didn't trust his character. What kind of man would let Emmie get so mixed up in this business? Besides, he had told Sheriff Drake it wasn't right that the old man had come out of those woods that night. He'd gotten the feeling he was involved. Now he knew he was. And Emmie thought this guy was so trustworthy.

"Your kind, trustworthy bootlegging friend not tell you, eh?" Silas asked, staring pointedly at Walt.

"Silas, watch the way you talk to him," Emmie snapped.

"She ain't got no reason to know about that," Walt said, leaning forward looking square at the younger man.

"I have no reason to know what?" Emmie asked but they were not listening to her.

"She already knows the truth. Except for you because I didn't think that was important. But now," Silas shrugged bringing his hands together, "now that I know you're the asshole that dragged her into this, I think she needs to know."

"Dragged her into this..." Walter laughed. "I didn't drag her into nothing. She's the one that found me... begged me... I have just been trying to protect her and get her a little money."

"Protect her? You call having her make you apple pie moonshine protecting her?" Silas shouted. "She will not be a part of your bootlegging."

Emmie opened her mouth to speak but Walt spoke up before she could get the words out.

"You think I want her in this? Hell, I came to pick up that 'shine to get it away from her. I don't want her near it. Then when I showed up she had spent hours decorating them jars... turning them into some girly drink. What the hell was I supposed to do with that? But because I was tryin' to take care of her... I took it anyway," Walter defended himself.

"Silas, I told you that I did that. It's not Walter's fault," she said, wanting to calm this discussion.

"Talkin' about bad influences. You better look in the mirror, boy," Walter said, chewing on his pipe.

"Yeah? Is that right?" Silas asked.

Throughout the whole conversation Gabe hadn't spoke until now. "Watch it old man."

"I ain't gonna be watchin' nothing. Ask her where she got the idea for that silly drink. It was from some speakeasy she went to. I'm guessing she didn't find that all by herself. If there is somebody no good for her at this table, it ain't me." He leaned back and puffed on his pipe.

Silas said nothing.

"Walt. That's not true either. I've not done anything I didn't want to do. You both need to calm down. I made my own choices here in both cases. And I'm sorry to both of you." she said, reaching a hand on each of their shoulders.

"Now, I want to know. How do you know each other?" she asked.

Silas looked at Walt waiting to see if he would speak. When he didn't, it was Silas who told her. "Walt was there the night your stepfather was killed."

Just like that, the wind was knocked out of her. She looked up at Walt, hurt and confused.

"You knew? You knew it wasn't a car accident?" she asked, her voice barely a whisper.

He nodded, looking down at the table. His mouth set in a grim line.

Chapter Forty-six

"Did you do it Walt?" Emmie didn't have to say what the it was. Everyone in the room knew. Gabe and Silas turned to take in her question as well. It was something they were initially curious about but Sheriff Drake had assured them Walt was not involved.

"No, child." He looked up at her with his tired eyes. They crinkled up as he spoke, "I wouldn't have killed Ronnie. Ya have to know that, right?"

She nodded, "But why wouldn't you tell me. I deserved to know the truth."

"I guess I didn't want to see ya scared. Didn't want to make you any sadder than you were. Plus I was afraid if you knew the truth you'd start sticking your nose in it. And when I saw them boys from out of town was involved." He pointed at Gabe and Silas. "There was another one too, younger but looked a lot like him." He pointed again at Silas.

"Trick?" Emmie asked.

"Yes," Silas confirmed.

Walter sighed, "I didn't want you to cross them. But I swear, girl, you got a talent for ropin' 'em in. If there was a nest o' snakes in fifty miles you'd jump right in it, wouldn't ya?"

Emmie frowned at Walter. But she knew maybe he was right. She shook her head to clear the emotions that were weighing down her mind. Secrets lead to nothing but lies and shame. It's all she'd seen over and over again. The moonshine, money, mama, Silas, Walter, her father… It was too much.

She felt Silas's arm pull her in close. He leaned over and brushed a kiss on her forehead whispering, "We're gonna fix this. We've almost got it."

She nodded.

"Oh Lordy, girl. HIM?" Walter spit. "You were so disgusted by that shopkeeper and you pick him?"

Silas started to stand but Gabe put his hand out. He wouldn't let him do something he would regret later.

"I'm going to let that go. But you need to watch it, old man," Silas said.

"No, you need to watch it. You better take care of her or you're gonna be answering to me through that shotgun over there, ya hear me boy?" Walter leaned across the table, his eyes never leaving Silas's.

"'Cause don't make no mistake, you're not good enough for her," Walt said to end his argument.

"I don't disagree." That's when Silas realized for the first time that Walt really was trying to protect Emmie. He acted like she was his family. "But I'm going to spend from here on trying to be."

Walt chewed his pipe. Then he nodded. "I guess that's all a man can ask."

Emmie was genuinely surprised at the turn of the conversation. It was weird and not at all what she had expected. But she did know she had a soft spot in her heart for each of those men. She felt in time they would grow to like each other.

"Well, what did you all drag an old man outta bed for?" Walter asked.

"Silas, I want you to talk to Walter about Sam Jones. Nobody around here knows more about moonshining or who does what than Walter," Emmie said. "I'd like to hear what he thinks about all this." She got up to pour some coffee while Silas and Walter talked.

He recounted the story from last week about the man coming in the pig saying he had some moonshine and knew they had lost their supply.

"We decided to let the jars come in just to see and as soon as he saw them, he knew right away they were Ronnie's. They roughed the guy up, found out who he was working for, and it was Sam Jones. They just found Sam last night. Do you have any idea how he would have got Ronnie's moonshine?" Silas asked.

"If you would have opened your eyes at the barn that night to anything but Bo you would have found your boy. He was sitting about three people to my right," Walter said. "First things first, boy. That is my 'shine, not Ronnie's. It's the recipe that has been handed down for generations and that's why your pig and speak costumers loved it. Ronnie might have been the smooth-talker but I was the maker. I'm the one that put those Xs on the jars. I'm guessing that's how you identified them," Walter said with pride.

Silas laughed and nodded. "Yeah. Well, you have any idea how he would have your moonshine?"

"No. I wouldn't give him nothing. I don't suspect Ronnie would have either. I think we was doing about all we could to keep your pig in business. Now, I didn't know for sure who he was selling to. Ronnie didn't give me no details much but I knew he wasn't just selling to normal folks. He needed too much 'shine too fast there at the end." Then Walter thought before he spoke again, "Like I told Emmie last night though, I do think he owed him money. I think he borrowed a little from him to keep your guy off his back for a while."

"Walt, Sam came by here and dug around in the barn for some tools one day after Ronnie died. You think he could have been getting the 'shine?" she asked.

"I say there's a good chance. The night before he died I'd just unloaded a lot of jars for him. He'd had us working overtime. It was so much I was afraid folks was gonna start noticing the white stains on the cave walls and trees from the smoke. That order would have been double or triple what you found in the pantry. I tried looking around for it a few months ago but never saw nothing of it," Walter answered.

Gabe and Silas looked at each other for a moment. It was Gabe who finally spoke up. "That would have been our order. I think James had just told him we were on the way to Chicago, so that would explain the rush. James gave him the *Three M Ultimatum*: money, moonshine, or murder."

"So it sounds like Sam was trying to sell you moonshine that was already yours," Emmie said.

"Yeah," Silas nodded then looked at her pointedly, "and so were you."

Emmie's mouth dropped open. He was right. She took a long pull from her coffee. That's when she realized how deep she had gotten herself in this mess. She couldn't even say how it had happened.

She looked at him. "I had no idea. I am so sorry."

"Yeah," Silas smiled down at her. "You're lucky I love you or you'd be in some serious shit right now." Was he teasing? Did he just say he loved her?

"Walter, did he ever pay you your part?" Gabe asked.

"Never saw it. I was going to confront him about it that night too but never got the chance." He shook his head.

"What would he have done with all that money?" Emmie thought aloud.

"It ain't hard to go through money. He was paying on this house. He also loved to go to the tracks… and we all know he liked his 'shine."

That's when the note popped back in her mind. He'd said he'd taken some of her money to live and paid it back a little at a time. She bet some of that money went to her secret stash. She would never understand why he was keeping it from her. What could he have been waiting for? It was probably something she would never know. At least she didn't have to feel bad about having Silas's money. She'd already given it back to him anyway.

"Thanks for your help, Walt," Silas said, holding out his hand to the old man. "I think I can take care of the rest if I find the money and the 'shine. I'll try to be sure you get what was coming to ya."

Emmie was pleasantly surprised to hear that last part.

"Yeah, well you just remember what I said, boy," Walter said, grabbing his shotgun and pointing at Emmie. But she knew him well enough to see his eyes sparked with humor.

Gabe walked outside with Walter, asking him a technical question about his shotgun. Apparently Gabe was a gun enthusiast, who knew?

"I'm going to use your phone to call Trick and James. It'll just be a minute." Silas walked into the living room to make his call. Emmie could tell he really didn't want her to hear whatever it was he had to say. And truth be told, she probably didn't want to hear it either.

The cuckoo clock chimed, announcing it was eight-fifteen. That's when it hit her. She had to work today. How could she forget? She ran upstairs, put on a little powder, grabbed her extra apron, and thumped down the stairs. She could hear Silas was still on the phone. If she walked, she would be late for sure. She saw Walt was just getting in his car; he could give her a ride. Flying out the door she called to Gabe, "I've got to go to work. Tell Silas, okay?"

Chapter Forty-seven

Emmie literally ran through the door of the shop right at eight-thirty. She had barely told Walt thank you as she flew out the door. She tied her apron around her waist and dropped her purse in the drawer behind the counter. That's when something out of place caught her eye on the counter. A small black box barely as long as a dollar bill and a few inches thick sat on top of a large white envelope. It was sitting right in the middle of the counter. It was really odd considering how obsessive Mr. Thomas was about things being in their place.

Emmie recognized it as the box that had been delivered to Mr. Thomas. It was the one he was so enthralled with. He carried it around for days. She picked up the box and turned it over in her hand. It was heavier than it looked. She opened it up and pulled out the smallest camera she had ever seen. Expo Police Camera was written in bold silver letters.

"It's interesting. Isn't it Emma?" Mr. Thomas startled her.

"Yes, sorry. I just was trying to figure out where it goes," she said, dropping the camera back in its case.

He stepped up behind her close, too close. She could feel his shirt on her back. She froze like a deer in the headlights.

His long willowy arms reached around her and pulled out the envelope. He pulled out a small desk calendar. It was the kind that looked like a book with spots for notes on each day. "Take a good look at that, Emma dear." His voice calm and collected.

Finally, he stepped back giving her a little more space. "Turn around and face me Emma," he said.

She turned around and leaned her back against the counter confused. She opened the calendar. The first several months were blank. Most of it made no sense, it was names, dates, and times entered/exited.

She scanned through several pages until she found names she recognized.

March 28 – Alexander DeCarmilla Entered: 8:45 p.m. Exited: 11:57 p.m.

"I think you know Ava's father." Mr. Thomas smiled. "But look at May 2… that's when things will be more interesting for you."

May 2

Patrick McDowell, Silas McDowell Entered: 7:35 p.m. Exited: 12:05 a.m.

Gabriel Del Grande, Vincent DeCarmilla Entered: 8:55 p.m. Exited: 11:43 p.m.

Emmie looked up at him, still confused. What ever this was, it wasn't good. She didn't want to see anymore. She handed him back the book.

"No, Emma. You really need to see October 22nd. Trust me." He smiled.

"Yesterday?" she asked.

He turned the pages and handed the book back to her.

October 22

Silas McDowell – Entered: 6:45 p.m. Exited: 11:52 p.m.

Patrick McDowell, Gabriel Del Grande – Entered: 7:02 p.m. Exited 11:52 p.m.

Ava DeCarmilla, Emma Talbot – Entered: 8:23 p.m. Exited: 11:52 p.m.

Emmie's hands began to shake. She looked up at him shaking her head. Why would he keep a log of when people entered and exited the blind pig? Before she could find her voice to ask he cocked his head to the side. Waving his pointer finger back and forth as he tsked. Emmie tried to step back away from him but she was already pushed against the counter.

"Emmie, I warned you about hanging around with that riffraff. And look what you have done. I had to put your sweet name in my book." He looked mockingly sad.

"Why are you doing this?" she asked.

"Because I am one of the few honorable people in this town. I've joined the United States Government in their fight on the evil that is alcohol. I am here to defend the 18th amendment. A few months ago my brother and I signed on as revenuers," he said with a proud smile.

"That's what Will meant about the money yesterday," she thought aloud.

"Yes, and it'll be coming to us real soon," he said.

That's when it clicked to her what he planned to do with the book. "Mr. Thomas, they will never believe you if all you have is some book. You cannot do this. There are good people in here." She touched the calendar.

"Good people." He laughed. "You are the only good name in that book. Which is why I will make a deal with you. Although, it is beneath me to do so, I do not want to turn you in."

She crossed her arms over her chest tucking the small book firmly under her arm as she spoke. "What kind of deal?"

"You probably haven't noticed but I have a soft spot for you Emma." His creepy smile gave her goose bumps. "If you agree to take me as a woman takes a man in front of God and everyone, I will erase your name from my calendar before I turn it in."

He was seriously off his rocker.

"Mr. Thomas what on earth makes you think the U.S. Government is going to believe what you wrote in your diary?" she spit.

"Oh, I've got more than the book." He moved close to her again and grabbed the envelope and the small camera. "It is amazing what you can get for under six dollars. I got the camera and these twelve film negatives," he said, holding up a tiny row of negatives. She took the negatives and held them up to the light. Was that a picture of the pig?

"They will never be able to make these out," she said.

"You're right," he nodded his head, "it would have been challenging. Which is why for three dollars I could also get an enlarger." Her reached inside the envelope and pulled out a stack of postcard sized photos and handed them to her. It was a series of photos showing the same people arriving at the door she'd walked through yesterday. One was the delivery she'd witnessed yesterday afternoon. Anyone who had entered that door in daylight was captured on film. When she got to the last one her breath caught in her throat. It was one of she and Silas talking yesterday on her lunch break.

"See, I knew in time you will be proud of me. Like I said, I really am the only one doing the honorable thing here. Emma, it would kill me for you to be a part of this ugly scene that is going to unfold very soon but the choice is yours, my dear."

Emmie slid the negatives and the calendar back in the envelope. After one last slow flip through the photos she put them in, also.

"You know I cannot marry you, Mr. Thomas. My heart is somewhere else," she said, crossing her arms over her chest, tucking the envelope in tightly as she did so.

His face darkened. "You must be talking about Silas McDowell." He took a step closer to her. She could feel his breath on her face. He gritted his crooked teeth. "They will use you and put you out, Emma. He can't give you what I can."

He grabbed her hair and pulled her face to his. His face was all mouth and teeth. Emmie picked up her heel and stomped his foot as hard as she could. She held the envelope tight and grabbed the small black box that held the camera and ran across the store. She slid on the marble tile near the door. His feet were closing in behind her. She felt him grab her shoulder and jerk her back, pushing her against a display of cans near the entry.

His breath was ragged from running after her. He pulled his hand and smacked her hard. Emmie could taste the blood from her lips.

"I'm sorry," she lied. "I panicked when you came at me."

His anger softened. When he reached up to touch her hair she took a step toward him. He wrapped his hands around her back. All at once she jerked her knee up as hard and fast as she could. He fell to the ground screaming and cursing.

Emmie flung open the door to the shop so hard the little chime flew off its rest. She ran across the street, past the fountain in the center of the square, and into the entrance of the law firm. The receptionist of the firm looked up startled. "My God, Miss Emmie, what on earth is going on?"

"Is Silas here? Trick, Gabe, anyone?" She asked, panting. She didn't know if Mr. Thomas would have the guts to follow her but she didn't want to wait around and find out either.

Chapter Forty-eight

"Yes, let me just call and let them know you are here," she said, picking up the phone.

Emmie had been in this building with Ava enough to know her way around. She bet Silas was using Al's office while he was away. She ran up the three flights of stairs. When she reached the last landing Silas was standing there waiting for her. At first he looked angry but as she drew nearer it turned to fear.

"What's happened?" he asked, grabbing her by her arm and leading her into an office. He sat her in a chair and propped himself up on the end of the desk.

"Emmie, you're bleeding." He reached out and touched her lip.

"Mr. Thomas." It was all she could get out. She was panting from the attack and her run. She thrust the envelope at him. "Forgot to tell you." She tried to catch her breath. "He's how I knew about the pig. He and his brother had a fight over watching it and something about money." She paused again. "Revenuers."

Without talking Silas pulled out the contents of the envelope and flipped through the pictures, nodding as he looked at each one. His face had set into a deep frown.

Beginning to compose herself, Emmie reached up and pulled the diary calendar from the envelope and turned to yesterday. His eyes were wide as he read the name of each person who entered and exited the joint. His finger stopped at her name and he looked up at her.

"And he did this," he pointed to her lip, "to you?" He kept his voice calm and gentle.

Emmie nodded.

"Because you were trying to leave with his evidence?" he asked.

"Yeah, and I wouldn't take his blackmail..." she said the last part quickly.

His eyes widened. He nodded to himself as if he was thinking through everything he had just learned.

"Well, you don't need to worry about this." He held up the envelope and calendar. "This is an easy fix." He smiled.

"What are you going to do?" she asked.

"I promised not to lie to you. So, please don't ask me questions you really don't want answered." His voice had a bite to it. "Just trust me, he is not the first asshole I have dealt with."

"Just don't overreact because you're angry and get yourself in trouble okay?" she said, wiping her hands on her skirt.

"Overreact? This," he held up the envelope, "this makes me angry. It pisses me off." He nodded his head. "But this," he brought up his hand, touched her cheek, and ran it down to her mouth, looking sad, "this crosses the line. For this he will pay."

Silas knew he was playing with fire by pissing off the shopkeeper that had a thing for Emmie but he didn't think he was dangerous. He had seriously misjudged that man but all of that would be corrected in time.

"Has anyone else seen these that you know of?" he asked her.

Emmie shook her head, "Maybe Will, his brother? But I really don't think he wanted to be involved."

Silas nodded, put the envelope and camera in his briefcase, and locked it.

"Will you wait for me one second?" he asked walking toward the door.

She nodded.

Silas was only gone for a minute or two and when he returned Trick was with him. "I see our little ball of trouble has returned." He smiled down at her.

Silas grabbed his brother by the arm. "Not the time, brother." He let go and walked out of the office. He tossed the keys to Trick and climbed into the back seat with Emmie.

"I'm taking you home to Ava's. Gabe is there and Vince is due back sometime today. I'm going to go take care of some things," he said, looking down at her.

"Other than this," he touched her mouth, "are you okay?"

She nodded, "I'm fine."

He leaned down closer to her face. "Did he do anything else?" He was hanging on the balance of control here. He looked down at her skirt and touched a spot where the fabric was ripped. Emmie hadn't noticed that. It must have happened when he grabbed her to pull her back from the door.

"No, honest. He just tried to kiss me. And I kneed him," she said.

This brought a huge grin to his face. He pulled her in close and cradled her head to his chest. Thumbing the hair down at her temple like you would a child. "Why does that not surprise me?" He actually laughed. Trick looked back in surprise.

Silas leaned forward and kissed her nose, her cheeks, her mouth. "I'm sorry this happened."

She shrugged brushing it off, "It is what it is, right?"

Emmie reached up and touched the scab over his eye. "Now we do look like fighting Irish."

****

When they got inside the house Gabe was waiting. "Are you sure you don't want me to go with you?" he asked.

"No. I won't be long. Emmie, let's get you cleaned up." He threaded his fingers through hers and led her to the bathroom.

"I will be okay," she said, trying to take the cold washcloth from him.

"Emmie let me take care of you," he said quietly.

She drew her hand back and nodded.

"I need to tell you something but being as you have had a rough morning, I'm not sure if I should," he said honestly and she appreciated it.

"Tell. You have to now that you've said that," she said.

"Trick got a confession. I called him from your house and he went straight to the jail where Sam was. He and Sheriff Drake got him to make a full confession."

243

"Why was he in jail?"

"Well, after an anonymous person wrote a letter saying they saw someone shoot Ronnie and then set his car on fire, the case was reopened." He smiled.

"Really, you've gotten all of that done in the hour since I saw you this morning?" she asked.

"More or less. Some of it may be happening right now or will happen very soon. Didn't I tell you once that timelines are subjective? And since Sam has confessed to robbing and murdering him it will be a very quick trial. Open and shut. Minimal stress on you. Walter and I talked after he dropped you off. He seemed to think this is the way you would want it handled."

She didn't really want to think about the alternative. Which made her think of Mr. Thomas.

Emmie nodded to agree with the trial. "Don't hurt him too bad, okay?"

"Is the him you're talking about Paul Thomas?" he asked, getting tense.

"Yes," she said.

"Define too bad and I'll see if we can compromise. I was thinking slow and painful death. Your turn," he said.

"Silas, really… I'm thinking don't hurt him past the point of recovery." She raised her eyebrows at him.

He grabbed his chin and rubbed his jaw thinking it over. "I'm not making promises but I'll try to go somewhere in the middle of those two things."

Emmie sighed.

"Okay. I'll try. I promise," he said.

When Emmie walked out of the bathroom door Ava was standing there. "I'd just let him kill him, honestly Emmie, that man has been a thorn in your side for years," she said nonchalantly then smiled.

By the time Silas made it back to Trick he was all business again. He could turn that off and on better than anyone Emmie had ever seen. She walked to the door to tell him goodbye.

"Be careful."

"I'll be fine." He smiled. "Will you be here when I get back?"

She nodded. He leaned down and gave her a quick kiss then reached on the table behind her, grabbed his other gun he'd left there this morning, and secured it in his holster.

Chapter Forty-nine

After Emmie had showered and changed she went to find Ava with the box from her house tucked into her arm. Throughout everything she'd been through last night and today, that letter was still on her mind. Last night, she thought she didn't think too much about the short note from her father. What did it matter who he was anyway? He'd never been there for her before so why should it matter now? But for some reason, she couldn't let go of it. It mattered that he sent her money she never knew about. It mattered her mother had kept it from her all these years. It mattered that Ronnie knew who he was. It mattered there were pictures hidden in her barn she had never seen. It mattered he was still close enough to someone she knew to "hear through the grapevine" she wanted to go to college. It mattered. All of it.

If there was one thing she'd gotten out of the last few days, it was keeping things to herself led to trouble. So, she decided to start by sharing it with Ava. She found her sitting on a couch. Gabe was standing behind her pacing like a tiger in a cage. He obviously didn't like being left behind to watch the girls.

"Whatcha got?" Ava asked, noticing the box right away.

"Well, Silas helped me find this." Okay, so that was a little half-truth.

She opened the box to find a stack of cash had been returned to the box. The stack looked thicker than before. As she reached the bottom she noticed there was a new note taped to one of the bills.

"I'm only going back to Chicago when you go with me. So, keep your cash. Love, S.C.M."

"Aww... I could die for how sweet that is." Ava grabbed her heart and pouted her mouth. "Gabe you have to see this. Silas has written Emmie to say..." she started.

He put his hands over his ears. "I do not want to hear this. I'm going to the porch."

"Got rid of him. Not we can talk." Ava smiled. "Seriously sweet letter though. Didn't I tell you he was carrying a torch for you?"

Emmie turned the note over in her hand and then laid it in the box next to the other notes. "This is actually the one I want you to see."

Ava took her time reading the letter from the mysterious M.V.D. and Ronnie. She flipped over and read the one from her father several times. "We can figure this out. We've got the initials. We know it's from Chicago. We'll figure it out."

"Chicago?" Emmie asked.

"Yeah, that money was wired. See that logo right there, L.C.B. It's Lake City Bank. My dad has an account there. We'll figure it out." Ava smiled.

Emmie nodded. "Thanks."

"No, I should be thanking you. Because this," Ava got up ran to the closet and pulled out her Halloween costume, "is absolutely stunning."

Emmie smiled at her friend's reaction to the dress. "How did you get it? I didn't have time to pack it last night."

"Gabe mentioned when he got home that you would probably be staying with us for a while. So, we went over and packed up some of your things for you. I saw this laying out in your living room and I had to bring it," she explained.

"Well, I'm glad you like it," Emmie said.

"I love it. It fits like a glove." Ava ran her hands along the bodice. "Yours looks nice too."

"Thanks," she said.

"But Emmie, it looks more like a nice black dinner dress than a Halloween costume. It isn't as special as the pattern I picked out for you," she said, holding up her friend's dress.

"Ava, that was really nice fabric. I couldn't bring myself to turn it into something I would wear once in my life," she answered honestly. "I'm going to make a witch hat fascinator, then it will look more like a costume. I'll carry a broom too."

"You will not carry a broom, people will think you're a housekeeper." Ava laughed.

Emmie grinned and then covered her mouth and stifled a yawn.

Ava hugged Emmie and tossed her the blanket she'd been wrapped in. "You're tired, it's been a long day. We can talk about the party later. Take a rest until he gets back."

Emmie tried to contest the idea but she couldn't. Her eyes were heavy and her brain grew foggy. Ava left the room quietly. She closed her eyes and relaxed for the first time in months. When sleep found her she wasn't sure she'd ever wake.

****

The frogs were croaking in the trees outside. Stars and a full moon lit the sky. It was cool but she was wrapped in blankets. She was tucked in so tight she could barely move. She could hear the creak of the rocker next to her. Even before she glanced over she knew who she would find. She could barely make out Silas's silhouette. But she could see the flame of his cigarette as he drew in a breath and the shadow of the smoke when he exhaled.

Emmie raised up slowly not wanting to inch out of the covers. "You might want to stay there, it's cool out here."

She took a quilt with her as she padded across the porch. He put out his cigarette as she got closer to him, spreading his arms for her. Emmie sat on his lap and pulled the quilt over both of them. They rocked and he hummed. She'd never heard him hum but it was deep and beautiful. With her head against his chest she could hear so well. She used to do that with her mama when she was a little girl. How could her mama have kept her dad from her? Her heart hurt at the thought. She felt like her world was shifting but she pushed all of that from her mind. She didn't want to think about that tonight. Emmie would think about that tomorrow.

"I got your note. I've always wanted to go to Chicago. I bet they've got some good schools up there too." She swallowed hard.

He smiled. "You just say when."

She nodded. "Did you mean what you said at my house today. That part about why it was okay I was selling your 'shine back to ya?"

He looked confused for a second then said, "Oh, that... I love you?"

She nodded.

He grinned and his mouth quirked over to the side. "Yeah. I love you."

"I love you too, Silas," she said.

He picked her up and carried her over to the bed. Swallowing hard he unbuttoned his shirt slowly and tossed it on the ground before sliding in next to her. "Let's pick up where we left off last night."

Emmie giggled as he ran his hands over her stomach and up her body until he grabbed her chin. He pulled her in for a long, painfully slow kiss and brushed his knuckles on her cheek. Something rough scratched her skin. It was then in the moonlight she noticed his knuckles were split.

"Silas, you're hurt." She brought them up to her mouth and kissed each spot.

"Not as bad as he is," he answered.

Emmie stilled next to him, not moving or speaking. She was still holding his hands next to her mouth. Frozen.

"He's still breathing, if that's what you're wondering. He's hurt but not beyond repair. His hands won't ever touch you again. They probably won't be touching a camera again either."

Silas looked down at her eyes. She was still tired. Exhaustion was marked on her face.

"Go to sleep, Emmie girl. I'll be here when you wake."

He pulled her into his chest and wrapped his arms around her. He hummed until he heard her breathing slow. She looked so beautiful asleep in his arms. Her lips, plumped from his kisses. Her eyes, closed and at peace. He pushed her hair away from her face. That sweet face, so full of hope, compassion and good. Silas stared out through the screened-in window. Taking in the glow of the moon, lighting the black night. That's what she felt like to him. A beautiful glow of light in a dark path.

"Shine on for me my sweet Emmie," he smiled and tucked the blanket around her shoulders, "Shine on."

Rise and Shine

Allison Jewell

Book two in the Shine On series is set to release July 2013.

Chapter One

Emmie's body was stiff as she stepped out of the dark car and onto the city street. It was busy and loud. Nothing like the small downtown square back home.

"This is it?" Gabe grabbed Emmie's old brown suitcase from the back of the car that took them from the train station to the hotel.

"Yep, that's it. Why?" Emmie asked.

"Ugh. I guess I'm just used to helping Ava with hers." Gabe nodded to the curb where Ava was talking with a bellhop for the Tealbach Hotel. The bellhop smiled and laughed at something she said while he loaded her belongings onto a gold cart.

"Bless her heart," Emmie laughed, taking in all six pieces of Ava's red leather luggage. "Gabe, we are only staying the weekend right? You know, there is no telling what all she had hidden in those cases."

He smiled and dropped her suitcase on the curb a few feet from where Ava's were. Emmie noticed one of the other bellhops reach down to pick it up.

"Thanks but I can get it," she said sweetly. The bellhop looked back at her confused. He still had one arm extended like he may take the suitcase right out of her hands. Pulling it closer to her body, she realized that she looked a little bit overprotective of her belongings. Really, she wouldn't have minded letting the guy take up her belongings but it had just now occurred to her that this man wasn't moving luggage out of the goodness of his heart. When he reached her room he was going to be expecting a tip and she refused to pay the man for something she could easily do herself.

"I don't mind, Miss," he said, taking a step closer to her.

"No…" she started but never got the chance to finish her sentence.

"Thank you, Sir. She's in room 233." Silas came up behind her, took the luggage from her hand and tossed it to the man. Then he handed the young man a crisp bill. She couldn't see the amount but from his smile she could tell the boy thought it a fair price.

Emmie turned around, trying her best to look annoyed but had a hard time keeping up the front. "The good Lord gave me two arms and I can carry my own bags."

He brushed a kiss on her forehead and pulled her in for a hug, resting his chin on the top of her head. She breathed in the scent. Emmie felt herself relax. All too soon he let go of her and took a step back saying hello to Gabe and Ava.

They shared pleasantries. Ava asked about his family and if they had settled in. Silas and Patrick had taken a train earlier in the week to Louisville to meet their family first. Emmie was going to be meeting them all tonight right before the Halloween party and her stomach was in knots. He'd asked her to come up early and meet his family but Emmie decided to wait until this evening. She didn't know why she was so nervous. Other than Trick, he rarely talked about his family.

If Emmie thought her train car had been elaborately decorated, it didn't hold a candle to the lobby of the hotel. From the outside, it looked like any other nice hotel they had driven past. But the inside was so unique; it was what set it apart. The windows were huge with pointy gothic arches. The chairs were deep hues of green, blue, and red. An elaborate staircase with a dark wooden banister cascaded down from the second floor. White marble floors echoed her footsteps. It was relatively empty and though it was elaborate, the feel was like a cavernous medieval castle.

"You like it?" Silas asked.

"It's the most beautiful place I've ever seen," she said, her voice barely above a whisper. She'd never in her life set foot in a place like this. She forgot how to walk in its beauty, so she stood and gawked at her surroundings while Ava, Gabe and Silas made plans for when to meet up that evening.

"Well, if it isn't Miss Emmie Shimmy," Vince's voice boomed. She'd missed his arrival. He was just releasing his sister and coming for Emmie.

"You better not." She laughed coming out of her stupor. There was no pool around but there was nothing Vince loved better than to find a way to razz her. She took a step backward to no avail. He was there in no time. He gripped her in a bear hug and whispered in her ear. "You've done good, Emmie."

She pulled back and looked at him surprised. *I've done good?* She didn't ask the question aloud but it showed in her eyes. He gave her a quirk of a smile that answered her question. She could see it in his face. Somehow, he'd been filled-in on everything that had happened in his absence and he was proud of her. That was odd. As quickly as he appeared, he slapped Silas on the shoulder and led the way to the stairs, heading off to his room.

Silas and Gabe walked the girls to their room and then headed to theirs. Emmie was meeting Silas early to get the family introductions out of the way before the party started. Although that was still hours away, her heart was already in her throat. When you live in a tiny town you rarely meet new people, much less new people who you hope will be your family someday. The thought caught in her stomach and swam around for a while making her feel more nauseous.

The hotel room was absolutely stunning. It was more of an apartment than a room and decorated in the same European-castle feel. The lush fabrics of the sitting area were so inviting. Ava squealed and clapped her hands, taking her costume from her luggage. She hung the dress in the closet and carefully smoothed out the nonexistent wrinkles.

"Can you believe it is actually here? Oh, Emmie I love my costume, thank you so much," she cooed.

Emmie smiled. "You'll be stunning."

Emmie found her suitcase was already in the bedroom. She pulled out her own lovely black lace dress. Ava was right, it didn't really look like a costume. Still though, she knew she'd made the sensible decision—black silk and lace should be worn more than one night. She smoothed out the dress mocking Ava's motions. She headed back to the living area and the small hallway closet. She hung her dress next to Ava's. She turned around and Ava was pouring something from a little silver flask. She poured a tiny amount in a cup and handed it to Emmie and then did the same for herself.

"What is this?" Emmie asked.

"Oh, just a special autumn drink to kick off the celebration." She grinned and held her hand out to clink glasses.

Emmie followed her motion and the girls tipped back the cup at the same time. She smiled before she even got the drink all the way down.

"How did you get it?" she wondered aloud.

"Silas. He left it hidden in the closet for us. They told me to check the closet for surprises while you were in your daze downstairs. I still cannot believe you made this," Ava said, touching her lips.

Emmie could still feel the warmth of the apple pie in her throat. He knew her well, she did need a shot of courage but more than that, she needed a shot of something that reminded her of home. She felt uncomfortable in her surroundings and that one sip of apple pie grounded her. How could he know that?

But, they'd come to know quite a bit about one another over the last few weeks. Just a couple of days before he left, he had taken her to the barn to search for the mysterious box of photographs that Ronnie's note had alluded to. Silas climbed into the rafters while she watched with bated breath. He'd found it relatively quickly. But then, she already knew he was a good snooper, didn't she?

She had waited until they got back to his car to open the box. They sat in his front seat and dug through the secrets it held. At first, she thought Ronnie had led her to a bunch of nothing. The top had a few photographs of her as a very young child. But as she dug deeper into the white tattered box, its contents got more confusing. There was a ticket to some dance at a local cave that doubled as a nightclub, a program from an event at St. Joseph, and a couple more letters from her real father. They were always signed with his initials M.V.D. One of the notes was full of beautiful words, flowers, promises. It was dated a full year before Emmie was born. The second was dated on Emmie's first birthday. It was short and to the point, pretty much saying here is the money and how to contact me if you need more. Her heart broke for her mother. She dug deeper into the box. That's when she saw it. A photograph dated the year before she was born. Her mother's young face was smiling back at her. She was seated at a table leaned back against a young man. He was handsome. Emmie was sure that she had his hair and maybe even his eyes. Their almond shape was reflected in her appearance.

Emmie walked over and picked up her purse off the coffee table, unzipped the side pocket and handed the photograph to Ava.

"What's this?" Ava asked, taking it from her friend. When she got a good look at it her eyes widened and she put her hand on her heart. But for once the move was authentic rather than dramatic.

"Your mom. Oh Emmie, you look just like her." Her eyes gazed down at Emmie and she gave a sad smile.

"Thanks." That really did make Emmie smile.

Ava looked back at the photograph. Her brow creased as she took a closer look. "This man is so handsome. He looks familiar."

"That's because I think he is my dad. See the hair... and the shape of his eyes? It's like me, isn't it?" Emmie asked.

Ava held the photo closer to her eyes, bit her lower lip and nodded. "That's true. You do favor him."

"Yeah, and if you flip it over the date was 1902. It's the year before I was born. So, the time makes sense," Emmie said. She was surprised how strong her voice was.

Ava put the photograph on the coffee table and walked over to hug her friend. She cradled her head and spoke softly. "We've got his picture and we know he lives in Chicago. We will find him." She pulled back and held her friend at arm's-length.

"Here." She pulled out the flask again and poured another generous shot. "Sip that and..." she trailed off and moved back to the closet and returned with an enormous black box with an orange ribbon.

"What on earth is this? Don't tell me you've already sent someone out shopping for you." Emmie laughed.

"Not me. You've already had someone shopping. See?" Ava showed Emmie the tag with her name on it.

Emmie carefully pulled the ribbon and lifted the lid to the box. "Oh, my." She covered her mouth with both hands.

"Told you he was carrying a torch for you. My family has great taste. I mean honestly, I am proud to call him a cousin after I saw this dress," Ava rattled on and on.

Emmie had already tuned her out. She was lost in the beauty of the costume. She pulled it all the way out of the box and held it up to her body. The bodice was similar to the one she had made for Ava. But it was a beautiful royal blue. The black underskirt wasn't as full as Ava's orange pumpkin but the soft peacock feathers that draped down from her waist made her costume just as showy. In the bottom of the box was a beautiful headband adorned with a few blue-green peacock feathers and a big silver gem where they crossed. It was the most beautiful costume she had ever seen.

"You think Silas did this?" Emmie asked, finally registering Ava's ramblings.

"Look for yourself," Ava said, pulling out a card from under the tissue paper.

Dear Emmie,

The blue made me think of your eyes. Ava mentioned (a few dozen times) that you didn't have time to make a real costume for yourself. Hope this one is okay.

Love,

Silas

****

The knock on the door came just as she put down her lipstick. She dropped the makeup in her clutch and headed to the door. She cautiously pulled it open. There he was. She was the one in the fancy headband, wearing a dress with feathers but he was the one that looked stunning. He was in a black three-piece suit with a hat pushed low on his forehead. She smiled up at him and her heart faltered when he didn't immediately smile back. His eyes were wide and unblinking and his

257

mouth was set in a straight line. She opened her mouth to suggest maybe she should change into the other dress but she didn't get the chance.

In one quick motion he pulled her in for a kiss. His mouth was on hers before she could take a breath. She tasted tobacco on his mouth; his hands slid down her bare arms and he quickly pushed himself away. The kiss was over before she was even fully aware it had started. He liked the dress.

He held a hand up and stepped away from her. "Sorry," he shook his head and leaned down to grab her clutch. She hadn't even realized she had dropped it. "You are beautiful."

Emmie smiled. "It's lovely. Thank you." She was surprised how quiet her voice had gotten.

"You're lovely," he said, passing her clutch back to her. "We better go. Ma and Pop are already on their way down."

Her heart beat up and she could feel her emotions warming her neck and chest. She grabbed her black wrap off the chair and yelled bye to Ava who was still working on her makeup.

"See you at the party," Ava sang from the bathroom.

As Silas and Emmie were walking out, Gabe came to the door. "She still getting ready?" he asked.

Emmie nodded and waved goodbye as Silas put his hand on her back to lead her down the hall.

"Surprise, surprise," Gabe said with a laugh as he entered the room.

"Oh, hush," Ava said, "I'm almost finished. Here." She rolled the flask down the hall. "Have a drink."

Gabe decided to forgo the glass and took his swig right from the flask. He sat down on the lush navy sofa and settled in for the wait. Ava's almost finished usually equaled to another half an hour. He didn't mind though. Gabe leaned forward and picked up an old photo lying on the coffee table. At first glance he thought it was a picture of Emmie with another man.

"She better keep that away from Silas," Gabe said with a laugh tossing the picture back onto the table.

"Keep what away?" Ava asked.

"That picture of her with another guy. Sort of weird that she's brought it with her," he mused.

"Oh, that's not Emmie. They look alike though don't they?" Ava shouted.

Gabe grabbed the photo again and looked at it a little more closely. Ava was right, it wasn't Emmie. "Who is it?" he called.

"It's her mom and some mystery lover," she said. "Emmie thinks that is her father but we don't know for sure. The date on the back seems right though."

For the first time Gabe turned his attention to the guy in the picture. He squinted and jerked the photo closer to his eyes. Ava walked out of the room just in time to see him turn the photo, look at the date on the back, and then drop the photo on the table like it was on fire. He stood and ran his hands over his face. Then he put the flask up to his lips and took another long swig with his eyes closed. He replaced the cap and put it in his pocket.

"What's wrong?" Ava asked as he paced the floor.

"Just getting ready for tonight." He tapped the flask he'd just put in his pocket. "You look beautiful, doll," Gabe said then pulled her in for a long slow kiss. She seemed to buy the act. He was glad that she couldn't tell what he was feeling right now. Anger, hurt, confusion. He didn't want her to feel any of this tonight. He didn't want her to question him about that photograph, so he kissed her until he was sure the word photograph wasn't even in her vocabulary. This was going to be her night. He refused to let some old photograph ruin what he'd worked months to plan.

ABOUT THE AUTHOR

Allison Jewell lives in southern Kentucky with her husband, two sons, and dog. When she isn't hard at work on her next novel, she can be found doing one of her favorite things: watching her oldest son chase the puck at the local hockey rink, secretly eating her mother's home-made brownies, hanging out at home listening to records with her husband, or making up silly songs with her youngest son. *Shine On* is her debut novel. She is currently editing the second book in this series, *Rise and Shine*.

Facebook: facebook.com/allison.jewel.56
Twitter: @AuthorAJewell